D0742460

The
Kindness
of
Strangers

**Center Point
Large Print**

**This Large Print Book carries the
Seal of Approval of N.A.V.H.**

Tales from Grace Chapel Inn

The
Kindness
of
Strangers

Susan Meier

CENTER POINT PUBLISHING
THORNDIKE, MAINE

This Center Point Large Print edition
is published in the year 2009 by arrangement with
Guideposts.

Copyright © 2005 by Guideposts.

All rights reserved.

All Scripture quotations are taken from
The Holy Bible, New International Version.
Copyright © 1973, 1978, 1984 International Bible
Society. Used by permission of
Zondervan Bible Publishers.

The text of this Large Print edition is unabridged.
In other aspects, this book may vary
from the original edition.
Printed in the United States of America.
Set in 16-point Times New Roman type.

ISBN: 978-1-60285-390-4

Library of Congress Cataloging-in-Publication Data

Meier, Susan.
  The kindness of strangers / Susan Meier.
    p. cm.
  ISBN 978-1-60285-390-4 (library binding : alk. paper)
  1. Sisters--Fiction. 2. Bed and breakfast accommodations--Fiction.
    3. Pennsylvania--Fiction. 4. Large type books. I. Title.

PS3563.E3463K56 2008
813'.54--dc22

2008045465
35306809 2·09

Acknowledgments

Behind so many good writers is a patient spouse. My husband Mike is no exception. He deserves at least half the credit for everything I do!

—Susan Meier

Chapter One

Louise Howard Smith sat at the kitchen table of Grace Chapel Inn studying Florence Simpson. Wearing a yellow dress with her brown hair fixed in a neat twist, Florence had dropped in that sunny May morning for an unannounced visit, and Louise wasn't quite sure what to make of it.

When Louise and her sisters decided to turn their family home into a bed-and-breakfast after their father's death, Louise immediately realized that she would have to adjust to the easy familiarity with which the residents of the small Pennsylvania town of Acorn Hill conducted themselves. Most of her adult life, she had lived in Philadelphia with her now deceased husband, Eliot, where neighbors were seen and heard, but personal connections were rarely made. Florence had been one of her greatest challenges.

Though stout, Florence was a reasonably attractive woman for her sixty-plus years. Unfortunately, she could be a bit aggressive and self-centered. She didn't seem to notice that Louise's sister Jane was cleaning the kitchen after having served breakfast to the guests, or that Louise herself was preparing to check out the ones who would be leaving after their weekend stays. "Would you like a sweet bun, Florence?" Jane asked, always a pleasant hostess. At fifty, Jane was the youngest of the three Howard sisters. She had long, dark hair that she wore in a ponytail, fair skin and blue eyes. A white bib apron covered her blue jeans and bright-pink shirt. An experienced chef, Jane was happy to serve her company.

"Why thank you, Jane." Florence reached for one of the warm buns on the plate Jane offered to her.

As Florence took a bite, a gentle breeze through an open window stirred the white curtains. They complemented the warm paprika paint on the cupboards, which, along with the rows of colorful tile on the backsplash, gave the room a welcoming feel to balance the professional look of the stainless-steel appliances and the black-and-white floor tiles.

"What brings you here today?" Louise asked. She smiled but was eager to get on with the conversation. She wanted a minute before a mirror to make sure that her beige skirt and matching sweater set as well as her hair were still neat before she checked out their latest guests, the Olsens and the McQuaids.

"I got a really great idea last night. Something I'm certain will attract guests to your inn for the Memorial Day weekend."

Jane smiled as she poured Florence a cup of coffee. "We're already booked for the Memorial Day weekend."

Florence's penciled eyebrows drooped when she frowned. "Really?"

"The bit of advertising we do and word of mouth worked very well to bring in guests for the holiday," Louise responded politely.

"That's great," Florence said, but her frown deepened.

Though Jane was sliding the breakfast dishes into slots in the dishwasher, she noticed Florence's unhappy expression and asked, "What's your idea?"

"Well . . ." Florence hesitated.

That brief pause confused Louise. She could only speculate that Florence had expected a much more enthusiastic reaction to the fact that her plan could potentially bring business to Grace Chapel Inn.

"I would like the residents of Acorn Hill to put on a talent show."

Jane turned from the dishwasher. "A talent show?"

"It could be something we do for free to entertain people who are visiting relatives here for the weekend."

Louise said nothing as she thought through the idea. Memorial Day weekend was only four weeks away, which didn't leave much time for practice. Also, a talent show required music. Louise was an accomplished pianist who had accompanied college students, mainly vocalists, while she lived in Philadelphia. Here in Acorn Hill she played organ for Grace Chapel and taught piano. Florence could want Louise to provide the music.

Jane lifted two cups from the counter and set them in the dishwasher tray. "But people who are visiting relatives don't need to be entertained. They'll be occupied with catching up."

Florence sat up straighter in her chair. "That's exactly my point. We always think we need an entire weekend for catching up, but by Sunday night everybody's all talked out. If we had a talent show, then everybody could bring their company to the elementary school auditorium and not have to be bored for three hours."

Louise's mouth fell open. *"Three hours?"*

Florence's hand fluttered to the collar of her white cotton blouse. "Well, yes. The town has plenty of people with talent. And I'm sure some of the acts, such as the singers, should perform two numbers."

Florence's "show" would run much longer than their community productions typically ran. That meant extended practice sessions. With only four weeks until Memorial Day weekend, they might be able to pull off a two-hour show if they rushed. A three-hour show would be a nightmare. To have any hope of success, they would have to get started right away.

Florence patted Louise's hand before she rose from her seat. "Just think about it. If three hours doesn't work for you, we could consider a two-hour show," she said as she headed for the kitchen door. "I'll be back tomorrow."

As Florence pushed open the screen door, Jane said, "See you tomorrow, Florence."

Louise watched their guest walk across the porch, down the steps and out of her line of vision, which also meant she was out of hearing range.

Jane turned from the dishwasher and faced Louise. "Why on earth does she want to put on a talent show?" she asked with a giggle.

"I have no idea."

"Well, *you* better believe she wants you to accompany the acts."

Louise nodded. "I realized that."

"Wonder why she didn't ask?"

"She probably didn't want me to say no," Louise said, rising from her seat at the table. "She's giving me twenty-four hours to warm up to the idea of how much fun it could be."

Jane's face puckered with confusion. "She thinks that after twenty-four hours you're going to think it will be so much fun to have a talent show that you'll agree?"

Louise shrugged. "Who knows what Florence Simpson thinks? We'll just have to wait until tomorrow to find out."

Alice Howard walked into the reception area of the Potterston Hospital dialysis unit, where she was filling in for a nurse who was on an extended vacation. Alice closed the door behind her, but as she turned toward the desk to pick up a chart, something slammed into her, knocking her back a step. She blinked to adjust her focus and saw a little boy.

"Jeff!" a voice called out.

Alice heard a woman's cry at the same time that she saw a man catch the little boy's arm and pull him away.

"Jeff, I've told you a thousand times—no running!" scolded the man who Alice assumed was Jeff's father. Tall and husky with dark brown hair, he smiled apologetically at Alice. "I'm sorry about Jeff."

"No problem," Alice said, smoothing her uniform. "No harm done."

Jeff's father nestled him against his side. "Jeff still hasn't learned the difference between outside manners and inside manners. We're getting there, but it's been slow going."

A blond woman stepped from behind Jeff's father and took the boy's free hand. "If he doesn't soon learn to be more careful around the patients and staff, we won't be able to bring him to any more of my dialysis sessions. I'm Myra Swanson, by the way." The woman offered her hand to Alice. "And this is my husband, Brett."

"I'm Alice Howard," Alice said, shaking Myra's hand, then her husband's. "I think it's a great idea to have your kids come with you so they can see there's nothing mysterious or frightening about dialysis."

"That was our thought," Brett agreed. "We don't

bring them every time, but we like to have them attend once a month to see that everything's still fine."

Alice nodded. "Sounds like you're old pros at this."

Myra laughed. "I've been having dialysis for three years now."

Alice couldn't stop herself from looking at the three children behind Brett. Two teenagers, a pretty blond girl who looked like her mother and a lanky brown-haired boy, appeared laid-back about the situation. But hyperactive Jeff couldn't be any older than six, and Alice wondered if his inability to sit still might mean he wasn't as accepting or understanding of his mother's situation.

"Okay, let's get going," Brett said to the children. He smiled at Alice. "Sorry again about Jeff crashing into you."

"Just an accident." Alice patted the little boy's head.

Brett pushed open the glass door and held it for his family as they exited. When they arrived at their red minivan, Alice waved good-bye, but as they drove out of the parking lot, her smile faded. As a nurse, she knew dialysis wasn't a cure for kidney disease; only a transplant was. She also knew there were about three times as many people waiting for transplants as there were kidneys available. But even more important, Alice knew that people on dialysis didn't lead easy lives.

Immediately after their treatments, most were full of energy, but as their next session neared, they became tired and listless.

A woman with a little boy who couldn't sit still probably had a very challenging routine.

When Alice returned home that night, she was exhausted. The regular dialysis-unit nurses had told her that Mondays were their busiest day, and now she had no reason to doubt them.

She stepped into the kitchen of Grace Chapel Inn, and the scent of beef and something fruity awakened her senses. Her mouth watered.

"I'm starving," she said to her sister Jane, who was setting dishes on the kitchen table. The sisters ate most of their meals together in the kitchen, as a family, rather than in the beautiful formal dining room.

"You only have about ten minutes before dinner," Jane said with a laugh. "Just enough time to freshen up."

"Great!" Alice said. She walked to the wide staircase of the front hall and up the steps to her room.

Her private space was a haven of peace and tranquility with walls painted buttery yellow. An antique patchwork quilt of pastel yellow, green and violet covered the bed. The rug of the same colors Alice had braided herself.

She quickly washed her face and hands, then changed out of her uniform and into jeans and a simple yellow blouse that accented her reddish-brown hair.

When she returned to the kitchen, Jane was setting plates of apricot beef with sesame noodles onto the table.

"I thought we were eating low fat," Alice teased as she took her usual seat.

"This isn't exactly low fat, but it's better fat. I used olive oil. It contains omega fats, which help with everything from brain function to maintaining healthy cells. I found a great recipe, then trimmed the beef and switched from regular vegetable oil to olive oil. We'll see if you can taste the difference."

Louise pushed through the swinging door into the kitchen. Wearing a simple cotton skirt with a sweater set, she looked proper and dignified, but comfortable. "The difference in what?"

"Jane made apricot beef with sesame noodles," Alice said. "But she made it with better fat."

"Better fat?" Louise questioned as she took her seat. "All I can say is if it tastes as good as it smells, we will be in luck."

Jane brought vegetables and a basket of fresh bread to the table, then sat. Louise said grace, after which Alice took a piece of the beef and passed the serving platter to Louise.

"How was your day, little sister?" Alice asked, reaching for the basket Jane handed to her.

Jane laughed. "My day was fine, but I think

15

Louise is being hoodwinked into one of Florence Simpson's schemes."

Louise rolled her eyes, and Alice glanced from one sister to the other. The oldest, Louise always looked picture-perfect in her cardigan and pearls. On the other side of the table, baby-sister Jane wore an orange T-shirt over trendy jeans. It wasn't unusual for Jane to find humor in things that Louise considered disastrous.

"So what's Florence's scheme?" Alice asked when neither sister said anything further.

"She wants to put on a talent show," Louise said resignedly.

Alice thought about that for a second, then said, "Why?"

"That's a very good question," Louise said.

"Yes," Jane agreed, "but the real problem is that she's probably going to ask Louise to accompany the acts."

"Oh," Alice said. She took a bite of her dinner and sighed in ecstasy. "This is scrumptious, Jane."

Jane grinned. "I knew it would be. Plus, the feeling of being full that olive oil gives you lasts longer."

"The meal is wonderful, Jane," Louise complimented.

"Much better than being forced to accompany a bunch of questionably talented people?" Jane teased.

"It isn't their talent that's the problem," Louise

said. She took another bite of her dinner, savoring it, then said, "The real problem is that this could take a great deal of my time, depending upon how much practice each person needs."

"That's true," Jane agreed.

Louise sighed. "But I also feel that I should participate in the community. If this is something everyone in town wants to do, I should be involved."

Jane frowned. "That's true too."

Louise turned to Alice. "What do you think?"

Alice glanced up from her dinner. "I'm sorry. I didn't hear what you said."

"I asked if you think I should be a part of Florence Simpson's talent show."

Alice opened her mouth to say something, but no words came out. As Jane and Louise were discussing the talent show, her mind drifted to Myra Swanson. Alice couldn't shake her concern over the poor woman's having to keep up with a young son. She had also remembered that the survival rate for patients with kidney disease dropped dramatically after five years of dialysis. The possibility existed that Myra could die from her condition and leave her little boy motherless.

She took a quick breath. "I'm sorry. My mind is wandering. I met a patient today who has been having dialysis for over three years."

Louise's expression turned sympathetic. "And how serious is that?"

Alice shrugged. "Everybody's different. Some people live great lives for decades on dialysis, but other people don't."

"And you think this woman is one of the ones who will have trouble?" Jane asked.

Alice shook her head. "I don't know. I never saw her chart. I only met her because her little boy bumped into me when I went into the reception area."

Louise perceptively said, "Her *little* boy?"

"*Very* little boy," Alice said. "He's only about six."

"I see why you're concerned," Jane said.

Louise took a long breath. "Alice, I think it's wonderful that you have such a big heart. But in this instance you may be looking on the dark side. As you said, this woman could be healthy for decades on dialysis."

Alice nodded. "I know. She could be doing very well. And she's only in her forties. Nine chances out of ten, she's healthy."

"Still," Jane said, "her son is awfully young. If he's six, I'll bet he's a bundle of energy. Worse, she has twelve years until he's eighteen. She must worry that she might leave her child without a mother."

Alice closed her eyes. She hadn't forgotten that Jane had been raised without a mother. It was more that she was so preoccupied with Myra Swanson that she hadn't made the connection sooner. "I'm sorry, Jane. I didn't mean to bring up something that would hit you so close to home."

Jane shrugged. "Actually, it feels sort of good to be the one who can comment the most knowledgeably on a situation for once." She grinned. "You two are so smart about people and life that I sometimes feel like a true baby sister."

"So, Jane, what *do* you think?" Louise asked.

"I think that Alice is 'looking on the dark side.'"

Louise groaned. Alice laughed. "You're teasing is just what I need to pull me out of this gloomy mood."

"I understand your mood, Alice," Jane said. "I would be concerned about that little boy growing up without a mom too. But I think Louise is correct. This is one time when you would be worrying for nothing if you fretted over this before you knew more of her story."

"You're right," Alice agreed. Then she burst out laughing. "So do you want to go back to talking about Florence Simpson's talent show?"

Louise sighed again. "You know what? After cautioning Alice about pessimism, I think I might be worrying for nothing too. After all, Florence hasn't even asked me to be an accompanist."

But that night when she was in bed, Louise knew Florence was going to ask her to provide the accompaniment for the talent show. There really wasn't anybody else in town who could spare the time for practices, and she inclined toward accepting the task if asked. Alice's news about the dialysis patient added a new dimension to Louise's decision. With so many people in the world having real problems, it seemed petty for Louise to refuse to help, particularly since she enjoyed being part of the small community.

Of course, Florence hadn't really given a good reason for her talent show. Providing something for visitors to do on Sunday night of a holiday weekend didn't seem like a realistic motivation, considering all the work necessary for a production like a talent show. Louise couldn't shake the feeling that there was more to this situation than met the eye.

Though she wouldn't say anything to her sisters, she had a suspicion there was a hidden agenda behind Florence's grand idea.

And Louise would bet her bottom dollar it benefited Florence.

Chapter Two

When Alice arrived at the dialysis unit just before noon on Wednesday, she saw Myra Swanson reading a magazine. Glad to see the woman who had been much on her mind lately, Alice strolled over to the chair in which Myra sat.

"Good morning," she said.

Myra closed the periodical and smiled. "Good morning. How are you?"

"I'm fine. You're looking awfully perky today."

Myra laughed. "That's because I'm finished with my dialysis. I'm waiting for my husband."

"He and the children didn't stay this time?"

"No. I was on my own."

At the troubled expression that stole across Myra's face, Alice sat on the plastic chair next to hers and asked, "Is something wrong?"

Myra smiled ruefully. "Actually, something could be very, very right."

"Something *right* made you frown?" Alice asked with a chuckle.

Myra took a long breath and hesitantly said, "Yesterday . . . someone offered me a kidney for a transplant."

Alice gasped. "Oh my goodness!"

"I know. It's unbelievable."

"Who was it? Someone in your family?"

"No. It's one of the volunteers at this hospital."

"Oh, you're friends with one of the volunteers here?"

"Rosalind Westwood and I aren't exactly friends," Myra replied. "We talked a few times when she was bringing around books and magazines or when she had the candy cart, and we became somewhat friendly. Then, yesterday, I ran into her when I brought my daughter to the hospital to check into the training to become a volunteer, and she told me she had decided to give me one of her kidneys if we're a match."

The magnitude of that act of generosity left Alice

speechless. Alice had met Rosalind Westwood a few times the same way Myra had—when Rosalind brought the candy cart or reading materials around to the unit in which Alice was working. But Alice didn't know her well enough to fathom why she would make such a generous offer to someone she knew only as a patient.

Myra laughed. "Believe me, I understand your surprise. Having somebody I barely know offer me her kidney is unreal."

"Are you going to have the transplant?" Alice asked, finally finding her voice.

"We haven't yet done the tests to see if she's a match. But our blood types are the same. So that's a good start."

"Well," Alice said, still at a loss for words. "That's wonderful."

"It is and it isn't." She paused, and when she spoke again her voice had been lowered to a whisper. "Really, Alice, to have someone I barely know offer me a kidney out of the blue like that . . ." She shook her head. "I have to wonder if her offer is even sincere." She lowered her voice again. "Or if she isn't a little odd."

Alice couldn't help it; she chuckled again. "I've met Rosalind. I don't think she's odd."

"Maybe not, but if I believe her and seriously consider her offer and she doesn't go through with it, I will have built up my hopes for nothing. We've been waiting for a kidney for as long as I've been on dialysis. My baby Jeff," she said, cringing as she probably remembered the way in which Alice had met Jeff, "is only six years old. With a new kidney I could do so much . . ."

Her voice caught and tears filled her eyes, but Alice knew what she was about to say. An active six-year-old boy needed an active mother, and right now she couldn't be the mother she wanted to be.

Myra composed herself and said, "I'm just saying it would be terrible for Rosalind to dangle the possibility of a normal life in front of me, and then snatch it away when she realizes she hasn't thought through all the consequences of donating one of her kidneys."

Alice nodded, not really able to comment on whether Rosalind truly had considered all the implications.

"At the same time, if this is a sincere offer, I want to accept it if only to be a part of Jeff's life the way I was with my other children when they were younger."

"I understand." Seeing Brett Swanson's red minivan pull into a parking space at the entrance, Alice rose. "Good luck with this."

Myra caught Alice's hand. "I'm sorry. I shouldn't have unloaded on you like that. It's just that it's so unbelievable to me that someone would be so generous that I couldn't stop myself from blurting out the whole story."

"I don't mind," Alice said. "I'm always available to listen." She wouldn't give advice. All the choices had to be Myra's, but from her years of experience as a nurse, Alice knew that sometimes talking out a problem gave a person a clear vision of what he or she should do. As long as Myra didn't ask Alice to make the decision for her, Alice would be happy to listen.

That afternoon, as Louise helped Jane prepare dinner, Jane said, "I may have forgotten to mention it, but the inspection for the inn is approaching."

"Did you get the notice in today's mail?" Louise asked.

"No," Jane said. "But the inspection is usually around Memorial Day."

Jane went on with an animated discussion of all the things she needed to do for the inspection, but Louise's mind drifted. The reference to the holiday reminded her of Florence Simpson, and she couldn't focus her attention on her sister's comments.

The fact that Florence hadn't contacted Louise as she was supposed to should have made Louise happy. Instead, she had the foolish sense that Florence was toying with her. She tried to tell herself to stop worrying, but even throughout dinner with her sisters that evening, Florence invaded her thoughts.

After the kitchen was cleaned and the sisters

retreated to the front porch, Alice quietly told them of Rosalind's offer of a kidney to Myra, and Louise forgot about Florence. Alice used only first names so that she didn't violate anyone's privacy, but that didn't change the impact of her story. Louise could hardly believe what she was hearing.

"My goodness!" she gasped at the same time that Jane's eyes widened in wonder.

"That was my reaction too," Alice said, setting the porch swing in motion with her foot. The sun was beginning to set, but the evening was warm as the town settled in for the night. "I have to admit I was careful about what I said to Myra. I don't want to influence her decision."

Louise frowned, studying her sister for a few seconds. Alice had changed out of the pants and smock she wore to work and into comfortable black shorts and a coral print blouse, but she didn't look relaxed. Also, from the way Alice's brown eyes softened with compassion when she spoke, Louise knew there was something more she wasn't telling them.

Louise asked, "You mean she actually has to consider whether she would get the transplant?"

"I would think she'd jump at the chance," Jane said.

Alice stopped the swing and Louise frowned. Alice only did that when the conversation was so important to her that she wanted to focus. Alice might want to avoid influencing Myra, but, just as

Louise had suspected, her sister already cared enough about Myra that this situation weighed heavily on her mind.

Though Alice had lived in Acorn Hill almost all her life, Louise and Jane had lived in Philadelphia and San Francisco respectively. They returned for their father's funeral, not expecting to stay. But the pull of settling in their hometown was strong. Transforming their family home into a bed-and-breakfast made it possible for Jane and Louise to remain in Acorn Hill and begin new lives.

Louise put up most of the money for the remodeling, but her sisters were equals in the venture. An experienced chef, Jane made the breakfasts that caused the wonderful "word of mouth" advertising that brought in many a new guest, and when the inn coffers ran low, Alice frequently deposited a portion of her nurse's paycheck into the bed-and-breakfast accounts.

When it came to family matters, however, as the oldest, Louise felt a strong tug on her heart to be a mentor and confidante to her sisters. With their father's death, they had found themselves without an anchor. Louise knew she could never replace Daniel Howard. His years of experience as pastor of Grace Chapel gave him a wisdom Louise would never attribute to herself. But she did feel she should be the person her younger sisters could come to for help or advice, and she was becoming quite skilled in reading their moods. She said a quick, silent prayer that Alice would confide her feelings and that Louise would be able to guide her.

Finally Alice said, "There are a few things to be considered, not the least of which is Rosalind's sincerity."

Jane gasped. "Myra thinks Rosalind offered her a kidney as a joke?"

Alice shook her head. "Not a joke. It's more that Myra worries that Rosalind hasn't thought everything through."

Especially attentive now, Louise said, "I can't believe that anyone who works at a hospital would be that negligent."

"Rosalind doesn't really work at the hospital," Alice replied. "She's a volunteer. I guess that's why Myra worries about whether she's considered all the facts."

"Because she might not know them?" Jane asked.

Alice nodded. "Yes. I think Myra's afraid that Rosalind could take back her offer once she gets all the facts and realizes she could be the one on dialysis if her remaining kidney fails. That risk is small, but it still may be something Rosalind never considered, something that might cause her to change her mind."

"Even if Myra doesn't get a transplant," Louise observed, "she is doing okay with dialysis."

"Yes. But a transplant gives her the hope of being able to be a bigger part of her son Jeff's life."

"Her youngest child?" Jane asked.

"Yes," Alice said. "The other night I told you that I thought he was six, and I was right. I'm guessing he's active in Little League, and I'm sure Myra wants to take him on vacations. Show him the ocean. Go to an amusement park. Take him to Washington, DC, to show him our nation's capital."

"She can't do that on dialysis?" Jane asked.

"She could if she sets up dialysis sessions at a facility near where she and her family are vacationing," Alice replied. "But even with dialysis, she'll always be more tired than she would be if she had a healthy kidney. That's the upside of getting the transplant. No more dialysis and lots more energy."

Louise tilted her head. "That makes sense."

"So with the transplant, she'll be able to do everything her son wants to do?" Jane asked.

"Just about," Alice said.

Louise tilted her head in question. It was obvious Alice was still troubled. "You want Rosalind's offer to be genuine."

"Yes. If Rosalind has a good family history, the chances of her remaining kidney failing are small, and the donor part of the transplant is fairly simple because they do laparoscopic surgery," Alice explained. "If Rosalind really wants to be a donor, there's no reason for her to be afraid."

"Maybe she isn't."

"Myra is the skeptic," Alice said, "not I. But I understand her thinking. Rosalind also has children to consider."

"In other words," Louise said, "the transplant decision is a process, and at any step of the way Rosalind could change her mind. That means Myra could get her hopes up for nothing."

"Yes," Alice said.

"So Rosalind's offer may not be as promising as it looked at first glance," Jane said.

"No."

The three sisters were quiet for a while. Louise hoped with all her heart that Rosalind wouldn't change her mind. Louise would have made any sacrifice for her husband, Eliot, if there had been a chance he could live a few more years. But she also knew that as a health-care professional, Alice couldn't interfere, and Alice's role in this was Louise's primary concern.

Louise peeked over at her sister and saw that Alice appeared more relaxed, as if talking out the situation had calmed her. She knew it for certain when Alice changed the subject.

"Speaking of decisions, did Florence show up today to see if you would help with her talent show?" Alice shifted her right foot and set the swing in motion again.

Louise held back a sigh of relief. Though she wasn't happy about discussing the talent show, she was glad that Alice felt free to move on.

"No, Florence didn't stop by, and the whole situation seems odd to me. First, I cannot shake the feeling that Florence has some hidden purpose for wanting to do this talent show. Then she told me that she would drop by on Tuesday to talk about it some more, but she didn't show up Tuesday or today."

"Maybe she changed her mind?" Jane said, a hint of hopefulness in her voice.

Alice laughed. "Not Florence. I know from my experience of working with her on the church board that when she gets a bee in her bonnet, you better believe she follows through."

"Exactly," Louise said. "That's why her not stopping by is so confusing."

"Have you decided what to do?"

"Half of me feels I should participate in the talent show because I'm part of the community. But the other half can't get past the feeling I have that Florence has an agenda of some sort, and I'm not sure I want to be a part of one of Florence's schemes."

"Good point," Jane agreed, rising from her seat next to Alice on the swing. "Are we ready for dessert yet?"

"Absolutely! What did you make?" Alice asked.

Louise was further gratified to see Alice brighten at the mention of dessert. If a little dessert could make her feel better, Louise was all for it.

"Chocolate cake."

Alice groaned. "Jane, I thought we agreed to be more careful about what we ate."

"This is a special treat. We've all been so good with our eating lately that I thought it was time we had a little splurge."

"But chocolate cake is *sooo* fattening," Alice said. "I'm going to have to increase the time I walk with Vera in the mornings."

"That's much better than depriving yourself of special treats," Jane said with a laugh.

"And it's only every once in a while," Louise coaxed.

"See, even Louise agrees that special treats are good."

Alice shook her head in dismay, then she grinned. "Okay, give me a piece of cake. Later tonight I'll call Vera and tell her that we have to add another fifteen minutes to our walk."

The next day, Louise was strolling along Chapel Road on her way to the Coffee Shop. It was a beautiful May morning, peaceful and quiet because school hadn't yet let out for the summer. A light breeze stirred dust on the sidewalk. The sun poured through the leaves of the trees that lined the street.

She was glad Alice had talked about the dialysis patient who was considering a transplant. She knew Alice probably missed discussing her patients and her feelings for them with their father.

So it was good she had become as comfortable sharing the good and the bad with Louise and Jane as she had been with him. In fact, Louise was beginning to like the position of confidante.

Satisfied that she had done the right thing for Alice the night before, Louise felt more strongly than ever that it was God's will that she be here in Acorn Hill.

Then she saw Florence leaving Fred's Hardware and stepping toward Chapel Road, which meant she still had to cross traffic to encounter Louise.

Louise increased her pace and tried to duck into the Coffee Shop before Florence noticed her, but she was two seconds too late.

"Louise! Louise!" Florence called, waving her hand. "Wait up!"

Louise stopped and Florence crossed Chapel Road and walked up to her. "I'm sorry I didn't get back to you on Tuesday like I said I would. But I had some plumbing problems. I only got everything fixed late yesterday."

"I'm glad you got your problems resolved."

Florence chuckled. "Me too! I thought I was going to have to rent a room at your inn to be able to take a shower."

Knowing Florence was only chatting this way now because she wanted Louise's help for her talent show, Louise merely smiled.

"Anyway," Florence said, finally getting to the point. "Have you thought about the talent show?"

"Yes."

"You've probably guessed I would be asking you to accompany the talent."

Louise nodded. "Yes. The thought did occur to me, but I haven't made a decision."

Florence shaded her eyes from the early morning sun. "We can't do this without you."

Louise said nothing while she reviewed the situation. Florence's motives might be self-serving, but this morning Louise was particularly happy to be a member of this community. Though it would be an imposition on her time, she appreciated that she had a talent that could be useful, and she knew she should volunteer.

In addition, she couldn't stop thinking about Rosalind, the woman Alice had told them was willing to donate a kidney to a stranger. If her offer was sincere, she was a good Samaritan to be sure. Going beyond giving time or money to help a stranger, she was giving a part of herself.

Counting her blessings and realizing that she could do so much more, Louise couldn't refuse Florence's request. If the people of Acorn Hill wanted a talent show, Louise would pitch in to do her share.

"Florence, I will be happy to be a part of your production."

Florence's eyes widened as if she had expected Louise to say no. "Great. Oh my gosh! I can't wait to tell everyone about the show."

"You haven't told anyone?"

"No. I wanted to be sure I had your support. But with you behind me, I will tell them now. Since this week is shot, tryouts will be on Monday night at the elementary school auditorium, where we'll have the show. I'll need for you to be there, ready to play anything that the people auditioning request."

"But on Monday nights, I . . ." Louise stopped herself, thinking again of Rosalind and her generous offer. Though Louise's stomach fluttered once again at the cavalier way Florence assumed Louise was "behind" her, Louise knew she could give up a few Monday nights of resting after mingling with the weekend guests at the inn. "I will see you Monday night."

"Seven thirty sharp. Be there!" Florence commanded, then turned and hurried away.

Louise stared at Florence's back as she walked down Hill Street. She couldn't believe Florence hadn't said thank you. Instead, she issued an order for Louise to "be there."

With a sigh, Louise turned and walked into the Coffee Shop, reminding herself that Florence wasn't the easiest person in the world with whom to work. But it didn't matter. Louise had made the commitment for reasons that had very little to do with Florence. She appreciated being home. She appreciated the gifts and talents God had blessed her with. But more than either of those,

Rosalind's amazing generosity inspired her to be a better person.

So what if it was a little extra work? So what if Florence was a tad difficult? Surely working with her wouldn't be *that* bad.

Chapter Three

A lice stepped out of the hospital cafeteria line and walked toward the crowded seating area. As cafeterias went, Potterston Hospital's was pleasant enough. The walls had been freshly painted in a soothing pale aqua color, and tables with peach plastic chairs provided diners with a comfortable place to enjoy their meals.

As Alice glanced around, searching for a place to sit, she noticed Rosalind Westwood only a few feet away, also scanning the room for a seat. Short and thin, with pretty dark hair that shone in the sunlight pouring in through the wall of windows, and wearing a green top over tan slacks, Rosalind was the model of a hospital volunteer—neat, capable and cheerful.

Her generosity to Myra was far from ordinary, and Alice couldn't stop the curiosity that bubbled up inside her about why she had made such an offer. She also couldn't quell her fear that Rosalind might not realize the full import of her proposal to Myra and could back out.

Something inside Alice nudged her to walk over

to Rosalind and suggest they sit together. Her father had told her that this odd feeling was sometimes God's way of speaking to us. But she couldn't believe God would ask her to overstep the boundaries of propriety. She didn't feel comfortable discussing patients, and that was what she would be doing if she began talking about Rosalind's donating a kidney to Myra.

She saw a group of X-ray technicians rising from their table. Without hesitating, she headed for the emptying space and set her tray on the table at the same time that another tray slid on across from hers.

She glanced up and Rosalind smiled at her. "You're Alice Howard, right?"

Alice nodded. "Yes. I've worked on your floor once or twice when I was filling in for someone," she said, referring to the fact that the hospital volunteers were assigned a floor, though they rotated duties.

"I remember you," Rosalind said as she sat.

Alice took a quick breath and sat across from Rosalind, wondering if dining together was a good idea. Still, it would be rude simply to leave Rosalind, even though another table was opening up. Besides, she knew enough about herself to have faith that she absolutely would not bring up the subject of Myra Swanson.

"So, how have you been?" Alice asked, unrolling her silverware from the napkin in which it was wrapped.

"I'm doing very well. I love volunteering here. I meet so many people I wouldn't ordinarily meet. It's great."

Seeing the sincerity in Rosalind's eyes, Alice smiled.

"But I don't envy you your job," Rosalind said. "Not only does nursing seem like a demanding profession with lots of responsibility, but also every time I turn around, *you're* in a different department."

"That's because I'm part-time. I don't have a permanent department. I float."

"That's got to be tough."

"No, I like it. I also meet all kinds of interesting patients, but more than that, I'm getting to know most of the hospital staff. I'm getting a chance to talk to people whom I would typically only pass in the hall."

"That's true. So how does your schedule work?"

"Usually, I get an assignment at the beginning of every week, but for the next four weeks I'm filling in for someone who is taking a long vacation."

"Oh, cool. After spending weeks in the same department you really will get to know the people who work there."

"Yes."

"So, what department is it?"

Alice hesitated. Once she mentioned the dialysis unit, the conversation could get awkward. But she also knew that being evasive might only make matters worse, or clue Rosalind in that Alice knew about her offer to Myra.

"I'm in the dialysis unit."

Rosalind's eyes widened. "Really? I know most of the patients there because they've all been on my floor at one time or another."

"Really?"

"In fact, I've come to like and admire so many of them. Do you know Myra Swanson and her family? They remind me of my family when my kids were younger. Like Myra, I have two boys and a girl."

"Yes, I know Myra, and the Swansons do seem like lovely people."

"Oh, you've met them too."

Alice nodded.

"It's such a shame that she's so ill when she has such a young son."

"You said your children are older?" Alice asked, attempting to change the subject without possibly offending Rosalind by reminding her that they shouldn't be discussing a patient.

"Yes." She laughed. "My *baby* is in his second year of college."

"Wow!"

"They grow up quickly." She paused, then hesitantly said, "That's part of the reason that after a lot of soul searching, I volunteered to donate a kidney for a transplant for Myra."

Alice wasn't exactly sure what to say, but she

knew that in the end honesty was always the best policy. She couldn't pretend not to know something she knew. At some point, the deception would come back to haunt her.

"Actually, I know. Myra told me."

"She did? That's a good sign. She was so shocked when I first spoke with her about it that I didn't think she'd ever adjust to the news. I'm glad she's coming to accept that I really want to donate a kidney to her."

Alice only smiled. As she and Rosalind began to eat, conversation about Myra's reaction was put aside. But now that Rosalind had freely disclosed her offer, Alice couldn't see any reason why they couldn't discuss Rosalind's being a donor, as long as they didn't tiptoe back into discussing Myra. At this point Alice's main concern was Rosalind's ability to keep the commitment. It was quite possible that through the right conversation Alice could get an indication from Rosalind whether she was the kind of person who kept her promises and who wouldn't disappoint Myra.

"I'm sorry. I don't mean to be rude. I know this is private, and you don't have to answer if you don't want to . . . but donating a kidney is a big step."

Rosalind chuckled. "Yes, it is. I can imagine that when this gets out, a lot of people in the hospital are going to be curious."

Alice grimaced. Was this another reason that

might cause seemingly happy-go-lucky Rosalind to back out? "Without a doubt," was Alice's response.

"There's really no mystery about my decision to be Myra's donor. Not only do I understand her life as a mother, but also I have an older cousin who was married to a woman who was on dialysis for years. Everyone in our family was tested—even in-laws—but no one was a match. Ultimately, she died from complications of her kidney disease."

"I'm so sorry."

Rosalind took a quiet breath. "It was very sad because her entire life had been a struggle. What made the situation even sadder, though, was that at her funeral we realized from talking to her father's side of the family that none of them had even been tested to see if they could have been donors."

"Donating a kidney isn't an easy decision," Alice gently reminded Rosalind.

Rosalind caught Alice's gaze. "I thought that, too, until I realized that the aunts, uncles and cousins who refused to be tested were desperately sorry they hadn't tried to save her. They were filled with a regret that made their grief nearly unbearable."

"But you don't really know Myra," Alice pointed out.

"You're right, but I do know that she has a husband and children who need her." Rosalind paused and sighed. "There are a lot of parallels between Myra's situation and the one in my family. But every day I go home and look at the pictures on my mantel of my three happy children. It doesn't seem fair that Myra's unable to be the mother that she wants to be."

"Aren't you worried that something might happen?" Alice asked.

She shook her head. "The surgery is the least of my worries. As a nurse, you know that the procedure for the donor has been improved. It's done laparoscopically now. I don't face a lot of risk."

"That's true," Alice said. "The incision is small, and the hospital stay is minimal."

"Yes. Some people are home a day or two after surgery. Lots are back to work within a week. My only real risk is that my remaining kidney could fail. Since there's no history of kidney disease, diabetes, or cancer in my immediate family, for me that's a minimal risk."

Fully understanding Rosalind's decision, Alice said, "Still, I think you're very kind."

"My cousin lost his wife. His children lost their mother. That alerted me to the fact that we all need to be more compassionate."

Alice smiled. "That's a wonderful way to look at it."

"If I'm a match, the surgery is on. I'm not going to change my mind. I *want* to do this. It's the right thing to do."

That night, Alice related the story of her encounter with Rosalind, and both Louise and Jane were as convinced as Alice that someone such as Rosalind, who had watched the wife of a family member die for lack of a donor, wouldn't back out. If Rosalind was a match, and Myra overcame her doubts about Rosalind and chose to have the transplant, Rosalind would do as she promised.

Feeling much better about the situation, Alice drove to the hospital Friday morning and entered the dialysis unit with a smile. She wasn't surprised to see Myra, who seemed to have a Monday, Wednesday, Friday schedule for her dialysis.

"Good morning," Alice said cheerfully.

"Good morning," Myra said wearily. "How are you today, Alice?"

"I'm fine," Alice said, "but you sound terrible. Are you okay?"

"No. I feel as terrible as I sound."

Alice quickly scanned the monitor on the dialysis machine and found nothing unusual. "Is something wrong?"

"Physically I'm fine. Emotionally, though, I'm a mess. One day I decide that Rosalind is serious, a transplant is worth the risks and I'm happy. The next day I'm riddled with doubt and overcome with worry."

"I understand."

Myra sighed. "And this horrible oscillating

could all be for nothing if Rosalind isn't a match. She's going ahead with the testing so that if she isn't a match, I can stop agonizing. But if she is, my decision comes down to one very important assessment."

"Whether she's committed?" Alice asked.

"First, I have to decide whether to take Rosalind's offer."

Working not to overstep the boundaries of her position, Alice carefully said, "But you already said you wanted a transplant because of Jeff. It's the only way to get the life you want to live."

"Sure, for me it's great." Myra closed her eyes. "But, Alice, how can I take another mother's kidney?"

"Oh, Myra, you're looking at this as if you expect something to go wrong."

"I have to. Rosalind has children too. They may be grown, but they need their mother strong and healthy."

Alice considered what Myra had said for a second, then said, "You know what? I think that's Rosalind's end of the decision. I think your best course of action would be to focus only on your end of things and let Rosalind's decision be her own."

"Even if I do leave that part of the decision entirely to Rosalind, I'm still left with the possibility that she could back out at the last minute."

Alice paused in her work. Rosalind's backing out had been her greatest fear until she spoke with

Rosalind the day before. Knowing she couldn't interfere, but still wanting to lead Myra down the right path, she said, "Have you spoken with Rosalind about why she's agreed to be a donor?"

Myra nodded. "She told me that she realizes she was lucky to be able to be a full-time mother to her children. She also told me about her cousin's wife dying for want of a healthy kidney."

"And you still worry that she could back out?"

"I'm not married to her cousin. I'm not any sort of relative at all. I'm not even a friend. I'm simply somebody she knows. She has no obligation to do this. In the last second, she could realize that, remember her own family and change her mind."

Alice studied Myra for a second. "Do you really think Rosalind would do that?"

Myra shrugged. "That's the problem. I don't know her. I don't know what she would do. And I don't want to get my hopes up and the kids' hopes up, only to have them shot down at the last second."

They were quiet while Alice checked Myra's blood pressure, then Myra softly said, "What would *you* do?"

Alice thought about the best way to phrase her answer, then said, "I don't know what I would do, but I also have to tell you, Myra, that I can't give you advice. It's not my place to make your decision for you, but more than that, I don't know you or your circumstances well enough."

Looking contrite, Myra said, "I'm sorry. I shouldn't have asked."

Alice refrained from breathing a sigh of relief. "That's okay."

"But that doesn't mean that you can't give me an opinion."

Alice laughed. "Now, you're walking along a fine line."

"I know, but I'm sort of desperate. I've heard the other nurses talking about how kind it was of you to fill in for the nurse who's out for a month. They say that you're supposed to be part-time but you fill in so much out of the goodness of your heart that you're almost working full-time. And since you work in every department of the hospital, you have to be on your toes all the time and know a little bit of everything."

Alice chuckled. "That's certainly true."

"The other nurses really like and trust you."

Taken aback by the high praise, Alice said, "Thank you for telling me."

Myra grimaced. "I'm telling you because it sort of suits my purpose. I'm not looking for advice. I'm looking only for an opinion. I won't quote you. I won't come back and say I told you so." She took a quick breath. "But if you've worked on Rosalind's floor and know her . . . what would you think? Would you have confidence in her?"

"Oh, Myra, I don't feel comfortable giving that kind of opinion."

"But you do know her?"

"I know her only because of having worked on the floor on which she volunteers."

"So do you think she's trustworthy?"

Realizing she could probably answer Myra's question as long as her reply was properly phrased, Alice said, "I don't know what your decision should be. I'm not giving advice, but Rosalind appears to me to be a kind-hearted person. If she made an offer to me, I would consider it sincere."

Chapter Four

Saturday morning Louise awakened to the sweet sound of birds chirping outside her window. Warm rays of sunlight poured into her bedroom. The floral wallpaper and green trim on the walls shouted of spring. The combination of the birds, the sun and her beautiful room instantly put her in a wonderful mood. The Rusnaks, guests who had arrived the night before, were only at the inn for one night, and Jane had volunteered to check them out after serving them breakfast. Louise had the entire morning to herself.

After dressing for the day in a simple beige skirt, which she paired with a sunny yellow sweater set, she made her way downstairs humming a bouncy tune that she suddenly realized could be the opening bars of a new song. Delighted, she walked to the reception desk in the front hall. Decorated with gold-and-cream wallpaper, the registration area for guests was elegant yet simple. She picked up a fountain pen and a tablet to jot down the notes from her song. As she did, she noticed a telephone message for her from Florence. When she lifted it from the small stack, she saw that the one beneath it was also for her from Florence. So was the one beneath that.

She let out a disgruntled sigh. She knew Florence could be persistent, but getting three messages from seven o'clock to eight o'clock was simply ridiculous.

"Have you seen these?" she said, waving the messages as she entered the kitchen.

Jane turned from the dishwasher. Louise's normally casual but still quite presentable sister was dressed in faded jeans, a baby-blue T-shirt and huge yellow rubber gloves.

"What on earth is going on with you?" Louise said before Jane could answer her question about Florence's messages.

"You know that the inn is to be inspected in a few weeks?"

"Yes," Louise said, "but you said you hadn't yet gotten the actual notice."

"Not yet. But I will soon, and the county has a new inspector. I heard from Clara Horn, who heard from a friend of hers who owns a bed-and-breakfast in Lancaster, that the new inspector is a stickler for details."

Louise glanced around. "I can't see what you are worried about. Your kitchen is sparkling clean."

"Yeah, well, if it isn't, we could be in big trouble. Clara was told that if he finds even one little thing wrong he takes it as what he calls 'probable cause' to inspect the rest of the inn."

Louise frowned. "We don't eat or cook in the bedrooms."

"No, we don't," Jane agreed. "But apparently this inspector is a clean freak of some sort who likes to inspect everything."

"Maybe he's just nosy," Alice said as she pushed through the swinging door to the kitchen. Louise remembered that because Tuesday had been Alice's day off that week, she had to work this Saturday. Wearing her nurse's uniform, with her hair tucked behind her ears, she looked ready for her day.

Shaking her head at Alice's guess, Louise chuckled and walked to the counter, which held a carafe of coffee.

Jane sighed. "Nosy or not, he's got the power to close us down."

Louise watched Alice glance around the kitchen, just as Louise had done a minute before. "I don't see how."

"That's just the point," Jane said, retrieving a bucket from the floor beside the sink and beginning to fill it with water. "This inspector claims that bed-and-breakfast owners get lazy because of

48

praise from their guests; they feel they do everything right."

"And he's out to prove us wrong," Louise speculated, pouring coffee into one of the cups beside the carafe.

"Yes."

"It sounds like gossip to me," Alice said. "I wouldn't take it seriously."

"It might be gossip," Jane said, "but I've decided I would rather be safe than sorry. After all, this is my area of expertise, my contribution. I don't want to let you guys down."

"Let us down!" Alice gasped. "My goodness, Jane, your cooking is a main attraction of the inn. You could never let us down. You're a major asset."

"I agree," Louise said, "but I also understand your wanting to make sure the place is in tip-top shape for the inspector. Do what you feel you need to do. I will help as much as I can."

Jane turned from the sink with a laugh. "Really?"

"Of course."

Jane laughed again. "It's eight o'clock in the morning and only the day after you agreed to help Florence, yet you already have three phone messages. I don't think you're going to have a lot of free time until after the talent show."

Alice gaped at Louise. "Three phone messages?"

"Since seven o'clock this morning," Jane said,

amusement in her voice. "Florence keeps coming up with wonderful ideas, and she wants Louise to 'jot them down.'"

Louise said, "She thinks I'm her secretary?"

"More like her assistant."

Alice grabbed her purse and headed for the door. "Well, Jane, you have fun today cleaning things that don't really need cleaning, and, Louise, it looks like you better get yourself a thick notebook and at least two pens."

As Alice left by way of the back door, Louise took a seat at the kitchen table. "This whole production is already getting out of hand."

"Florence has a way of making things more work than they need to be."

"Then I will simply have to rein her in."

"Good luck with that," Jane said. "What would you like for breakfast?"

Louise tilted her head as she thought about that. "How about leftovers from the guest breakfast?"

"Sorry, since we had only Mr. and Mrs. Rusnak, I made them individual platters of eggs and bacon." Jane grinned. "But a positive way to look at that is that I can prepare anything you like."

Louise rose from the table. "That's okay. I think I only want a bagel."

"Getting down to your fighting weight for when you face Florence?" Jane asked with another grin, this one even more devilish.

Louise shook her head in exasperation. "I'm not

going to fight with Florence. I will explain that perhaps she's getting a bit carried away."

Jane laughed. "As I said. Good luck with that."

As Louise prepared and ate her bagel, she listened to Jane take inventory of cleaning projects in the kitchen. The first order of business was to make the kitchen so clean the inspector wouldn't feel the need to go into the guest rooms, but—just in case—she also added cleaning projects outside the kitchen to the list she was keeping in her head.

With her bagel eaten and her place at the table tidied, Louise went to her room to freshen up, then said a quick good-bye to Jane before she headed off to see Florence.

The Simpsons' house, a handsome red brick dwelling surrounded by flowers in a well-tended yard, suggested that Florence and her husband were financially comfortable. Louise pressed the doorbell, and Florence answered on the first ring.

"Oh, Louise! Thank goodness you're here. We have a million things to do."

"Actually, Florence," Louise said, accepting Florence's invitation to step inside her foyer. "That's why I'm here. I don't really have time to function as a personal secretary."

Florence frowned. "I never asked you to be my secretary."

"No. You didn't ask me to be your secretary. However, the three phone calls this morning lead me to believe you will be giving me tasks beyond what I agreed to do as accompanist."

Florence waved her hand in dismissal. "Oh pish-posh! Those were nothing important. Just me thinking out loud," she said with a laugh. "Forget I called. Sometimes I get overenthusiastic."

Knowing that was true and also knowing from having participated in many productions that enthusiasm can make more work, Louise said, "I think that's true. A talent show can be a won-derful way to showcase everyone's talent and also for everyone to have fun. But," she added, being careful to say this in such a way it didn't hurt Florence's feelings, "having worked on many programs, I can tell you that it's always better to keep amateur productions as simple as possible."

Florence gasped. "Simple? What fun would that be?"

"I'm just saying that even a simple show can have big complications and problems. Because this is your first attempt at putting one together, my advice is that a simple show done well will be much better received than a complicated show where many things go wrong because you didn't have time to anticipate them."

Louise watched as Florence considered that. "I see what you're saying."

Louise relaxed. "Good."

"But I'm still going to do the fancy show. I have

a good feeling about this, Louise, like everything's going to be just wonderful."

Louise opened her mouth to argue, saw the determined look in Florence's eyes and closed it once again. There was no point in arguing any further, particularly since Louise knew that enough things would likely go wrong and Florence would be forced by circumstances to pare down her production.

"I have a lesson this morning," Louise said, turning to the door.

"Don't forget our first tryouts are Monday night at seven thirty."

"I haven't forgotten," Louise said as she twisted the doorknob. She left Florence's house thinking about how odd it was that as much as Florence was convinced things would work out okay, Louise was equally convinced something terrible was about to happen.

Still, having something happen would actually be good. Florence would be forced to pull back on her plans and then, perhaps, everything would be okay.

Or at least that was what Louise told herself as she headed back to Grace Chapel Inn for her piano lesson.

That evening, when Alice returned home from work, the house was in chaos. Everything that was usually neatly arranged on the desk in the front hall was scattered in disarray on a nearby table, as if Jane had been in the middle of dusting when she was needed elsewhere and never got the chance to return. The same was the case in the living room. The ferns had been removed from the marble-topped table. The throw pillows had been taken from the burgundy-colored sofa and matching overstuffed chair, and they sat on a side table, as if Jane had been vacuuming the upholstery but then scurried away. The Queen Anne chairs had been pulled away from the table in the formal dining room, and the violet-and-ivory velvet shawl had been removed from the piano in the parlor.

It looked as if someone had ransacked the place.

Alice finally ended up in the kitchen, where she found Jane fanatically scrubbing an old pot.

"What are you doing?" Alice asked in amazement.

Jane wiped the sweat from her brow as she turned from the sink. "At the moment, I'm not sure."

Alice laughed. "I can believe that. You've got projects going in every room of the house." She glanced around. "Where's Louise?"

"She took a walk out to Fairy Pond to enjoy this beautiful weather."

Alice cautiously said, "What's for dinner?"

"Oh my gosh! I didn't even get anything out of the freezer."

"That's okay—" Alice began, but Jane interrupted her.

"No. It's not okay. But I have some chili in the freezer and a loaf of onion bread that I can thaw."

Alice patted Jane's shoulder in an effort to calm her. "I'll get the chili and the onion bread. You sit and catch your breath. While I prepare these, you and I will create a list of things you really need to do."

Jane glanced forlornly at the old pot in the sink. "I guess I didn't need to try to make that shine."

"Do you ever use it?"

Jane shook her head.

"That's why we're going to make a list. There's no sense cleaning things the inspector won't care about."

Jane nodded as Alice opened the freezer and pulled out a container marked "chili" and a loaf of bread. Reading the little tag, she saw that it was the onion bread, and she brought both to the table.

"The chili can be thawed in the microwave."

Alice smiled. "You may have been our primary cook since we opened the inn, but I can still throw together a supper."

"I'm sorry, Alice."

Alice laughed. "I wasn't offended by your comment."

"No, I mean about you having to make dinner after working all day."

"I'm not upset about that either," Alice said with another laugh. "What I'm upset about is your being so frantic. This inspector really will frazzle you if you don't get organized."

Jane straightened in her seat and Alice knew she had challenged Jane just as she had planned to do. In the past, Alice had seen that Jane didn't respond well to the kind of vague threat that the inspector presented, so Alice subtly got her to see the inspector's visit instead as a challenge that could be met successfully with the proper preparation.

Jane rose to grab a tablet from a holder by the wall phone and returned to the table. "Okay, let's see. First off, I need to make sure the kitchen is spotless and organized."

"Exactly. Everything you get done after that is gravy."

"Except for the dining room, since that's where we serve our food."

Sliding the chili into the microwave, Alice grimaced. "Oops! Forgot that the place we serve the food is also included in his inspection."

"He really isn't supposed to go into the guest rooms or baths unless he feels he has a reason to."

"So maybe the smart thing to do is simply not give him a reason to?" Alice suggested, undoing the tie of the plastic bag for the bread.

"Yes."

"And that means focusing on the kitchen."

Sounding relieved, Jane said, "Yes, focus on the kitchen."

• • •

When Louise returned from her long walk, Alice had the kitchen smelling of delicious chili and warm bread. Jane also had a written list of things to do before the inspector's appearance. The tasks were listed in order of importance with kitchen items first.

After they ate their chili, Louise volunteered to bring dessert to the front porch so both Jane and Alice could get a rest. She set plates of angel food cake with fresh strawberry slices and a dollop of low-fat whipped cream on the small wooden tables beside the comfortable outdoor furniture, then sat down.

"So how was your day, Alice?" Louise asked before she took her first bite.

Alice hesitated, then said, "It was . . . okay."

Hearing the note of uncertainty in Alice's voice, Louise asked, "Did something happen with your kidney patient?"

Before Alice could reply, Jane groaned with misery. "I'm terrible! I've been so wrapped up in the inspection I forgot all about your patient."

"No, Myra is fine. But I talked with Rosalind again."

"To make sure she hadn't changed her mind?" Louise asked.

"No. To make sure my impression of her was correct. When I saw Myra on Friday, I didn't give her advice, but I did give an opinion. I told her that if Rosalind offered me something, I would believe her offer was sincere. Unfortunately, the more I thought about it, the more I realized that spending one lunch hour with Rosalind didn't mean I knew her enough to say for sure she wouldn't reconsider. But luckily, when I was taking my afternoon break, so was Rosalind. I decided to sit with her and have another conversation to see if I still felt as comfortable."

Jane asked, "And did you?"

"It's the oddest thing," Alice said. "When I talk with her I have absolutely no doubt she is committed to helping Myra, someone she barely knows."

"That's impressive," Louise said.

"She really lives out her faith," Alice said.

They spoke for a few minutes of Rosalind's incredible generosity, and when the conversation about Rosalind died out, Jane turned to Louise. "How about Florence?" she asked. "I never got a chance to ask about your visit with her this morning. Did you convince her to simplify her plans?"

"Sadly, no."

Alice looked from Jane to Louise. "I feel as if I missed something."

"I explained to Jane this morning and then tried to explain to Florence that productions like this are best kept simple because there are many things that can go wrong, and during the week before the production, you can't be polishing dance numbers.

You need your time and energy for last-minute problems." She paused and frowned. "Hearing myself say that, I realize I wasn't that clear with Florence this morning. So if she doesn't understand that I was protecting her from problems down the road, it's my fault."

"Maybe you should talk with her again tomorrow."

"I think I will wait and see what happens at the audition and take my cue from that. Florence is a smart woman. She may see from the auditions that she needs to scale down her plans."

"And if she doesn't?" Alice asked with a grimace.

"Then . . ." Louise paused. "I'm not sure. Florence is a woman who knows what she wants."

"You mean she's stubborn," Jane interjected with a giggle.

"Let's say determined," Louise clarified kindly. "And sometimes it's best not to interfere with a determined person."

Alice smiled. "Louise, you are a very smart woman, and I know you can take care of yourself. But I have experience with Florence on the church board, and I know that if you don't convince Florence to put a lid on things, you might find yourself accompanying a production the size of *The Ten Commandments*."

Though Louise experienced a flutter of fear, she said, "Thanks for the heads-up, but I still think I'll wait until after I see Florence's behavior at the audition before I say anything."

Chapter Five

Monday morning the mailman delivered the official notice of the inspection for Grace Chapel Inn. James E. Delaney was scheduled to arrive on Monday one week before Memorial Day, which gave Jane a couple weeks to prepare, plenty of time, especially since, thanks to Alice, she had a concise list of things to do.

Walking to the hardware store to purchase some steel wool, Jane congratulated herself on being well prepared and decided to downplay the fact that she had been panicking. It was a new day.

Pushing open the door of the hardware store, she didn't see Fred Humbert, the store's owner. She glanced into the corner of the 100-year-old building, then down the aisle to where garden supplies were displayed, but again didn't see Fred.

Finally she called, "Hello? Fred?"

Fred emerged from a door behind the counter, wiping his hands on an old cloth. A middle-aged man with sandy-colored hair, Fred was head of the church board and the town's unofficial philosopher and weather prognosticator.

"Good morning, Jane. What can I do for you today?"

"I'm just looking for steel wool. I know where it is, but I wanted to say hello before I picked it up."

"Steel wool?" Fred frowned. "Are you preparing to paint something?"

"No. Doing a little pot scrubbing."

Fred nodded knowingly. "Ah, must be inspection time."

"Yes."

"You nervous?"

Jane took a breath. "I was. But this morning I got the official notice, and I have time before the inspection to get everything shipshape. Plus, Alice and I made a to-do list, so now I have time *and* I'm organized."

"Sounds good to me," Fred agreed.

Jane walked back to the aisle, grabbed a packet of steel wool and returned to the counter.

Fred rang up her purchase and slid the steel wool into a bag as Jane counted out the necessary payment.

"I'm glad you're not frantic about this," Fred observed as the register door opened. "I'm one of those people who believe that if you keep up with things on a daily basis, you have nothing to worry about when someone wants to check up on you."

"That's true," Jane agreed, taking her change.

"It's the same philosophy Vera uses with her students. At the beginning of the year, she explains that if each person in the class keeps up with the lessons, there won't be any need to cram for tests or get excited about midterms or finals."

"Kind of like the seven wise virgins in the Bible

who were prudent enough to have oil for their lamps."

"Exactly." Fred beamed. "Though the seven foolish virgins who didn't bring enough oil for their lamps were surprised by the bridegroom's arrival, the arrival of the bridegroom was no surprise to the seven who were prepared. And you're prepared, Jane. You treat your guests like royalty. Each time I've been to the inn I've seen that the place shines. This inspection should be a piece of cake."

Hearing Fred's praise, Jane stood a little taller. He was right. Even if an inspector dropped by today, the inn didn't have any major problems. She kept her kitchen in excellent shape. The guest rooms were immaculate. The bathrooms were spotless. All as a matter of course. Cleanliness wasn't something they sought only for the benefit of inspectors.

She grinned at Fred. "Thanks. You know, you made me feel so good I think I'm going to stop at the Coffee Shop for a treat."

"Attagirl," Fred said, waving as Jane walked to the door.

Outside, Jane took a breath of the fresh Acorn Hill air. She kept forgetting that her small hometown wasn't like a lot of other places. People in Acorn Hill and most of Lancaster County in general used common sense and reason. She might go through the inn to make sure it shined when the inspector showed up, but tearing everything apart was silly.

Her thoughts took her across Chapel Road to the Coffee Shop. As she entered, Hope Collins, the waitress, looked up from the book she was reading. By the time Jane had slid into one of the red faux-leather booths, Hope was at her table with a glass of water.

Though Hope was well known for experimenting with hair colors, today her short hair was a natural-looking dark brown. As always, her pink uniform was neat as a pin. Today she wore a white ruffled apron.

"What can I get for you?" Hope asked, pulling her order pad and pen from her apron pocket.

"I think I'm in the mood for a banana-nut muffin," Jane said, waving her hand to indicate that she didn't need a menu.

"Yum. I love the banana-nut muffins. How about some coffee to go with that?"

"Coffee sounds great."

Hope scurried away and Jane turned to look out the window. It was almost ten thirty, so the Coffee Shop was empty. Most children were in school. Mothers pushed strollers or held the hands of toddlers as they ran their day's errands. The peace of the scene relaxed Jane even more.

Hope returned with Jane's muffin and coffee.

"Coffee's hot. Muffin's warm. Can I get you anything else?"

"No, thank you."

"It's not like you to take a break in the middle of the morning," Hope said, obviously looking for conversation in the empty diner.

"I needed to get out for a minute to chill out. Saturday night Alice told me I was panicking for nothing over an upcoming inspection."

"Inspection?" Hope said. "The inn has to be inspected?"

"Yes, because we cook and serve food there."

"Well, I hope you don't get the same inspector who does the Coffee Shop."

Jane frowned. She didn't think they would have the same inspector. After all, there was a huge difference between an inn and a coffee shop. Still, both had a kitchen.

"James Delaney is inspecting the inn."

Hope gasped. "Oh, Jane!" She didn't say another word, but the sympathetic tone of her voice spoke volumes to Jane.

"Oh no. What have you heard?"

"Once," Hope said, her voice dropping to a conspiratorial whisper, "he shut down a restaurant because there were footprints under one of the booths."

Jane's face scrunched in confusion. "Footprints?"

"Apparently someone had walked in with muddy shoes on a rainy day."

"Didn't Mr. Delaney take the rainy conditions into consideration?"

Hope shrugged. "All I know is that he said if there were footprints in the dining room where the restaurant employees should be trying to impress diners, then who could say what was in the kitchen."

"Didn't he look in the kitchen?"

Hope shrugged again, and though Jane's initial reaction was to become alarmed, she forced herself to relax. Hope was a wonderful person, but she was also a conduit for others' stories. Sometimes those stories got embellished. This appeared to be one of those cases. No inspector under the sun would shut down a restaurant without going into the kitchen.

She smiled at Hope. "Well, there are no footprints anywhere in the inn. And if it's raining the day he arrives, I'll simply keep a mop on hand."

"Good idea, because the other thing I've heard is that if he finds something he doesn't like in one area he's inspecting, he considers that probable cause to go into areas he shouldn't have any reason to go into."

Jane froze. That was exactly what she'd already been told.

"In other words," Hope continued, "for all you know, he could end up in your attic and write you up for cobwebs."

Though the last comment bordered on absurd, the logic behind it was sound. If the inspector found something he didn't like in the kitchen, he could go into the guest rooms and bathrooms, and that meant those had to be every bit as clean as she intended her kitchen to be.

And *that* meant she was back to needing more than one list. She now needed lists to cover all of Grace Chapel Inn.

Suddenly there didn't seem to be enough time to get ready.

When Alice spotted Rosalind walking toward the cafeteria at the same time Alice was scheduled to eat, the coincidence of running into her didn't seem so coincidental anymore. It almost appeared as if Rosalind was timing her breaks to "run into" Alice.

"Fancy meeting you here," Alice said, trying not to make too much of it, but she couldn't help it. Rosalind knew Myra was skeptical about her offer, and Alice knew Myra. It almost seemed Rosalind wanted to be around Alice enough to nudge Alice into convincing Myra to accept. And that made Alice uncomfortable.

"This won't be much of a meeting," Rosalind replied with a smile. She held up a dollar. "One of the patients on my floor had a sudden craving for gelatin."

Alice frowned. "Excuse me?"

Rosalind laughed merrily. "It's the silliest thing. She loves the gelatin here and keeps dollar bills stashed in her bedside table. The second I arrive with the candy cart, she pulls money from her drawer as if she's doing something illegal and whispers to me to run down here and get her some gelatin." Rosalind lowered her voice to a whisper. "And fresh. Not like the stale stuff they sometimes keep in our unit's refrigerator."

Alice burst out laughing. "That *is* about the silliest thing I've ever heard."

Rosalind laughed too as they both entered the cafeteria line. Alice took a tray, but Rosalind simply walked behind her toward the gelatin.

"I'm sure you've heard sillier," Rosalind said as Alice took a salad from an assortment on shelves above them. "I know I have."

"You're sort of in a unique position," Alice pointed out.

"Yes, I am." Rosalind grinned. "I'm not exactly hospital staff, but I know my way around."

"Which makes you the perfect candidate to run errands."

"I don't mind," Rosalind said with a small smile as she took a dish of lime gelatin from the shelf. "I've got a pretty good life—great husband, great kids and the ability to work at something I really like, volunteering, rather than being forced to get a job because I need the money." She smiled at Alice. "Do you mind if I go ahead of you?"

"Of course not," Alice said, stepping out of Rosalind's way. "Please."

"I don't like to keep her waiting."

Rosalind paid for the gelatin and gave a small wave to Alice before she made her way through the lunch crowd and out into the hospital corridor.

Alice stared after her. Every time she tried to evaluate Rosalind, Rosalind only seemed to prove her sincerity and kindness. Alice was beginning to wonder if Rosalind wasn't being tossed in Alice's path by Someone higher up, Who wanted Alice to be convinced of what a good person Rosalind Westwood really was.

At seven thirty sharp, Louise walked down the center aisle of the auditorium at Acorn Hill Elementary School, where Florence had received permission to hold her talent show and where auditions were about to start.

At least Louise *thought* they were about to start. The lights of the small stage brought the little area to life, showing off the hardwood floor and velvet stage curtains. But Louise didn't see any people. Not even Florence.

"Hello?" she called, using a tentative voice in order not to disturb anyone in case Florence was behind the curtain giving instructions to the people planning to audition.

Florence peeked out from behind the royal-purple velvet curtain. "Hello, Louise! Isn't this exciting?" Walking out onto the stage, she spread her arms wide as if embracing an audience. "It's such a thrill just to stand up here . . . even without an audience."

Shaking her head, Louise chuckled. She knew exactly what Florence was saying. The first time she got on a stage she felt that thrill, but it was coupled with anxiety. It was one thing to perform, quite another to please an audience. The two were not synonymous.

"It's very different when you're standing in front of a hundred people or two hundred or three hundred, knowing your performance has to entertain them."

"You're much too serious, Louise," Florence scolded as she made her way to the right of the stage, where she began walking down the steps. "We're doing a talent show. It's supposed to be fun. Even the mistakes are supposed to be fun."

Louise's eyes narrowed as she considered what Florence had said, and certain things began to fall into place for her.

Florence had made no secret of the fact that she had recently had counseling sessions with Rev. Thompson. The result of those sessions was that Florence had decided to work toward getting along with everyone. Florence's enthusiastic attitude about the production bore that out, and Louise was beginning to see that maybe Florence had thought up this production as a way to ingratiate herself with the community.

Deciding that had to be the unexplained reason

for the talent show, Louise relaxed somewhat. Florence's desire to get along with her community was a positive incentive. With that motivation figured out, Louise might not have to worry that something unpleasant would jump out at her when she least expected it.

Relaxing even more about this production, Louise looked around. "Where are the people?"

Florence waved a hand in dismissal. "I'm sure nobody wanted to have to wait to perform. They'll probably be here in a half hour or so thinking they avoided waiting in a line. Nobody likes to wait for anything anymore."

"I can't argue that," Louise said, walking to the piano. "This will give me time to get set up."

"Great," Florence said, following Louise to the piano.

"You may go back to what you were doing," Louise said as she slid her briefcase onto the piano bench. "I'm fine."

Florence shrugged. "I'm sure you are," she said, but she continued to peer over Louise's shoulder.

"Maybe you should stand by the front door and make sure everybody knows where to go," Louise suggested kindly.

"Oh, Louise, everybody knows where the auditorium is. I don't need to stand by the door."

"Then perhaps you would like to take a seat over there," Louise said, pointing to the first row of audience chairs.

Florence looked at the seat, then back at Louise. "But you and I could pick the talent together."

"You don't have to sit in my pocket to do that," Louise said, trying desperately to get her point across without being harsh, but Louise was just about certain she was going to have to spell out everything.

"In fact," Louise continued, "it's always better if the performers consider the accompanist to be 'on their side,' so to speak. We form a sort of bond. Accompanist and performer working together in the tryout." She paused, then pointed at Florence. "For you, the director."

Florence seemed to like that explanation, because she nodded, her eyes shining. "Yes. For me. The *director*."

As Louise continued to prepare for the auditions, bringing out copies of sheet music for the tunes most often chosen for this kind of affair, Florence took a seat in the front row, then bounced out again.

"I'll need my pen and paper."

Louise reminded herself to be patient, because if her conclusions from a few minutes ago were correct, Florence was trying very hard to do something good. In addition, Louise couldn't forget the sacrifice of Alice's friend Rosalind. Her generosity made Louise's having patience with Florence seem like the least she could do.

Florence hurried back to her seat, showing

Louise her tablet and pen. Louise smiled and Florence settled into her seat. Five minutes quickly ticked off the clock as Louise arranged the music for a variety of popular tunes.

Another ten minutes passed. As she practiced a couple of numbers, her companion began to fidget.

Engrossed in familiarizing herself with the songs, Louise hardly noticed that fifteen more minutes went by, and Florence had begun to pace.

Louise gave Florence points for not disturbing her as she prepared. But when the auditorium clock indicated eight o'clock and no one had come racing down the aisle to the stage, Florence sighed heavily.

"This is ridiculous," she said, raising her arms and letting them fall against her sides in disgust. "Try to do something nice for people and this is how I'm repaid. Nobody shows up."

Louise stifled a sudden sense of hope that she might not have to become involved in Florence's production because of nonparticipation. No, that kind of thinking wouldn't do. If she wanted to emulate Rosalind, she couldn't be happy that Florence's efforts were failing. In fact, she had to see that Florence's efforts didn't fail.

She rose from the piano bench and walked to the area where Florence paced agitatedly. "Perhaps no one showed up because they're afraid."

Florence's face puckered in confusion. "Afraid? Of what?"

"Performing isn't easy. A person can have a beautiful voice, practice for hours and still feel uncomfortable singing in front of people."

"*Hmm.* That makes sense."

"Not only that," Louise continued, "but also it has been my experience that some of the most truly talented people don't know they are."

Florence caught Louise's gaze. "What are you saying?"

Louise took a second to think through her words. What she was about to suggest meant that she was committing to working more closely with Florence, but in for a penny, in for a pound. If she was to follow Rosalind's example, then she needed to be fully committed to this project.

"I think what we need to do is have a recruitment campaign."

"Recruitment campaign?" Florence echoed.

"Yes. We'll chat up people at the Coffee Shop or after church services on Sunday, and not only drum up interest in the program, but also do a little bit of confidence building. After all, I would have expected at least a few members of the church choir to be here. Yet they are not. That probably means they're shy about performing alone."

"Yes," Florence agreed. "That makes perfect sense."

"I'm glad you agree."

"Absolutely."

Louise walked to the piano, lifted her briefcase to the bench and began collecting her music.

"I think we'll start at the General Store, move on to Nine Lives Bookstore—" Florence stopped and shook her head. "You know what? The simple thing to do would be to start on Berry Lane and make the loop down Acorn Avenue and up Hill Street."

"That makes sense."

"Okay, I'll see you at nine o'clock tomorrow morning in front of Nine Lives."

"I'm sorry, Florence, but we have guests tonight. Jane was already checking them in when I left. I need to be available . . ."

Florence sighed and put her hands on her hips. "Louise, I thought you were with me on this project. If you can't be committed, maybe I should find myself another accompanist."

Louise struggled to control her reaction. She nearly told Florence that she could have easily kept the recruitment campaign idea to herself and simply bowed out when no one showed up. But she didn't want to do that. Florence was struggling with her interpersonal skills, so part of Louise's role in this production could be to give a good example to Florence.

Louise gave herself a second to consider how to reply without offending Florence and also without being a doormat. Finally, she said, "What about nine thirty?"

"Nine thirty?"

"Yes. I'm sure I can be out of the inn by nine thirty. I will see you at Nine Lives then."

Florence tugged at the bottom of her suit jacket. "Well, okay. That's a good compromise."

Seeing Florence's easy acquiescence, Louise felt very good about the resolution of the problem, until she got out into the warm Acorn Hill night. Then it hit her that with the recruitment campaign in addition to participation in the show, she would be spending an extraordinary amount of time with Florence until the talent show on the Sunday before Memorial Day.

Three long weeks.

Chapter Six

When Alice arrived at the dialysis clinic at seven o'clock on Tuesday morning, the entire place was buzzing.

"What's up?" she asked Judy O'Malley, a short, slim brunette with brown eyes, who was one of the clinic's regular nurses.

"You haven't heard?"

Shrugging out of her light jacket, Alice laughed. "I just got here."

"Well, rumor has it that Rosalind Westwood has offered a kidney to Myra Swanson." Judy leaned closer. "Not only that, but Rosalind's a match."

Alice looked shocked.

"I know, I was amazed too. These two women don't even really know each other. Rosalind's a volunteer. She met Myra during one of her stays. That's it. That's their only connection."

Alice said nothing; she simply stared at Judy.

"That was my reaction too. I was shocked speechless," Judy said.

Alice finally spoke. "Has anybody heard if Myra's accepted?"

"It's the darnedest thing. That's where the story dies. It's like a soap opera, and we're all waiting to tune in tomorrow and get the rest of the story."

"Yes, you'll have to wait until tomorrow," Alice said absently, remembering that Myra usually came in for dialysis Monday, Wednesday and Friday. "She'll be in around ten."

Judy perked up. "This is great!"

Alice sighed. "Judy, don't you think we should tread lightly with this?"

Judy gaped at her. "Are you kidding? Every one of our patients prays for a chance like this. Myra should be walking on air when she arrives."

"She may not have heard that Rosalind's a match," Alice cautioned.

"*We* wouldn't have heard if Myra hadn't yet been told."

Alice said nothing.

"Besides, Myra's such a wonderful person, you can't blame everybody here for being happy for her."

Grimacing, Alice nodded. "I know. I can see how all the nurses and staff get close to the patients, working with the same ones week after week. They're regulars here as much as the staff."

"We love them and care about them," Judy agreed. "And Myra's especially wonderful. Her children are adorable. Her husband is the salt of the earth. No family deserves this break more than Myra's family does. I can't wait for her to have the transplant so they can all have a happy life."

Alice knew exactly what Judy was saying, and she hoped that when Myra arrived, she was ready for the nurse's enthusiasm.

Louise arrived at the Coffee Shop a little after nine on Tuesday morning. Though they had originally planned to meet at Nine Lives, Florence called just after Louise had returned home the night before and said that she had changed her mind—they should start with the Coffee Shop first, because that was where most people congregated in the morning.

After a horrible, nagging premonition about Florence's pushing her way into the Coffee Shop and doing more damage than good in terms of enticing Acorn Hill residents into participating in the talent show, Louise had rushed through checking out the guests so that Florence wouldn't enter the Coffee Shop first.

When Florence came walking down the street at

the same time Louise was reaching for the door into the Coffee Shop, Louise was glad she had decided to show up early.

Florence smiled brightly at Louise. "Let's go!"

Louise caught her arm before she could open the door. "I was thinking last night that perhaps we should have a strategy for approaching people."

Florence's brow furrowed in confusion. "A strategy? To get people to participate in a talent show? This is Acorn Hill, Louise. We don't need a strategy."

With that, Florence turned and pulled open the door. She marched to the counter, lifted an empty cup and spoon and clanged the spoon against the cup.

"Good morning, everyone," she said happily, as the small crowd quieted down and looked over to see who was demanding their attention.

Louise surveyed the people to ascertain if anyone in the group could be easily offended. Hope Collins stood at the far end of the counter refilling Fred Humbert's coffee cup. Because it was a weekday, Fred's wife was at school, and though Fred would ordinarily be at work at the hardware store, this was probably a morning break.

In the booth behind Fred, Zack and Nancy Colwin, a slim man with light-brown hair and his smiling wife, were eating sweet rolls. Nancy helped run the bakery that provided most of the treats for the Coffee Shop, and Zack ran Zachary's, the town's supper club. Both had plenty of experience with Florence, and Louise wasn't worried that either of them would get the wrong impression from anything Florence said.

Nia Komonos, the town librarian, a tall woman with dark hair, stood by the counter looking at the baked goods, probably choosing her morning snack. Patsy Ley, wife of the assistant pastor of Grace Chapel, Henry Ley, stood next to Nia with a bag of pastries, apparently waiting for Hope to come over so she could pay her bill.

Sylvia Songer, proprietress of Sylvia's Buttons entered behind Louise. "Good morning, Louise."

Louise absently said, "Good morning," as she decided that no one in the Coffee Shop that morning would be too surprised or offended by anything Florence did. However, she also didn't believe any of them would necessarily be very interested in a talent show.

"Okay, everybody, listen up!" Florence continued. "Louise Smith and I are putting together a talent show, and we wish to welcome everybody to join us."

Though Florence made it sound as if she and Louise were partners, Louise didn't correct her but simply smiled at the Coffee Shop patrons.

"We hope to put on the show the Sunday before Memorial Day as a little something entertaining, especially for those of you who will have guests.

We're not charging admission. It's not that kind of show. We simply want to showcase our town's talent at the same time that we give you all a way to entertain your visitors."

Louise watched Nia's brow furrow in confusion and Sylvia glance at her watch, clearly more interested in getting to her shop than hearing about a talent show.

"We had auditions on Monday night," Florence went on, smiling as she slowly walked down the aisle, looking each patron in the eye. "But we still have plenty of room available for talent. So I brought this pad and pen," she said, producing a small tablet and pen from the side pocket of her full skirt, "to give everybody here an opportunity to sign up for a second audition we're having Friday night."

Louise took a deep breath. She hadn't agreed to another audition, but, realistically, she didn't have anything else scheduled and she could do it, so there was no point arguing.

"Knowing how many people intend to show up will help Louise and me to prepare."

There was a short silence in the room as everybody stared at Florence. Then, as if everyone simultaneously realized she was done, they all nodded or smiled and went back to their own conversations.

Sylvia said, "I'm sorry to rush you, Hope, but I really need to get to my shop." She faced Louise and Florence and smiled apologetically. "Sorry, ladies, but I do have to get going. I have a special project I'm working on."

"Me, too," Nia said as she turned to leave. Hope brought her coffeepot back to the counter. She poured a container of coffee to go and walked to the cash register, where she took the change that Sylvia had ready for her, then got Nia a doughnut and rang it up. Finally, she rang up Patsy Ley's bag of goodies.

Florence watched all three women walk out of the Coffee Shop. She turned to Louise. "We can stop by Sylvia's Buttons and the library to get signatures later."

Aware that Florence didn't realize that Sylvia and Nia clearly weren't interested in participating, Louise nonetheless said nothing.

Florence walked to Zack and Nancy's booth. She smiled brightly and set the tablet on the table. "So, do you sing? Do you dance? Play an instrument?" she asked, nudging the tablet toward Zack. "We're happy with absolutely anything because we're looking for variety."

Zack glanced down at his coffee cup, and Nancy said, "Actually, Florence, Zack and I are a little too busy to participate in a talent show."

"Oh, don't be silly. There won't be that many practices."

Zack chuckled. "Florence, we don't even have time for one practice."

Florence gasped. "Well, you can't perform without practicing."

Nancy grimaced. "I think that's Zack's point. We can't perform."

"How do you know you can't perform if you don't try out?" Florence slid the tablet a little closer to Nancy. "Just write down your name and an audition time that's convenient for you, and I swear Louise will be kind to you."

Nancy quickly slid the tablet back to Florence and said, "Let me rephrase what Zack was saying. No time is convenient for us. We both work."

Finally getting the message, Florence blinked, pasted on her happy smile again and said, "Of course." She waved her hand as if dismissing the situation. "I'm sorry."

Picking up her tablet, she smiled one last time, then pivoted and tapped Fred on the shoulder. When he turned, she thrust the tablet at him. "Since you're first to sign up, you get to choose whatever audition time you want, Fred."

Fred leaned away, refusing to take the tablet. "I can't sign up for anything without talking to Vera first, and she's at school. Will be all day," he said, obviously uncomfortable.

That was when Louise stepped in. She walked over to Florence and diplomatically took the tablet from her. She tore off the top sheet and walked back to the cash register. "How about this, everybody? I'm going to create a sign-up sheet that we'll leave here by the register." As she spoke she wrote SIGN-UP SHEET FOR TALENT SHOW TO BE HELD THE SUNDAY BEFORE MEMORIAL DAY. Then she numbered the lines from one to twenty-five. She faced Hope. "If that's okay with you," she said politely.

Hope shrugged. "Sure."

Louise turned to the Coffee Shop patrons again. "If you wish, you can sign up at your leisure, and you can also tell your friends that if they wish to sign up, the sheet will be here."

Hope took the sheet with a smile. "I have a clipboard in back."

"That's great!" Louise said.

"Yes, absolutely!" Florence gushed. "Thank you, Hope . . . and you know, of course, you can sign up too."

"Oh, Florence, I don't have any talent."

"Pretty girl like you? Of course you have talent."

Louise chuckled. "Florence, good looks and talent aren't necessarily synonymous."

Florence straightened. "I know that. I'm just saying that lots of times the two go together. Look at all those beautiful singers on TV."

Louise only smiled.

Florence turned to Hope again. "I know you've often talked of acting, but have you ever tried to sing or dance?"

Appearing unhappy with Florence's reminder of her unfulfilled dreams, Hope flushed. "Believe me,

I've tried everything. Emphasis on *tried,* because when I sang I always made a fool of myself. My friends were so much better than I was."

Florence's expression became genuinely sympathetic. "Oh, honey!" she said, reaching across the counter to take Hope's hands. "That kind of comparison is not going to happen here. We're only doing this show to have a chance to have a good time and showcase our abilities. The last thing we want is for anybody to feel she's not as talented as somebody else."

"That's good, because when it comes to singing or dancing, I'm not."

"But that doesn't mean you can't perform to the best of your ability and have a good time."

Louise was very proud of Florence until she added, "Naturally, of course, some of us are going to be better than others. That's the way all of life is. Some people are just inherently better. But no one will care. The audience still claps as hard for you as they will when I perform."

With that Florence turned toward the door, but as if suddenly inspired she faced the small group again. "If that's what has the rest of you hesitant, let me say one more time from the bottom of my heart that this is not a competition. It's all in good, clean fun. So please don't be afraid to sign up just because you can't sing as well as I—as well as someone else."

In that moment, Louise suspected another motivation behind why Florence wanted to have a talent show. She wasn't doing something for the people of the town. She wanted to showcase her own talent.

Chapter Seven

Wednesday morning Alice pushed aside the curtain to enter the cubicle where Myra reclined, reading a magazine. Two needles had been inserted into her arm. One carried blood to the dialyzer, where a dialysis solution pulled waste and extra fluids from her blood. Filtered blood returned to her body through the second needle.

"Good morning," Alice said brightly, determined not to give away that she had heard the rumors running rampant through the unit about Rosalind's being a match. "How are you today?"

Myra set the open magazine aside. "I'm good."

"That's great."

"Yes, I guess," Myra said, then she sighed. "Look, there's no sense in our pretending everything's fine. I know the news has gotten around that Rosalind's a match."

Alice flinched. "Unfortunately, it has."

Myra shook her head slightly. "I wouldn't mind, except now I feel even more pressure about my decision."

"You still haven't decided?"

Before Myra could say anything, Dr. Allen, the physician listed as Myra's family doctor, entered the cubicle.

"Good morning, Myra," he said, smiling broadly as he picked up Myra's chart. A tall man with a booming voice, his commanding presence filled the small space. He quickly reviewed the chart, then crossed his arms on his chest. "Looks like we've got some talking to do."

Alice moved toward the cubicle opening. "I'll just leave you two alone."

"I'd rather you stay," Myra said quickly.

Dr. Allen shrugged. "You're fine here, Alice." He waved his hand toward Myra. "I have confidence in you and so does Myra."

"I appreciate that."

Dr. Allen pulled a chair next to Myra's bed. He seemed upbeat as he talked to his patient. "My partner at the office told me she called you and conveyed the news that Rosalind Westwood is a match."

"Yes," Myra said.

Dr. Allen took a long breath. "She also told me that you said you needed time to think about the transplant."

"I have time." She inclined her head toward the dialysis unit. "It's not like this isn't working."

"It's working, and you do have a certain amount of time . . ."

"But?" Myra prodded when he fell silent.

"But you don't want to let an opportunity like this one pass you by."

"I'm not sure I understand that," Myra said, her face clouding with confusion.

"Wise people strike while the iron is hot. You have a donor. She's willing and able right now. Don't let too much time pass." He rose and slid Myra's chart into its holder at the foot of the bed. "You don't know what tomorrow is going to bring."

"You mean you think she could change her mind," Myra said, jumping on his comment as if he had just verified her worst worry and also vindicated her procrastination.

Dr. Allen shook his head. "No. I mean Rosalind's husband could transfer to Timbuktu. *Your* condition could change. Something in her family circumstances or your family circumstances could change. So I'm saying exactly what I said before. Wise people strike while the iron is hot."

With that he smiled at both women, then left.

"I seem to be trying everyone's patience."

"I understand why you're hesitating," Alice said sympathetically, making the notes on the chart that she couldn't make while Dr. Allen had held it. "But I also understand Dr. Allen's point that you can't wait forever."

"I'm afraid Rosalind is a nice woman with good intentions who could change her mind at the last minute. I'm afraid of getting everybody's hopes up for nothing. Those two things are why I'm hesitating."

"Now that Rosalind's gone this far, those aren't really good reasons anymore," Alice said, fluffing the pillow behind Myra's shoulders. "Actions speak louder than words, Myra. And right now Rosalind's actions are saying she's committed to following through."

"Okay, then, let's get to the real bottom line. The truth is I'm bewildered regarding her motives."

Not understanding that at all, Alice stepped away from the bed. "Her motives?"

"I just don't get it," Myra said quietly. "I don't understand *why* she would do this."

Alice thought about that for a moment, and as she did, she remembered how often her father's best counsel to a member of his congregation was, "Sometimes you're not supposed to understand." She took a moment, then quietly said, "Sometimes you're not supposed to understand."

"But I *need* to understand."

"Why?" Alice asked.

Myra's face puckered in confusion. "What do you mean, why?"

"What happens if you don't know? What happens if you don't have all the facts? If you don't understand?"

"If I don't understand, I can't trust."

Alice fluffed Myra's second pillow. "Maybe that's the real bottom line here." She stepped away from the bed and smiled at Myra. "You don't trust. I can't help you with your decision because it's not my place, but from what you just said about not trusting, I realized there's only one thing that can help you. You need to pray about this, Myra."

"I have been praying," Myra said, then she shrugged. "Sort of. I probably don't pray as long or as hard as I should."

Alice laughed. "You don't have to pray long and hard. Simple cries for help are sometimes the best prayers when it comes to making decisions. Just ask for help and keep on asking. The answer will come."

Myra nodded. "I guess."

Alice walked to the curtain, but inspired, she turned and faced Myra again. "Just remember the answer doesn't always come the way we expect it to. And sometimes when there's so much confusion and so much distraction, we don't realize the answer has been in front of us all along. Don't forget to listen for the still, small voice."

"Explain to me again what we're doing," Alice said, pressing her foot against the gardening shovel to loosen the dirt in the flowerbed in front of the house.

Louise bent over a tray of colorful potted flowers from Wild Things, Craig Tracy's shop. Jane had purchased everything from yellow and white daisies to purple pansies and something short that looked like brown-eyed Susans.

"You and I are assigned to garden detail."

Still confused, Alice glanced over at her. "Why?"

"Because the comments Jane heard from Hope about the inspector really rattled her."

"But the list she and I made gave her such confidence."

"She still has the list. She has, unfortunately, expanded it."

"Maybe I should talk to her again."

Louise reached for one of the pansies. She ran a thin blade between the dirt and the container and gently lifted out the flower, dirt and all. "I'm not sure it will do any good. She's positive that there's trouble brewing with this inspection. She's calling her feeling an intuition. I don't think a talk will help her this time."

Alice sighed. "I hate gossip. Yesterday morning I walked into the dialysis unit and everybody was buzzing about how Rosalind was a match for Myra."

"But that's good news." Louise tilted her head in question, then added, "Right?"

Alice anchored the shovel into the ground beside the flowerbed and took the plant from Louise. "Yes and no."

"I understand the *yes,* but not the *no.*"

"Myra hasn't made up her mind. So with the latest development she has the added pressure that everybody knows about the transplant offer."

"She feels that she can't say no?"

Alice shrugged. "Something like that."

Louise chuckled. "Why don't you explain what her reluctance is exactly?"

"She told me this morning that she's been praying and hasn't gotten an answer."

Louise laughed again. "Please don't tell me this is the first time she has had to wait for an answer to a prayer."

"I'm sure it isn't. I think the problem is that she's being given an answer, but there's so much confusion around her and so many people with opinions that she can't hear God's answer."

Louise considered that, then said, "That makes sense."

"Yes, it does. I told her to listen for the still, small voice, but that's about all I can do. No one can help Myra with this decision. She's the one who has to make it."

"Yes, she is," Louise agreed, then she sighed. "I'm sure Florence and I are going to be the subject of some gossip ourselves soon, if we aren't already."

Alice grinned. "Uh-oh. What happened?"

"You remember that I told you we were going to recruit talent yesterday?"

"Yes."

"Well, we started off the day by going into the Coffee Shop, where Florence issued a blanket offer for anyone who wanted to audition. No one took her up on it."

"Really?"

"The silence was painfully embarrassing. Not just for Florence but also for the customers, who didn't know how to handle the situation." Louise sighed. "I managed to salvage everybody's feelings by giving the customers the benefit of the doubt. I thought that they might be too shy to sign up right away, so I left a sign-up sheet with Hope."

"Good idea."

"I thought it was, and I also think it might have worked, except Florence made a remark about everybody's not worrying about not being as talented as she is. Her comment was *not* well received. She almost made it sound as if she was daring people to compete with her. I wouldn't blame Hope if she tore up the sheet after we left."

Alice took another plant from Louise. She set it in the small hole she had prepared, then covered the roots with the dirt she had scooped out and patted it down. "I'm sorry to hear that."

"That was actually the good part of our day."

Alice glanced up at Louise. "Things got worse?"

"Yes. When we stopped at Time for Tea, she told Wilhelm she knows no one will do as well as she will with her solo performance of 'Memory' from the musical *Cats*, but everybody should participate anyway, because it's all in good fun."

"She isn't making it sound like fun."

"No, she isn't. She managed to insult all the shop

proprietors and even some people we met on the street."

Alice frowned. "I don't understand. I mean I know that comment was a tad presumptuous, but all in all, we know that Florence is good-hearted. Yet it sounds as if she went out of her way to insult people."

"And in insulting people she reminded everybody that if they sign up for the project, they have to deal with her, and nobody wants to deal with her. I can just imagine them thinking that if Florence is already criticizing them *before* tryouts, how difficult will she make everybody's life after tryouts?"

Alice's frown deepened. "She does have a tendency to nitpick."

Louise reached for another plant but stopped and faced Alice again. "The truth is I didn't think she consciously intended for her comments to be mean. Because I was with her every time she insulted someone, I very clearly saw that it had been her intention to encourage."

"But the encouragement came out as insulting."

"Yes." Louise shook her head in exasperation. "It was the oddest thing. Almost as if she doesn't know how to encourage or compliment."

"That is odd."

"And it's going to ruin her show."

"Maybe you could help her with that."

"I'm already going beyond what I signed up to do by assisting her with tryouts."

Alice smiled kindly at her older sister. "It won't take any extra time to show her how to be more pleasant and complimentary. You can do it during the auditions."

"I suppose."

"And you know the saying, 'In for a penny, in for a pound.'"

"So I keep telling myself."

Chapter Eight

Louise met Florence the next morning at the Coffee Shop. Normally, she would have suggested they have tea on the front porch of Grace Chapel Inn for this discussion, not just for comfort and privacy, but also because Florence had inadvertently alienated the Coffee Shop regulars. She didn't think she and Florence would get a warm reception. But Jane continued to be in a tizzy about the upcoming inspection, and Louise didn't want to upset her schedule.

On top of that, Louise needed to be tactful with Florence. Sitting in a room full of people, some who could accidentally overhear what Louise was saying and some who would deliberately try to listen in, Louise knew she wouldn't be tempted to say anything inappropriate and would bridle her tongue.

"Hello, Louise," Florence said, sliding onto the bench seat across from her friend. Dressed in a pretty blue blouse over a white pleated skirt, Florence looked fashionable yet ready to go to work.

"Good morning, Florence."

"Why the emergency meeting?" she asked as Hope walked over and set a place mat in front of her.

"Just coffee, dear," Florence said to Hope, who smiled stiffly and ambled away.

"My goodness! What's wrong with her?"

"That's actually what I wanted to speak with you about," Louise said, jumping on the providential opening. "Things didn't go very well in our recruitment of talent on Tuesday."

Florence frowned. "Really? We were everywhere. After two days, I expect our sign-up sheets to be filled." She turned around in her seat so she could see the area of the counter where they had left the clipboard for their sign-up sheet. "In fact, I should go get the sheet right now—"

"Don't," Louise said, stopping Florence before she could rise.

"But we need to get organized."

"I took the liberty of glancing at the list before you arrived." Louise paused and gently said, "No one has signed up for the show."

Florence cocked her head in confusion. "No one?"

"No one." Louise paused again to gather her thoughts, then continued in a voice that she kept soft and gentle. "Florence, I know your heart is in the right place with this talent show. However"—Louise folded her hands on the table in front of her—"we ran into some problems on Tuesday, and I think that's because—"

"I know, everybody's shy," Florence said, patting Louise's hand. "You're so sweet to worry about me, but I'm not offended or upset."

"Florence, I feel it's my—"

"I know. I know. You feel it's your place as assistant director to keep my spirits high."

Louise nearly choked. "Assistant director?"

Florence grinned broadly. "I decided last night to promote you. After all, you did come up with the good idea of the sign-up sheets that keep everything nonconfrontational and give our shy Acorn Hill residents the opportunity to sign up in secret."

Louise stared at her. "These people have to get on a stage and perform. Signing up in secret only takes them so far."

"Then why did you suggest it?"

Louise took a deep breath to mask the fact that she was counting to ten. "All right. Florence," she said, forcing herself to be patient, "let me begin again. I asked you to meet for a discussion this morning because, though I understand that shyness may be keeping some people from signing up, true performers would be eager for an opportunity to display their talents."

Florence considered that. "So you're saying we

simply haven't presented our idea to the right people yet?"

Louise shook her head. "No. We spoke with nearly everyone on Tuesday. I'm saying that part of the reason that they may be standoffish about performing is that they are a bit hesitant to work with you."

Florence's mouth dropped open. "Oh, I get it. You're taking over. As if I haven't been good to you, Louise Howard Smith. Why, for heaven's sake! I just promoted you this very morning."

"Florence, I don't wish to take over," Louise quickly corrected her. "What I'm saying is that you came on too strong when we were recruiting."

Florence lifted her hand to her neck and played with the pearl button of her blue blouse. "I'm a leader," she said defensively. "Leaders have strong personalities."

"Very true," Louise agreed, happy to have found something positive to use to state her case. "But artistic people don't always respond well to typical management and leadership techniques."

Florence drew a breath. "I never thought of that."

"Exactly," Louise happily agreed.

"So what are you suggesting?"

What she wanted to suggest was that Florence take more of a backseat role, but Florence was already worried that Louise intended to take over her production, a situation that couldn't be further from the truth. Not only did Louise not want the responsibility of the show, but also she didn't want the spotlight that Florence longed for.

"Perhaps you need to use a lighter hand."

"A lighter hand . . . *hmmm*." Florence chewed the side of her lip as she considered that.

"So that people realize they can decide what they wish to perform." A terrible thought struck Louise, and she leaned across the counter to get closer so she could whisper. "You don't intend to tell everyone what to perform, do you?"

Florence laughed. "Heavens no!"

Louise breathed a sigh of relief.

Florence jumped up from her seat at the booth. "Attention, everyone!" she called, waving her hand. "Louise has just indicated to me that I may have sounded a bit pushy when we were here Tuesday, and I just want everybody to know that I hadn't intended to come across that way. Everyone gets to choose his or her own song, or dance, or whatever." She waved her hands again, as if indicating she was open to anything.

Though shouting through the busy coffee shop wasn't the best way to apologize and clear up any misunderstanding, everybody knew Florence's personality, and Louise could see from the facial expressions of the patrons that no one was offended.

"So tryouts are tomorrow night at seven thirty. I won't tolerate anyone being late. You must have your own sheet music," she said, sternly rattling off orders as if giving an assignment to a group of rowdy high school students. "And anyone who misses two practices is o-u-t . . . out!"

Florence took a long, satisfied breath and sat across from Louise again. Louise only stared at her, unable to believe that she'd given a reasonable facsimile of an apology, then ruined it by issuing commands.

Thoroughly embarrassed, Louise couldn't have even spoken if she had known what to say.

"There," Florence said with a smile. "Problem solved."

Louise remained silent. She knew Florence was aggressive, opinionated and all too often bossy. She couldn't believe that someone who was basically kind could come across as being totally mean-spirited.

The door opened and Louise's aunt Ethel Buckley entered with her beau, Lloyd Tynan, Acorn Hill's mayor. Ethel was in her seventies and still an attractive woman with her pale-blue eyes and bottle-red short hair. Standing next to Lloyd, who wore a beige suit that complemented Ethel's sunny yellow dress, Ethel looked pretty and contented.

Louise realized that Ethel's arrival was just what she needed.

"Excuse me, Florence. I'm going to say good morning to my aunt." She rose from the booth and walked over to the entry, where Lloyd and Ethel stood looking down the line of booths as if trying to decide which one to choose.

"Aunt Ethel, Lloyd," Louise said. "Why don't you sit with Florence and me?"

Ethel smiled hesitantly as if surprised by Louise's offer. "How very sweet of you, Louise."

"I'm simply happy to see you this morning," Louise said honestly.

Lloyd said, "Why? What's Florence done? I've heard all about how she tried to bully people into trying out for her talent show. Is she threatening dire consequences if no one signs up?"

Louise lowered her voice to a whisper. "Florence's heart is in the right place, but I'm afraid she doesn't have the personality to attract the acts."

Ethel glanced at Florence. Louise saw understanding and a hint of compassion in her aunt's eyes as she said, "I know. Poor thing. Sometimes she can be like a bull in a china shop."

"She does have some leadership characteristics that she hasn't quite refined," Louise said kindly.

Lloyd chuckled. "That's one way of putting it."

"And I believe," Louise continued, "that people are afraid of working with her."

Ethel nodded. "You're probably right."

"What she needs is someone to help her smooth out the rough edges."

"Can't you do that?" Ethel asked.

"We're not equals," Louise said. It was true.

Louise respected Florence as her aunt's friend and didn't feel it was appropriate to scold her or argue with her. Even when she tried to counsel her in a kindly manner, Florence often wouldn't take her advice seriously.

Ethel sighed. "You're asking me to help her, aren't you?"

"Yes."

Ethel sighed again, this time more heavily.

"This morning Florence made me assistant director," Louise said. "But if you agree to help, that title goes to you. I will simply be the accompanist."

A smile slowly lifted Ethel's lips. "Assistant director?"

"Yes."

"My name will be in the program?"

"Absolutely."

She spun to face Lloyd. "Well, that is tempting. I would have somewhere to wear that gorgeous peach dress I bought. Still, it just seems like it will be so much work."

"Well, I was about to ask Lloyd to be master of ceremonies, so the two of you would be working together."

Lloyd looked surprised. "You want me to be master of ceremonies?"

"Well, of course she does," Ethel said, playfully tapping Lloyd's arm. "You're the mayor, after all."

Florence walked up behind them. "What are you

three doing over here? Louise, if you want to talk with your aunt you should just invite her and Lloyd to join us."

"I was asking them to join us when we got into a discussion of the talent show," Louise said. "I hope you don't mind, but I asked Lloyd to be master of ceremonies."

"Of course he would be master of ceremonies," Florence said with a laugh. "He's the mayor."

"And I'm going to take over some of Louise's duties," Ethel quickly jumped in. "I'm going to be assistant director."

Florence faced Louise. "Louise?"

"I'm sorry, Florence," Louise apologized because she knew how this must look to Florence. "I should have asked you first before offering Aunt Ethel my job. But I'm so busy I thought you would do better to have someone who could really help you." She smiled hesitantly. "Again, I'm sorry."

Florence frowned, then said, "No, Louise, I'm sorry. All along you've been trying to tell me you're busy, and I've been giving you extra work." She turned to Ethel. "Do you mind helping me?"

"No. I think it will be fun."

"And I think I'll send my tuxedo to the cleaners," Lloyd said as Louise directed everyone away from the door and to the booth.

When Ethel and Lloyd were settled on one side and Florence was settled on the other, Louise told them she had errands to run and made her escape.

She hated to think of it that way, but as she paid her bill and left the Coffee Shop, that was exactly what she felt like she was doing—escaping—not because she didn't want to be part of the production, but because she and Florence had such different styles of dealing with people. Ethel really would temper Florence's zealousness and smooth out some of her rough edges.

Louise stepped out into the sunny May morning, feeling free for the first time since she agreed to help Florence. She turned to walk back to Grace Chapel Inn, but remembering how Jane was fussing over the inspection, she stopped.

Jane really took the bulk of the responsibility for the inn, though Louise and Alice hadn't planned it that way. But now that Louise was back to having a little time on her hands, there was no reason for Jane to be overburdened by the inspection. She knew Jane wouldn't let her get involved in any of her major housecleaning projects. However, she also realized Jane had been neglecting her flower gardens. Which was why Louise and Alice had found themselves planting flowers the day before.

Suddenly, Louise knew what she could do to help her sister.

Switching directions, Louise made her way to Wild Things, where Craig Tracy, a short, slender man with light-brown hair, stood behind the counter creating an arrangement.

"That's beautiful," Louise said as she entered the shop.

"I love tulips with roses." Craig tilted his head toward the arrangement in the crystal vase. "It's for Patsy Ley's dining-room table."

"Really?"

"Yes. I didn't get all the details, but apparently she did something exceptionally nice for one of the parishioners from Grace Chapel." He fussed with the bright pink tulips, shifting them between the white roses. "This is how she's thanking Patsy."

"That's a lovely gesture."

Sliding a new tulip into the vase, Craig said, "So what can I do for you, Louise?"

"First, I would like some advice."

He spread his hands in a gesture of submission. "At your service."

"Jane is a bit busy with an upcoming inspection. I was going to surprise her by doing something special with her gardens. Jane already has them in fairly good shape, but I think I would like to add some shrubs and flowers to them so that Jane doesn't have to worry about her gardens when the inspector arrives."

Craig gave her a confused look.

Louise chuckled. "I really don't think that the inspector is going to inspect the gardens. Primarily, he will be inspecting the kitchen and dining room. But Jane has the impression that he'll go through the entire property. In her really panicky moments she's sure he'll close us down for a minor infraction."

"Hmmm," Craig said. "If this is the guy from the county, I've heard a thing or two about him from Hope when I've stopped at the Coffee Shop for my morning pastry."

"So has Jane."

"I can see why she's concerned."

"That's why I want to perk up the flower beds. I want her to look outside and smile, knowing that no matter where the inspector looks on our property, he'll find everything is beautiful."

Craig laughed. "You're a good big sister. What kind of advice are you looking for?"

"I would like to hear what I *can* do before I decide what I *want* to do."

Craig pondered that. "Let's see. There are lots of flowering shrubs, such as azaleas, hydrangeas, roses, butterfly bushes." He paused, crossing his arms on his chest. "Begonias seem to be pretty popular, but they're too much work for me. They come in annual form, which of course means they won't grow back the next year, but that also means there's no rootstock that you have to dig up in the fall and replant in the spring. Dahlias are like that too. Hollyhocks, pinks, mums . . . there are perennial mums, which is what I have. You could try daisies, geraniums, pansies, and," he smiled, "one of my favorites, snapdragons. Though they're technically an annual, they do reseed and come back the next year. I have one now that I planted four years ago."

"My goodness," Louise said, beginning to feel overwhelmed by the choices.

"At home, I have a couple of nifty perennials called ice plants that spread over the ground. They have spiky, daisylike flowers in hot pink and yellow. There aren't lots of those around, but that's part of the reason I like them." He grinned. "They're different."

"I think I might want something different. Something that will make Jane smile because she didn't think of it."

"Delphiniums are nice, and so are lupines. Neither of those are staples around here. So those would be different too. Or phlox, which are a perennial and have a wonderful scent. Plus, they're just gorgeous. They come in white and pink and some other colors too. Poppies are getting a little more popular around here as well. They come in all sorts of varieties, annual and perennial, and lots of different colors."

He grinned again. "How's that for a start?"

Louise shook her head. "That's not a start. That's where we end. I have enough ideas."

"Let me get a pen. We'll write down your choices and I'll order them for you."

"Thank you, Craig," Louise said as he rummaged through a drawer in the desk behind the counter.

"How did you want to begin?"

"Let's start with the ice plants."

Craig began writing. "Good choice."

Craig and Louise worked for most of an hour drawing diagrams to get an idea of what shrubs Jane already had in place and what flowers would complement them. By the time they were done, Louise had spent more money than she had intended, but she also knew that after the plants arrived, she would turn the back flowerbeds into showplaces. And that would delight her sisters.

Louise left Wild Things satisfied and happy, but as she headed up Hill Street, she heard Florence calling her.

"Louise! Louise!"

Louise stopped. "Hi, Florence. Did everything go well with Aunt Ethel?"

"Yes," Florence said nervously. She glanced to the left, then right, then caught Louise's arm and nudged her to the edge of the sidewalk out of the way of passersby. "Yes, I appreciate you soliciting her help, but . . ."

"But what?" Louise asked. Seeing the pleading look on Florence's face, Louise felt a sinking feeling in her stomach.

"I think I know what you were trying to tell me this morning."

"You do?"

"Yes, I wouldn't let you say what you really wanted to say because I realized that I had been too pushy about how good I was."

Confused about what Florence was saying, Louise said only, "Oh?"

Florence lowered her voice and looked down at the pavement. "Louise, this is very hard for me, but I have a confession to make. I'm not as good of a singer as I told everyone."

"Florence, I'm not sure why you are telling me this."

"I had planned for us to work together so that I could more or less trick you into giving me extra practices."

Finally understanding, Louise stared at Florence. "You wouldn't have to trick me into extra practices. Only ask," she said, studying Florence, who didn't look like herself at all. With shoulders hunched and her eyes downcast, she looked forlorn and weary. Louise put her hand on her companion's shoulder. "Are you okay?"

Florence glanced up. "Sure. Of course. I'm fine. I'm just apprehensive because I know that while I need help with the show, I'm afraid that without a buffer—someone like you, Louise—Ethel will take over. On top of that, I need extra practices." She fluttered her hand as if frustrated. "I'm just a mess today. Your aunt is strong, but she doesn't have your patience. And I think things are going to get all confused."

"You want me to continue helping."

Florence nodded.

Louise drew a quiet breath. She now had several

flats of flowers arriving in a week, *and* she was back to being Florence's right-hand person.

"Florence, I'm sorry that you have concerns about Ethel's being part of your project. I genuinely believed that she could be a better helper than I could be."

Florence gave Louise a sheepish look. "Oh, it's just that sometimes we're too much alike."

"As long as you realize Aunt Ethel will have to remain as assistant director, I will come back and help. Especially with your practices. I think Aunt Ethel could be a great help to you."

"Great!" Florence said, then she unexpectedly hugged Louise, and Louise closed her eyes. Every time she thought she had an answer to her troubles, she seemed to dig herself in deeper.

Still, she had promised to work with Florence, and she was now committed to the flowerbeds for Jane. Louise intended to honor her commitments. Somehow everything would work out.

Chapter Nine

Walking down Chapel Road on their way to Nine Lives Bookstore for an evening book discussion, the Howard sisters were unusually quiet. Considering Myra's transplant, Jane's busyness with the upcoming inspection, and Louise's concerns about the talent show, Alice realized that each had a good reason to be lost in thought.

"So how was your day, Louise?" she asked, smiling at her older sister.

"Don't ask."

Alice laughed, but Jane said, "Uh-oh. Something happened with Florence?"

"That's right. You're recruiting talent with Florence for the talent show," Alice said, remembering the discussion she and Louise had in the garden about how Florence had alienated everyone in town. "Did things get any better?"

"Only if you think my getting promoted to assistant director makes things better."

This time Jane laughed, but Alice was intrigued. "Really? The program is so involved that it needs an assistant director?"

"It is now." Louise drew in a quick breath. "Let me tell you something, Alice. I'm trying to be a good Samaritan, but being a good Samaritan isn't as easy as it sounds, and lots of people have second thoughts about good deeds. I hope that won't apply where Rosalind is concerned."

"Rosalind won't back out. For her, donating a kidney goes beyond helping one person. She's helping a family."

"Maybe if the talent show had a cause, like aiding a family," Louise said, "I could be more committed to Florence."

"I think it's a little too late for introducing that sort of thing," Alice said.

"This isn't like you, Louise. What's happening

with Florence that's making this so difficult?" Jane asked.

"Every time I try to set a boundary with Florence, she somehow flips things around. Instead of holding the line, I end up with more work."

"How is she flipping things around?" Jane asked with a laugh.

"At first, she simply made assumptions," Louise explained. "For instance, I agreed to be the accompanist, but the next morning she called and wanted me to 'jot things down' as if I were her secretary. I spoke with her about that and she acted as if I had made a mountain out of a molehill."

"That does sound like Florence," Alice agreed. "So what happened today?"

"I tried to get Florence to see she was inadvertently insulting people, and just like with the confusion over her treating me as her secretary, she acted as if I had everything confused." Louise glanced at Alice. "I knew I didn't."

Alice nodded her understanding.

"When I recognized that I couldn't make her understand what I was saying, and that therefore she wouldn't change, I convinced Aunt Ethel to help Florence, and Florence seemed okay with that. But she met me outside Wild Things later and drew me back in by saying she and Aunt Ethel could work together, but only if they had a buffer."

"And you're that buffer," Alice guessed.

"Yes."

"Well, I have to say that Florence might be right this time," Jane said. "She and Aunt Ethel are friends, but they are both strong, independent women. Without a third party to act as referee, they could get into some battles or, worse, lose their friendship completely."

"I know," Louise agreed. "And I don't want that to happen. I also don't want to hurt anybody's feelings, but I'm back to having those strange suspicions about Florence."

Jane asked, "What suspicions?"

"That there's something more to this show than meets the eye."

As Louise said that, the sisters approached the white building with the swinging sign over the door that identified Nine Lives Bookstore.

Jane grasped the handle of the beveled-glass door, and the sisters walked in.

Books filled the wooden shelves labeled POETRY, TRAVEL, BIOGRAPHIES and so on. Brown carpet covered the floors, and portraits of the favorite authors of Viola Reed, the store's owner, hung on the pale taupe walls.

As soon as they entered, Alice saw the top of Ethel's head. She couldn't miss the "Titian Dreams" hair color as Ethel moved along the back shelf, probably looking for one of her beloved romance novels.

Before Alice could turn and inform Louise that

their aunt was already in the bookstore, Ethel saw them and, waving her hand, called out, "Girls, I'm back here."

Alice's gaze swung to Louise, who smiled graciously. "Hello, Aunt Ethel," she said as their aunt approached them.

"Hello, Louise." She caught both of Louise's hands in hers and squeezed lightly. "I just wanted to thank you for giving me your job as assistant director for the talent show."

"You're welcome."

"I'm so excited! Do you know that before Florence and I left the Coffee Shop, I had three people sign up for the show?"

"That's great," a surprised Louise responded.

"I hope you don't mind, but I replaced the sign-up sheets you placed in the businesses around town with sign-up sheets I made from poster board."

"They sound perfect," Louise said.

"Well, I don't know if they're perfect." She paused to smile broadly. "But mine are definitely much easier to see. I also added some fancy designs with bright markers so they look happier and more inviting than yours did."

"Mine were made on the spur of the moment," Louise said, "from the tablet Florence had brought. Nothing special."

"See? That's why mine are better."

"I'm sure they are."

"Oh, look, there's Viola," Ethel said, pointing to Viola Reed. "I'm going to try to talk her into singing for the talent show. I need to plant the seed now, so she can be thinking about it while we discuss this month's book. Then when we're done, I'll give her my real pitch, and by this time tomorrow I'll have four people signed up for the show."

With that Ethel left, and Alice stared after her for a second before she turned to Louise. "She certainly knows how to get people to do what she wants."

"Which is exactly why Florence needs her," Louise agreed.

The door opened again, and Vera Humbert entered. Wearing navy-blue slacks with a baby-blue blouse that matched the blue of her eyes, Vera looked relaxed and ready for the discussion.

"Hi, girls," she greeted as she walked up to Alice, Jane and Louise. "Why, Jane, I'm surprised to see you here. Are you becoming a bookworm?"

"Not really. I came as much to escape my kitchen as I did for the discussion."

Vera looked ready to say something else, but Lloyd walked over from behind a bookshelf. "Louise, I have to thank you for getting Ethel involved in the talent show." He gestured toward Ethel, who was animatedly speaking with Viola, very obviously trying to talk her into singing for the talent show. "When it comes to assignments like this one, your aunt shines."

"Yes. She does," Louise agreed.

"She loves to be a part of things," Alice said.

"Speaking of being a part of things," Lloyd said, "I heard a rumor from the hospital today. Someone came into the Coffee Shop late this afternoon and said a janitor at the hospital had announced he was donating one of his kidneys to an orphan boy."

Jane burst out laughing, but Alice shook her head in dismay. "Oh, for heaven's sake."

Lloyd frowned. "So it's just a rumor?"

"Yes."

Lloyd's frown deepened. "That's odd, because I heard this from Pastor Ken." Lloyd grinned. "Sources don't get much more reliable than the pastor."

"Did I hear my name?"

Alice turned to see Rev. Kenneth Thompson approaching from behind her. Rev. Thompson was a tall man with short, well-groomed dark hair, hazel eyes and patrician features. Originally from Boston, he had been looking for a pastoral assignment in a small town with a slower pace, and he was humbled to have been chosen to replace Daniel Howard as pastor of Grace Chapel.

Vera said, "Lloyd was just telling us about the story you told this afternoon at the Coffee Shop about the janitor who was donating a kidney to an orphan boy."

"That's right," he said. "What a shining example. The story goes that the janitor knew from working at the hospital that donor procedures have been simplified and that the risks and problems for the donor are now almost nil. So when he met this sick child, he really wanted to help him."

Alice stared in amazement. Being familiar with hospital gossip and how a story can be twisted and turned, she knew she shouldn't be surprised that there were such extraordinary inaccuracies in the story, but she couldn't help being amazed all the same.

Lloyd smiled at the minister. "Sorry, Pastor Ken. It's a great story, but from the look on Alice's face, I'll bet it isn't quite accurate."

The pastor turned to Alice. "It isn't?"

Alice flushed. Just enough of the story was true that she knew she couldn't say it was a total fabrication and let it go at that. She had to clear up the misunderstandings.

"Part of the story is correct. Someone is donating a kidney to one of the dialysis patients, but it isn't a janitor giving a kidney to an orphan boy."

The pastor looked abashed as he grasped Alice's hand. "Oh my goodness, Alice. I'm so sorry. It was simply such a wonderful good-Samaritan story that I couldn't resist retelling it."

"It is a good-Samaritan story," Alice agreed. She smiled at the thought of Rosalind's commitment and knew that because Rosalind's truly was a good-Samaritan story it should be retold. Still, she didn't think it wise to begin telling this story without getting some counsel on how to approach it.

"Pastor Ken," she said. "Could I talk with you for a moment?"

"Sure." He glanced at his watch. "Looks like we've got five minutes before the official starting time, and with your aunt Ethel keeping Viola busy, we may actually have more."

Alice led the pastor outside to the wrought-iron bench beside the door. As they sat, he apologized again. "I'm sorry for bringing up something that's potentially sensitive for you, Alice. I know you can't really discuss patients, and since you're working in the dialysis unit, I probably put you in an uncomfortable position."

"Actually, that's why I asked to speak with you. You're right. I don't talk about patients as a general rule. But in this case, it really is a good-Samaritan story. The donor is a woman whose children have grown. She is helping a mother whose children are still young."

"The donor must be a wonderful person."

"She is," Alice said, smiling. "That's what causes the dilemma. Her generosity is so inspiring, it's very natural to want to talk about this."

"I agree. That's why I was so quick to tell the story myself. When an example like this comes up, we're all inspired by it."

"But there's another side to this story."

"Ah," Rev. Thompson said knowingly. "The recipient."

"She's reluctant, and I'm beginning to understand why." Alice drew a breath and glanced at the minister. "She's a quiet, sweet person who probably doesn't want her life under a microscope."

"You know what, Alice? I think this calls for a few actions. We need to pray for both the donor and the recipient. Why don't you talk to them and see if they are comfortable with us starting a prayer circle." He paused and thought for a second. "Once you get permission, I'll ask Vera to think about the prayer circle idea, and I'll use the church bulletin to make sure that everybody involved talks about the good-Samaritan aspects and stays away from gossip."

"I think that sounds like a wonderful plan."

"I thought you would. Now, let's get back in and talk about our book."

"I'm much more ready to do that now than I was five minutes ago," she said. Then, remembering Louise, she touched the pastor's sleeve to keep him from rising. "One more thing."

"What's that?"

"Would you please remember Louise in your personal prayers?"

He frowned. "Is there a problem?"

"Not a big one," Alice said. "Just a little good-Samaritan issue she's dealing with herself."

"Helping Florence with the talent show?"

"You've heard about it?"

The pastor shook his head. "I hate to say this,

Alice, but it's the talk of the town. It seems to be the perfect opportunity for people whom Florence has hurt, no matter how unintentionally, to snub her."

Alice's face fell with regret. "Oh, that's awful."

"I'm doing what I can to combat it, but unfortunately people have very long memories when it comes to being offended."

"Florence doesn't mean the things she says the way they come out."

"And she's changing," he agreed. "But change takes time. Louise's working with her is the best example people can get for dealing with the new and improved Florence, even if she isn't entirely new and improved yet. So you're right. This isn't about Florence. It's about Louise. We need to pray that your sister doesn't lose heart."

"Thanks."

"You're welcome. Now, let's go inside and discuss our book."

Alice, Jane and Louise returned from the book discussion around nine o'clock. Streetlights illuminated their way and led them back to Grace Chapel Inn.

As they entered, Jane said, "Pastor Ken's coming over to discuss the menu for a meeting he's hosting for local Red Sox fans. I've agreed to help him with it, so I'm making a pot of decaf if anybody's interested."

"Not for me, thanks," Louise said. "I'm going to bed." Wishing her sisters a good night, she went up the stairs.

Alice accompanied Jane to the kitchen. "I'll be going up soon," Alice said, sliding out of her sandals. She placed her hand against the countertop to keep her balance, and as she did, she saw the inspection letter Jane had received for the inn. When she straightened again, she lifted the letter from the counter and read the name at the bottom outloud.

"James E. Delaney? Why do I feel I know that name?"

Jane poured water into the coffeemaker. "I don't know. Except that he nitpicks. He's such a pain that the proprietor of every inn he inspects talks about him. Everybody's sure he's trying to get promoted."

Bending to pick up her sandals, Alice couldn't stop thinking about the name James E. Delaney, and suddenly she realized why it rang such a bell with her.

"I know why I recognize the name. A patient with that name was admitted today."

Jane laughed. "Really? There are two of them? It's hard enough to believe there's one man in Lancaster County with that name, let alone two." As she said that, Jane frowned. "It *is* hard to believe."

"Well, if our patient is your inspector, you might

120

as well fold up your to-do list for the inspection and save it for a few weeks."

Jane spun from the counter to face Alice. "Really? Why?"

"I can't tell you what's wrong with him," Alice said, but she knew that James E. Delaney had come into the hospital by ambulance because of severe pain. His appendicitis was so far advanced that he wasn't a candidate for laser surgery, and he had undergone traditional surgery. He wouldn't be back to work in a day or two as laser patients usually were. "But I can tell you that he will still be recovering the Monday before Memorial Day."

Jane's eyes widened. "I'm off the hook?"

"If it's the same person, yes."

Blinking as if she didn't quite know how to process that news, Jane could only shout, "Wow!"

"I'm sure this doesn't cancel your inspection," Alice said with a laugh. "But it probably postpones it. You might want to check with his organization."

"Yes," Jane agreed. "I'll call them tomorrow."

"And maybe we should say a prayer for Mr. Delaney."

Jane squeezed her eyes shut. "I feel awful. I was so wrapped up in my own problem, I didn't even consider that this poor man is sick."

"We'll fix that now," Alice said, and she led Jane in a short prayer.

Chapter Ten

By the time Louise entered the kitchen for breakfast the next morning, she had prepared the front desk to check in that weekend's guests, and Alice had left for the hospital.

"Did you hear the good news?" Jane asked excitedly.

On her way to the coffeepot, Louise chuckled. "Jane, you're the first person I've seen today. I haven't had time to hear anything."

"Alice recognized the name of the inspector on my letter."

Pouring her coffee, Louise said, "Really? She knows the inspector?"

"She knew that someone with that name was admitted to the hospital yesterday. So I called the hospital desk this morning. I didn't ask for information, just his room number, and guess what? He's on the surgical floor."

Louise brought her coffee to the table and sat. "Jane, it's too early for games. What does all this mean?"

"Alice couldn't tell me what was wrong with him." She sighed. "But she recognized his name when she saw it on the inspection letter because he has an unusual middle name, and he used it when he was admitted. That's why we think it's the same man. It's pretty hard to believe there could be two people with the name James E. Delaney in Lancaster County."

"True," Louise agreed.

"Anyway, Alice suggested that I call the inspector's office and casually ask if the inspection is still on, but I'm afraid of giving them the impression that I'm worried about it or trying to get out of it." She sighed. "I don't want a new inspector to be as focused on trouble as Mr. Delaney always seems to be."

Louise chuckled.

"Since I couldn't call the agency, I called the hospital."

"And you're assuming he won't be well in time to do your inspection."

"Most surgical recoveries take four weeks or more. He's scheduled to inspect the inn much sooner than that." She grinned. "I'm home free."

"I'm sure he's not the county's only inspector."

Jane shrugged. "He may not be the only inspector, but I'll bet he's the only tyrant inspector. As far as I'm concerned, as long as I don't give them reason to think I'm trying to get out of my inspection, my worries are over. The kitchen is spotless, and the rest of the inn is in excellent order. My big problem with James E. Delaney was that he seeks out unusual things. Since I couldn't guess what those things would be, I felt I had to overclean everything. Now," she said with another wide grin, "I don't have to. I'm fine. The inn is *ready*."

Louise smiled. "It's very good to see you so happy."

"I'm just so relieved," Jane said, bringing a cup of coffee to join Louise.

"And you have time to have coffee with me again. You are back to normal."

"Because I cleaned the most important stuff first, I have time on my hands."

"You do?"

Jane shrugged. "Yeah. Can you believe it? I have time. Which means I could help you with the talent show, if you want."

Louise thought about Jane's offer. She had planned to spruce up the back flowerbeds as a surprise for Jane. Now that she had done the preliminary planning with Craig and purchased the supplies, she very much wanted to complete this project. She knew she couldn't get out of the regular talent-show practices or the special practices with Florence, and with two weeks left before the show, running around with Florence and Ethel promised to be tiring. Having Jane's help would be a blessing, and working in the garden would give Louise a break from her duties.

Not only that, but getting Jane out of the house for a few hours over the next few days to go with Ethel and Florence recruiting talent would give Louise a chance to get the soil ready for planting, and she could also plant without Jane's being aware of it.

Actually, having Jane take over as referee seemed like the perfect way to get the garden done as the surprise Louise wanted it to be.

She smiled. Maybe all things did work for the good after all. "If you have time on your hands, I could really use a favor."

"Uh-oh. Because you said favor instead of help, I know that means you want me to be the one to referee for Aunt Ethel and Florence."

"I'm sorry, Jane," Louise said quickly. "If you don't want to do this . . ."

"No, I'm happy to do it. In fact," she said with a grin, "I think it will be fun. I'm so much younger than they are that I can have a sense of humor about this and maybe even make them laugh a bit."

"This is true."

"So I'll be happy to help Florence and Aunt Ethel recruit talent." She paused long enough to take a sip of coffee, then gasped excitedly. "Hey! Maybe they'll even let me sing."

Louise groaned. "Oh no."

Jane burst out laughing. "I was kidding, Louie. What I'm going to do is try out as a dancer."

Louise's eyes widened in horror and Jane laughed again.

"All right! All right! I'll be a strictly behind-the-scenes person."

Humming as she pulled a tray of chocolate-chip cookies out of the oven a couple of hours later,

Jane reminded herself that both Louise and Alice had cautioned her about thinking the inspection would be canceled. Louise reminded her that another inspector could show up. And Alice stressed that, no matter how remote, the possibility existed that there were two James E. Delaneys in Lancaster County.

Still, Jane couldn't help feeling ecstatic. It seemed as if a great weight had been lifted from her back. As she told Louise, even if the inspection wasn't canceled, a different inspector would be assigned the job, and for a normal inspector, someone not as nitpicky as James E. Delaney, Jane knew she and the inn were ready.

She heard the buzz of voices coming from the back porch and knew that Ethel and Florence were approaching the kitchen door. She glanced at the coffeepot. The last drops of freshly brewed coffee dripped into the pot. The cookies were warm from the oven. The kitchen smelled like heaven. There was absolutely no way Ethel or Florence could get into an argument in Jane's warm, sweet-smelling kitchen.

She walked to the back entry and pushed open the screen door. "Come in, ladies."

"Thank you, Jane," Ethel said as she entered, Florence right behind her. "Oh, yum. Chocolate-chip cookies. Did you bake those just for us?"

"Just for you," Jane said, working the plan she had established to get the trio of talent scouts off on the right foot. She intended to make Ethel and Florence feel special so that both would be more accommodating and more accepting of the fact that Louise had shifted this duty to Jane. Considering Ethel's enthusiasm about the cookies, Jane decided she had made the right move.

"Have a seat."

Florence took the seat at the head of the table, and though Ethel glanced at Florence oddly, she didn't say anything. She took the seat beside Florence, and Jane immediately handed her the plate of warm cookies.

Hoping to keep things moving, she hurried to the counter to pour the freshly brewed coffee into a brightly painted carafe. The fluorescent red, orange and yellow design was happy and fun and Jane felt it added to the upbeat mood she was creating.

She brought the carafe to the table, where mugs, spoons and napkins awaited beside the cream pitcher and sugar bowl that matched the carafe. She sat across from Ethel, to the right of Florence.

"These cookies are wonderful, Jane," Florence said, closing her eyes in ecstasy. "How on earth do you get them so soft?"

Jane grinned. "Trade secret. But if everything goes well with the talent show, it's a secret I would be happy to share as a way to celebrate."

Florence appeared pleased, but Ethel wasn't so easily swayed. Her expression tended toward a frown. She was clearly catching on to the fact that Jane was operating with an ulterior motive.

As Jane poured coffee into the mugs, she turned to Florence. "So what did you have in mind for today?"

Florence straightened in her chair as if she were the CEO of a major corporation, not someone planning a local talent show. "We need to get out into the community and spread the word about the upcoming auditions."

Ethel waved her hands in dismissal. "I think auditions are a sham." She faced Jane, looking for support. "It's almost an insult to say you're putting on a talent show, but then add that you're the person who's going to judge whether an individual is talented enough to perform." She picked up her coffee. Before she took a sip, though, she said, "Right, Jane?"

"It is a talent show," Jane agreed. "And from my experience with that title, I would get the impression it's open to anyone who wants to display any talent he or she has." Florence's eyes narrowed and Jane quickly added, "But I can also understand why you would want to screen the talent."

"Screen the talent?" Ethel said with a laugh. "So far we have four people signed up. It's not going to take two hours to have four people sing."

"I intend to sing too," Florence put in.

"By yourself? For two hours?" Ethel countered.

"I think I just figured out our problem," Jane said

quickly, jumping in before either woman could move from standing her ground to getting angry. "All we're talking about are singers. Maybe we've accidentally, inadvertently, certainly not on purpose, given people the impression that we're only looking for singers. Maybe what we need to do is to get out into the community today and let everybody know that tonight's auditions are canceled and that all talents are welcome. I for one love a good stand-up comedian. We must have at least one of those in Acorn Hill. And dancers," she said, snapping her fingers as she got an idea. "Maybe Alice's ANGELs group would like to put together some kind of dance routine."

"The school majorettes already have a dance routine," Florence said slowly. "They use it for special competitions."

"Why, yes, they do," Ethel agreed. "And it's quite stunning. I'll get in touch with their coach."

"And since we're talking about kids from school," Jane said, "maybe it would be fun if Vera could get her fifth-grade class to do a skit."

"That would be fabulous!" Florence said.

"And maybe Nia Komonos would like to do a reading?" Ethel said, speaking of the librarian. "It would be a way for her to participate and get in a plug of sorts for the library."

"This is great!" Florence said, shaking her head with wonder. "I can't believe I didn't think of these things on my own."

Jane patted her hand. "I'm telling you, it's the cookies. My chocolate-chip recipe can work miracles."

"Well, the sugar's certainly got my brain going," Ethel agreed. "I just thought of another idea. The church choir. We haven't had any word from them."

Florence gasped with appreciation. "We could get them to open the show with something uplifting and close it with a traditional song that the audience could sing along with."

"Exactly," Ethel said, beaming.

"This is coming together wonderfully," Jane said.

"Okay, since we're creating something of a structure," Florence said, pulling a tablet from her purse, "let me write this down." She listed "uplifting choir song first," then at the bottom of the page wrote "traditional song from the choir." She put Nia's reading three lines above that and put Vera's fifth-grade class skit in the middle. The dance team from the majorettes was slated right before the final song.

"Let's pencil the ANGELs group in here," she said, writing their name two lines below Vera's fifth-grade class. "Though we don't know what they will do, if we ask Alice, I'm sure she will come up with something special."

Then she glanced from Ethel to Jane. "Now all we have to do is find the stand-up comedian you suggested and check out those other possibilities."

"Things are looking up already," Ethel said with a satisfied smile.

"And you're going to sing, Florence," Jane reminded her with an encouraging look.

Ethel nodded. "We really only need four more acts."

But Florence frowned. "I want this to be a long, special production. I don't want it reduced to a math equation."

Jane laughed. "It's not a math equation. We're simply working to figure out how many acts we really need."

"I just want to go with the flow on this," Florence said hesitantly. "I feel I'm being led to something, but I don't know what."

"I think you were listening to the wrong voice, Florence," Ethel said primly. "Until I came on board, you were being led straight to disaster."

Jane jumped in before things got sticky. "That's not really true. Florence had signed on Louise, and she was only in the beginning stages of finding talent. We're lucky to get you, Ethel," Jane said. "I think if Florence feels she's being led to something, we need to trust her instincts."

"Thank you, Jane," Florence said. She rose. "Now, shall we make the rounds of the shops that have our sign-up sheets and see if we have any more takers?"

"That's a great idea," Jane said, silently congratulating herself on a successful first meeting. She said a quick mental prayer of thanks, grabbed a light sweater and followed Ethel and Florence out into the mid-morning sunshine.

"By the way, ladies, you don't mind my getting involved like this?" Jane asked.

"Why, of course not, dear," Florence answered, and Ethel added with a knowing look at her niece, "Besides, this will lift some of the burden from Louise."

Walking down the hall to a patient's room, Alice had her head down as she read a chart. She nearly bumped into Brett Swanson, who caught her by the shoulders to stop her.

"Whoa!" he said, with a deep, rumbling laugh. "We just about had a meeting like you had with Jeff the first time around."

Alice felt her face redden. "Oh! I'm so sorry. I was preoccupied with this chart." She paused, drew in a quick breath and smiled. "Hello, Brett. How are you?"

"I'm fine." He squeezed his eyes shut. "Actually, I'm great."

"Sounds like you have good news," Alice said carefully.

Brett grinned broadly. "Myra agreed to the transplant."

"Oh, that's wonderful!" Alice said. Myra had told her in their last conversation that she had decided to take Rosalind at her word, so Alice knew agreement to the transplant wasn't far behind, but this was the first official word that Myra had agreed.

"Yes, it is, but what's even better is that I feel she's really accepted the notion."

Alice tilted her head in question. "Really accepted it?"

"Myra isn't exactly a private person, but she's sensitive." He shook his head. "And sometimes when she doesn't understand her good fortune, she questions it."

"That's understandable."

"Especially for someone who has had as much trouble as Myra has," Brett agreed. "The past few years have been so difficult that she had begun to expect bad things to happen. Having Rosalind extend such generosity is bringing her back to the optimistic person she used to be."

"That is inspiring," Alice said softly, her heart constricting as she realized the truth of what Brett had said. Sometimes life did push some people down so far that only a true act of mercy and kindness could bring them back.

"The really wonderful part is that Myra has agreed to talk about this with anyone who will listen."

Confused, Alice said, "I don't understand."

"Part of what upset Myra was that Rosalind had no trouble discussing this. She talked about it so much that Myra really had to wonder about Rosalind's motives."

"I remember. But Myra didn't have any trouble talking to me about it."

"Because with you her story sort of tumbled out accidentally. After that, you were such a good listener that she began to trust you. Then Myra met Rosalind for lunch and they talked it all out. Now, Myra is so happy she's talking about the transplant. She's hoping that some other generous soul might be inspired to help an additional person who's in need of a kidney."

"That is certainly possible," Alice said. "But it's still a difficult decision."

"Yes," Brett agreed. "That's why we feel so blessed that Rosalind came into our lives."

"So what happens now?"

"I'm on my way to meet with the doctor and Myra to discuss just that."

"Please keep me informed," Alice said. "By the way, my pastor suggested a prayer circle for Myra. He's asking a dear friend of mine to be in charge."

Overcome with emotion, Brett swallowed. "Alice, that's wonderful."

"I still have to get permission from your wife and Rosalind."

"I don't think you'll have any trouble there."

"Good. Maybe you could steer Myra my way when you're done with your appointment."

Brett reached out and squeezed Alice's hand. "Thanks. I'll do that."

· · ·

Louise had just finished showering after changing out of her gardening clothes when Jane returned from an all-day jaunt with Florence and Ethel. Feeling particularly good about the work she had started in the back flowerbeds, and also totally relaxed for the first time in days, she quickly dressed in a white linen skirt and a three-quarter-length sleeve, light-weight, blue knit top. She also donned her pearls, if only because she felt like celebrating, but she couldn't actually suggest a celebration without giving away the secret that she had a reason to celebrate.

As Louise came down the front stairs, Jane looked up from reading the mail that was sitting on the front hall desk. "Wow! You look great."

"I *feel* great. Rested."

"Well, I'm glad I could help. We had a blast today."

Louise frowned. "You had a good time with Florence and Aunt Ethel?"

Jane laughed. "Absolutely. You would be surprised what I can convince those two to do."

Louise shook her head. "Only you, Jane."

Jane grinned. "Don't I know it." She dropped the mail and headed for the kitchen. "Now I have to come up with something for dinner."

She began walking toward the swinging door and Louise followed her.

Approaching the refrigerator, Jane said, "It's

such a warm day that I'm thinking we should have all cold things."

"You mean sandwiches."

"Special sandwiches," Jane qualified. "*Hmm . . .*" She paused and thought. "I'm thinking something like pesto veggie panini."

Louise grimaced. "What's that?"

Jane laughed. "Don't look so skeptical, Louie. You're going to love it."

"I'm reserving that opinion until you tell me what it is."

"It's eggplant, squash, zucchini and carrots with fresh cucumbers, Roma tomatoes, spinach and low-fat provolone cheese. I'll serve it with garlic and low-fat mayonnaise on a French roll." She grinned. "As I said, you're going to love it."

Louise considered that. "It does sound good."

"It's fabulous." She opened the refrigerator door. "And for dessert . . . cherry gelatin and low-fat whipped topping."

"Alice will love you for that."

Louise stayed in the kitchen to assist Jane as she mixed up the dough for the French rolls. They prepared the vegetables for the sandwiches while the dough rose, and then Louise left the kitchen to teach a piano lesson she had scheduled. By the time the lesson was completed the entire house smelled of fresh bread.

"I sort of defeated the purpose of having all cold foods by heating the kitchen to make these buns."

Jane laughed as she opened a couple of windows to draw out the heat.

Louise inhaled, then said, "Yum. You may have heated the kitchen, but I think it's going to be worth it."

"That's what I love about living here," Jane said, returning to the counter, where she arranged the vegetables for the sandwiches. "Instant gratification. You and Alice love the scents of my cooking as much as the finished product itself."

"Maybe more," Louise agreed. "Because the scents aren't fattening."

Jane laughed again as Alice opened the kitchen door and entered. "What's going on?"

"Jane and I were just discussing how good she makes the house smell."

Alice sniffed the air. "Yum! You are so right." She sniffed again. "Fresh bread."

"French rolls," Jane corrected. "For pesto veggie panini."

"It's a cold eggplant sandwich," Louise said, deliberately making the dinner sound silly so Jane would correct her.

"It's a great deal more elaborate and mouthwatering than my *oldest* sister might have suggested, and we serve it with low-fat mayonnaise."

Alice nodded. "As I said, yum! Let me change out of my uniform, and I'll be all set to tell you whether you deserve a gold star."

Ten minutes later, Alice returned to the kitchen

wearing comfortable white shorts and a sleeveless pink blouse. Louise had set the table with dinnerware that matched the red, orange and yellow carafe Jane had used earlier in the day.

"Everything looks so bright and pretty," Alice commented as she took a seat.

"I love these dishes," Jane said. "The colors remind me of summer."

"Well, it's getting close. Only a little over two weeks before Memorial Day," Louise agreed.

"Speaking of Memorial Day, Louise," Alice said, "did you do any work with Aunt Ethel and Florence today?"

"No. Jane very nicely volunteered to help me in that regard."

Jane grinned. "I had a blast."

Alice frowned. "With Aunt Ethel and Florence?"

"She played precocious child."

"And it worked perfectly," Jane said, not the least bit offended. "Louise said they needed a buffer, and I played a role that allowed both of them to be the adults and compromise."

"Wow!" Alice said.

"Yes, wow!" Louise agreed.

"The first thing we did this morning was set up a list of acts we thought we could get. We're going to ask the choir to open and close the program. Florence is also going to ask Vera if her class will do a skit. Aunt Ethel will get in touch with the coach for the majorette dance squad to see if they can do their dance number. And, Alice, if you can arrange it, we would love the ANGELs to do something."

"That's a wonderful idea," Alice said. "I'm sure we can work out some kind of performance."

"We're using those acts as our pivot points," Jane continued. "We'll put the other singers and dancers in between them." She took a bite of her sandwich, then added, "And we're eliminating the auditions. Aunt Ethel thinks there's no point to them, and I agree. We told Florence that we think anybody who wants to perform should be able to perform. By the end of the day, Florence agreed with us."

Louise nodded approvingly. "Very good."

"Now we just have to fill up the other slots."

"I'm impressed," Louise said.

"Me too," Alice agreed. "And I also have some good news."

"What's that?" Jane asked.

"I ran into Brett Swanson . . . in fact, I nearly did, literally. Myra has not only agreed to the transplant but she's so excited about it that she's talking to everybody who will listen."

"That's wonderful news," Jane said.

"It's even better news that she seems to be getting comfortable with it," Louise said.

"Yes," Alice said, "it is good, because while things may be easier for the donor, the recipient still has surgical risks as well as the possibility that her body will reject the organ."

"So Myra still faces some unknowns," Louise said.

"Nothing that she can't handle."

"Good," Louise replied, but she got an unexpected tug at her conscience. It was Rosalind's unselfish gesture that had prompted her to offer to help Florence, and Louise believed that if things got problematic for Rosalind, that determined woman would not back out. Though Louise reminded herself that she was still accompanying the talent for the show and hadn't completely backed out, she also knew she had to fulfill her role to the utmost.

"I think I will call Florence tonight and talk about scheduling practices."

Chapter Eleven

It's so nice of you to agree to practices at Grace Chapel Inn," Florence said as Louise led her into the parlor while Jane and Alice cleaned up the kitchen after supper. "I didn't realize they would be doing maintenance work on the elementary-school auditorium."

Wallpapered with green ivy and pale lavender violets, the parlor held Louise's baby grand piano, which was draped with a violet-and-ivory piano shawl, a gift from Alice to Louise. The piano bench had a tapestry-covered top, under which Louise kept her sheet music and composition folder. An antique, brass-faced clock sat on the fireplace mantel. Three Victorian Eastlake chairs, curio cabinets and a metronome completed the room.

"It's not a problem."

"They promised it will be ready for us the night of the show, but all of the acts will need to practice here," Florence reminded her apprehensively.

"It's still our pleasure," Louise said graciously. "This weekend's six guests don't arrive until around nine this evening. And most guests are normally out of the inn all day. Besides, I don't expect most of the practices until next week."

Florence frowned. "All your guests will arrive around nine? What a coincidence that they're all arriving late."

"Not at all," Louise said. "The Rosenbergs invited their two sons and daughters-in-law to spend the weekend with them here. It's a family visit."

"Oh," Florence said. "That's a handy way to fill up the inn."

Louise smiled. "Yes. Sometimes we're blessed that way." She lifted the lid off the piano keys. "Where would you like to begin?"

"Well," Florence said, removing the sheet music from a manila folder. "I would like to do two numbers. 'Memory' from the Broadway musical *Cats*," she said, handing that music to Louise, "and Elvis Presley's 'All Shook Up.'"

Louise sighed as she looked over Florence's choices. Florence had told her that she was worried about her performance because of bragging about her abilities at the Coffee Shop the day they first went out to recruit talent, but here was a separate problem. Though "All Shook Up" didn't put any unusual strain on a voice, "Memory" was a very difficult piece for even seasoned performers. "This combination will require a lot of practice."

"I know, but I think I have a very good range, and that combination will allow me to show it off."

Florence's casual attitude was such a switch from the fear she had exhibited when she asked for special practices that Louise wondered if maybe Florence had only given into momentary panic that day.

Not wanting to insult Florence by reminding her that she had been questioning her own abilities, Louise decided to pretend that conversation hadn't taken place and let Florence's singing dictate how Louise approached her performance.

Louise opened the sheet music for "Memory." "This is a beautiful song."

"Very. It's one of my personal favorites."

Louise then opened the music for "All Shook Up" and frowned. Though the range posed no difficulty, the song itself seemed an odd choice for someone in her sixties. "This is a little"—she paused, trying to think of the right way to phrase her observation—"bouncy."

"That's the point," Florence said. "I'm trying to show that I'm versatile."

Tapping her fingertips together, Louise considered Florence's reply.

Finally she asked, "Are you trying to show that your voice is versatile or that as a performer you are interested in different kinds of music?"

Florence took a breath. "Well, let me see. I guess I'm trying to show that I'm interested in all kinds of music."

"Okay," Louise said, pleased with Florence's response because there was logic to it. "That makes perfect sense. I'm assuming that you'll want to sing 'All Shook Up' first to open the show in an upbeat, fun way."

Obviously pleasantly surprised by Louise's comment, Florence gasped. "You want me to open the show?"

Louise shook her head quickly. "No. I'm sorry. Jane told me the choir is opening the show, and I think that's a wonderful idea. But I'm assuming you will be one of the first acts. Since the show will open with something upbeat, then the audience will be prepared for the dance group from the majorettes. 'All Shook Up' would be a perfect way to keep the energy high."

Florence nodded her understanding. "You are so smart about these things, Louise."

Louise chuckled. "I don't know about *smart,*" she said. "But I'm experienced. I've worked with everything from symphonies to wacky college productions. I have experience in a little bit of everything."

Florence sighed. "We are so lucky to have you."

"Actually, Florence, I feel very lucky to be in Acorn Hill. That is one of the reasons I volunteered to help with the production." She set up the sheet music so that she could begin playing. "So what do you say we get started?"

Florence beamed. "Great!"

Louise played the first few bars of "All Shook Up" and Florence all but shouted the first line. Louise stopped.

"Let's try that again, Florence," she said gently. "And this time sing a little softer."

"You want me to sing rock-and-roll softly?"

"No. Not sing softly. Sing a little quieter than you were."

Florence drew a preparatory breath. Louise positioned her fingers over the keys and played the introduction. Florence began to sing again—still loudly—and this time slightly off-key. Louise stopped again.

"What's wrong?" Florence asked.

Louise considered the situation. Florence had admitted to overstating her abilities, and Louise now tended to agree that she had. Florence wasn't as talented as she wished she were. Still, that wasn't unusual; every performer wished to be more talented. In addition, there was something about Florence's voice that told Louise it wasn't as bad as one might think from hearing those first few lines. Louise surmised that in her nervousness Florence was probably overcompensating, and Louise wouldn't get a clear picture of her voice or her talent unless she was singing something a little more subtle.

"You know what? Let's start by practicing 'Memory.' It's a soft song that builds to a strong ending. It might be a nice way to work you into the practice."

"Good idea," Florence agreed.

Louise rearranged the sheet music. She played the opening bars of "Memory," and Florence began to sing every bit as loudly and every bit as off-key as she had been with "All Shook Up." Again, Louise stopped her.

"Florence, I probably didn't give you enough time between songs, because you were still in the more bouncy, more energetic mode. So let me play the song the whole way through, and you listen to it and let the music sink into your soul. Then we'll try it again with you singing."

"Okay," Florence said and took a seat on one of the Victorian chairs.

"Close your eyes if you want," Louise suggested, then began to play.

The soft notes of the opening of the song drifted through the room in the haunting way that couldn't help affecting anyone who has ever experienced a significant loss. Louise closed her eyes and allowed the music to move her as she thought of the lyrics that told of lost love, lost opportunities and the solace of memories.

When she finished playing, the room was poignantly silent. Finally Florence said, "That was beautiful."

"I agree."

"And I want to do it justice."

Florence spoke with such reverence that Louise turned on the piano bench. "Then we will practice until you do."

Florence smiled sheepishly. "Thank you."

They practiced the song for an hour with Florence showing at least slight improvement with every repetition. Louise knew Broadway wouldn't be storming Florence's door, but she had a solid voice, if not an irresistible one. She had undoubtedly heard herself sing well more than a few times. She'd probably also been able to hit and hold hymn notes that others around her could not. So—with luck—she could perform this song.

The problem was that they had only two weeks until the show. Unless Florence listened to absolutely everything Louise told her to do, she might not improve quickly enough.

Worse, Florence's wanting to do two songs might be out of the question because Louise wasn't sure they had enough time to perfect one song. But Louise decided to cross all bridges when she came to them. For now it was enough to know that she and Florence could have amicable practices.

As Louise walked Florence to the front door, she said, "I'll need a schedule for the practices for the other acts."

Florence grimaced. "We don't have one. Can they call you and set up times?"

Louise said, "Yes. That way I will be able to portion out my time on a day-by-day basis."

With her practice behind her, Florence said good night and left. Ten minutes later the phone rang. The majorette dance team coach quickly explained to Louise that the dance team *could* use a tape for their music, but they liked live music so much better. So they were wondering if Louise could have a practice or two with them. They knew their routine. They simply wanted to get the timing down with Louise.

Louise thought about the small parlor and reminded the coach that the auditorium wouldn't be available until the day of the production.

"There are only four girls on the team," the coach assured Louise. "And they don't do anything like backflips. It's a soft number. A scarf dance."

"Those are lovely," Louise said, then, considering that they could move the chairs out of the way, she added, "What time tomorrow can you and the girls come over?"

They set a time for the next morning, which surprised Louise, who thought that teenagers would want to sleep late. But the coach told her that their regular practice time was every Saturday morning anyway. Louise agreed to see the girls at nine and hung up the phone.

It immediately rang again.

"Grace Chapel Inn," she said, answering the call.

"Louise! Fred Humbert, here. I've agreed to do a number for the talent show, and Florence told me I needed to call you ASAP to set a practice time."

Louise quickly grabbed her calendar from the desk and asked, "What time is good for you, Fred?" as she listed the nine o'clock practice for the dance team from the majorettes.

"Well, I don't have to be at the hardware store until around eleven tomorrow, and I'm going fishing after closing. So it would be nice if I can get my practice in before I go to work."

"How does ten sound?"

"Ten is great."

"Good. I'll see you then."

She hung up the phone and took two steps toward the kitchen before the phone rang again. This time it was the choir director. He called to discuss the musical selections that would meet the requirements for the show, and to tell Louise that she could count on their practicing on their own. Louise sighed with relief, then graciously said, "I'm really looking forward to a special performance by the choir."

When the call was over, she walked to the kitchen.

Jane was arranging a plate of hors d'oeuvres and a plate of cookies for their soon-to-be-arriving guests. "Wow! You got done just in time."

"I needed every second I could get for practice with Florence."

Jane raised her eyebrows. "I know. I'm sorry, but I sneaked into the room to get a book I left there last night and heard her. I'm afraid she isn't that good."

"Actually, that's not so. Florence's voice has a lot of potential. With enough practice she could be a very special part of the show. But if she doesn't get enough practice—"

Jane held up her hands in a defensive position. "Don't even say it. I heard enough for myself to know what kind of trouble we could be in for."

"There won't be any trouble. If she doesn't get enough practice, I'm going to have to talk her out of singing."

Jane's eyes widened. "You could do that?"

"As someone who has accompanied hundreds of performers, I know how devastating it can be for someone to be poorly received. I won't let her go through that."

"What if she doesn't agree with your assessment?"

Louise sighed. "She'll have to agree."

The next morning about ten thirty, Alice stepped out of the shower after tending to myriad chores upstairs and heard someone singing. After dressing in beige pants and a white blouse for her meeting with the ANGELs after lunch, she went downstairs. By then the sound of the lone singer had been joined by others. Two different singers were warming up in the front hall, and someone was practicing a musical instrument in the living room. Sliding past the singers, she made her way to the kitchen, where Jane was at the dishwasher, emptying it and putting away the breakfast dishes.

"What's going on?" Alice asked, but Jane didn't even look up. "What's going on?" she asked again.

When Jane still didn't answer, she walked over and tapped her on the shoulder. Jane clutched her chest and gasped as if Alice had scared the breath out of her.

"Sorry."

Jane, somewhat embarrassed, took earplugs out of her ears, then said, "Sorry. I didn't realize you were in here."

Alice laughed. "Hey, if I had known that I would be listening to this I would have earplugs too. Who is that singing?"

From the parlor they could hear lyrics—"Why there's a change in the weather, there's a change in the sea, so from now on there'll be a change in me . . ."

Jane listened and shrugged. "I didn't see him

arrive, but that sounds like Fred. Certainly the lyrics are right for him."

"How did so much activity get started at the same time?"

"All I know is that after the Rosenbergs headed out around eight, Louise made some phone calls, and she's had somebody from the talent show in the parlor practicing ever since with the door open to keep the parlor cool."

"Wow. Louise isn't usually *that* regimented."

Jane agreed. "I think she may be trying to make sure she has enough spots open in her schedule for Florence to practice."

Pouring herself a cup of tea, Alice glanced at Jane. "Why?"

"Let's just say she wants to make sure Florence's performance is as good as it can be."

"Florence is that talented?" Alice asked excitedly.

Jane prudently said, "Only potentially."

Alice laughed again. "I get it."

The sound of something resembling song drifted into the kitchen from the front hall. Jane flinched. "Wow!"

"Poor Fred. I'm sure Louise will help him to be the best he can be," Jane said, her voice filled with hope.

Alice nodded. "No offense, but I think I'll grab my second cup of tea at the Coffee Shop."

"No offense taken," Jane said, "but if you don't mind, I'm putting these back in." She waved her earplugs. "I have a whole morning of this, and I'm not taking any chances."

Shaking her head, Alice chuckled and left by way of the back door. She took her time walking to the Coffee Shop, enjoying the warm, sunny morning and the peace of Acorn Hill. By the time she got to the Coffee Shop, she had forgotten all about Louise's significant task of turning the residents of Acorn Hill into performers. She ordered tea from Hope, then chatted with her for a few minutes. When the conversation turned to the talent show, Hope indicated that customers were now talking about it in terms more accepting—even more enthusiastic—than before. So, Alice realized, progress was being made after all. She thanked Hope for the tea and the talk, paid her bill and left for the ANGELs meeting in the Grace Chapel Assembly Room.

Vera had asked to speak to the group about the prayer circle for Myra and Rosalind. When Alice reached Grace Chapel, Vera was waiting for her. Wearing a bright-pink jogging suit that hid her slight plumpness, Vera smiled happily as Alice approached.

"Hi."

"Good morning," Alice said. "All ready for the meeting?"

Vera brandished a stack of index cards. "I have information about kidney transplants and prayer circles. I'm ready for anything."

"Great. I got permission from Rosalind and Myra for us to use their names in the prayer circle. So it looks like we're all set."

They stepped into the room, which was filled with noise and activity. Alice said, "Good morning," in a slightly raised voice, and all the girls quieted and turned to face her.

"Take a seat please," she said, motioning to the chairs around the tables. "As I told you when I called this special meeting, we need to plan an act for the talent show, but first Mrs. Humbert— whose class will be putting on a skit, by the way— is going to speak to us about a few things of importance."

Vera said, "Thank you, Miss Howard," then walked to the center of the room with her index cards.

"Pastor Thompson has asked me to organize a prayer circle for a very special need. A patient Miss Howard met at the hospital is about to have a kidney transplant. The kidney is being donated by a living donor, which means that the donor is able to give a kidney and still go on with her life."

A small gasp issued from the crowd of about sixteen girls ranging in age from eleven to fourteen.

Sarah Roberts said, "How do they do that?"

"I'm glad you asked," Vera said with a laugh. "Actually, the procedure is rather simple." She went on to explain the laparoscopic surgery involved in removing the kidney and how the donor's remaining kidney was sufficient for good health.

"The procedure for the recipient of the new organ isn't quite as easy," she said as the girls sat in rapt attention. Watching the kids, Alice began to realize that the latest information about transplants hadn't yet become common knowledge for the general public, and people were curious.

"The process is still major surgery," Vera continued, "and not only does the recipient potentially face organ rejection, but she must take antirejection drugs for the rest of her life."

Sissy Matthews whispered, "Wow! That's awful."

Vera shook her head. "No, it's actually wonderful," her voice softened with compassion. "The person needing the kidney has usually spent years on dialysis, an involved and often wearisome procedure that allows machines to do the work ordinarily done by a healthy kidney. Dialysis makes it possible for patients to lead something of a normal life, but a transplant gives them significantly more energy and eliminates visits to the dialysis center. Without a transplant, some patients need dialysis three times a week, and the procedure is time consuming. With the new kidney, they regain their energy and the time they spent on dialysis, and their lives change for the better."

"So," Jenny Snyder said, "our prayer circle will be for the health of the two patients?"

"Yes," Vera said, "for their physical health and their mental well-being."

The girls broke into discussions among themselves, and Alice clapped her hands to regain their attention. "How do we want to handle this?"

"I think we should pray before and after our Wednesday meetings," Lisa Masur suggested.

"I think we should all pray privately," Kate Waller said.

"I think we should meet at the church," Sarah added.

Jenny said, "I think we should meet once a week at church too."

Again, the girls broke into discussions among themselves, and Alice turned to Vera. "What do you think?"

"Well, first off, I know a lot of these kids are busy, so I think the extra time at church might turn into a problem, and we don't want that. We want their experience with this prayer circle to be positive."

"How about if I suggest that we pray before and after our meetings and that everybody remember Myra and Rosalind in her private prayers?"

Vera nodded approvingly. "Sounds good to me."

As Alice made the suggestion to the girls, she suddenly realized that each and every one of them was now a big part of this transplant, not simply as people who prayed, but as people who could make a difference by spreading the word.

If everything went well with the transplant, Rosalind's generosity really could inspire other qualified people to consider donating.

Chapter Twelve

Sunday evening Louise was going over some papers in her room, and she found the receipt for the plants she had ordered for the back flowerbeds. She groaned, realizing that the garden would have to be better prepared to receive new flowers and shrubs.

With a sigh, she left her room and went downstairs for a cup of tea and discovered that Alice had also gone to the kitchen for a treat, a cup of hot chocolate.

"Need some chamomile?" Alice asked with a chuckle.

"Is it that obvious that I'm stressed?"

"Yes," Alice said. "I'm guessing that all the practices you've been having in the past two days are making you crazy."

"Yes, that and . . ." She paused and walked over to the pantry just to make sure Jane wasn't in there taking inventory or looking for ingredients for tomorrow's breakfast for the departing guests.

Alice burst out laughing. "What are you doing?"

"I'm checking for Jane."

"She's at Aunt Ethel's. More strategy sessions for gathering talent for the show. They still need two more acts."

Louise said, "Peachy. More practices."

"Louise, you never get stressed out over anything that has to do with music. Something else has to be bothering you. What is it?"

"I'll tell you, but you must keep it a secret."

Alice raised her eyebrows.

Louise sighed. "You remember how panicked Jane was over the impending visit of the nitpicky inspector?"

"Yes, I remember all of Jane's instructions about the gardens. Until the inspector arrives, we keep them up so that she doesn't have to worry about them. Is that what this is all about? You're worried we won't keep up those gardens?"

"No, I wish that is all that it was." Louise sat at the table. "Alice, when we were working on the gardens, I realized that we only have perennials in the back flowerbeds."

"That makes them easier to care for."

"Yes, I knew that, but I also thought it would be a nice surprise for Jane if I could really spruce up that section for the inspection and the holiday. So I went to Wild Things and talked with Craig, and we came up with a plan to really revitalize the back."

Alice's mouth fell open slightly. "Oh no. What did you do?"

"I ordered flats of flowers and a few new shrubs." She shrugged. "I kept telling myself I could work it all in. I forgot about them until tonight when I was looking through this week's papers and saw the receipt."

"How far did you get with preparing the beds?"

"Not very far I'm afraid. I had intended to do an hour or two of digging every day when Jane was off with Aunt Ethel and Florence, and that would have worked, except I didn't keep it up and now I'm committed to practices."

Alice turned her attention to the hot chocolate she had left cooling on the counter. "Tomorrow I'll pick up where you left off."

"Oh, Alice, I couldn't ask that of you."

Alice faced Louise with a smile. "You didn't. I volunteered. Besides, it will be fun. Working in a garden is very therapeutic. I like to think and pray when I'm out there."

Louise frowned. "Me too. That was part of my motivation. Digging for the sake of stress relief." Her voice became serious. "Alice, are you sure this isn't too much for you?"

"Positive. As I said, I'll enjoy it." She grinned mischievously. "Besides, I like being part of a secret. Deciding to spruce up those gardens was a wonderful idea and a sweet thing for you to do, Louise."

"Even if I can't do it?"

"You are doing it. You're simply sharing some of the hot, dirty, backbreaking work, and I'm your humble servant."

Louise smiled. "Thank you."

"You're welcome," Alice said, then handed Louise the cup of tea she had prepared. "Go sit on the front porch. I'll join you in a second, and you can give me complete instructions."

"First I'll get the sketch that Craig and I drew up for the gardens." Alice was wonderful. Once again Louise thanked God that she was in her family home and that she had two extraordinary sisters.

Unfortunately, Alice's kindness also served to remind Louise that every time she offered her services of late, she couldn't finish the project involved. Jane was helping Florence and Ethel, and now Alice was helping with the back flowerbeds.

On Monday morning Jane received a letter from the department charged with inspecting the inn.

"Listen to this," she said as Louise poured herself a cup of coffee and Alice reached for a mug to make tea. "We are sorry to inform you," she read, "that the inspection schedule has been changed because of an unexpected illness."

"That would be Mr. Delaney's emergency surgery," Louise speculated.

Jane continued reading. "We are sorry for any inconvenience this causes you. Please direct questions to me at the number below. Sincerely, Irwin Penberthy."

Alice frowned. "What's so unusual about that? After all, we've sort of been expecting it."

Jane quickly reread the letter, looking for a statement that specifically said the inspection was called off. "When I called them after you told me about Mr. Delaney's surgery, the clerk told me to expect a letter, but this letter doesn't exactly say that the inspection is canceled."

"That's because they still have to inspect the kitchen and dining area," Louise put in. "So it hasn't been canceled, but it has clearly been postponed, probably until Mr. Delaney is well enough to work. That's why they didn't set a new date. They probably don't know when he will return."

Jane sighed. She couldn't shake the feeling that it was odd that Irwin Penberthy didn't actually spell out that the scheduled inspection was off. Yet she also suspected that she'd blown this inspection out of proportion and turned the situation into something more than it really was. After her time of working with Ethel and Florence, she'd come to see how easily something could be exaggerated, and to see how often she had to talk Ethel or Florence down from a metaphorical ledge. She knew she'd been every bit as fanatical about preparing for the planned inspection. Still, it was better to be safe than sorry.

"Let me check this out," Jane said, walking to the phone. She dialed the number given on the letterhead. "I'd like to speak with Mr. Penberthy, please."

"I'm sorry, ma'am," the operator said, "but he's out of the office today. I'll connect you with his secretary."

The operator clicked off and a chipper voice said, "Mr. Penberthy's office. Ginny speaking."

"My name is Jane Howard. I understand Mr. Penberthy is out of the office today."

"Yes, he is out nearly every day," Ginny said, "doing his inspections."

"Do you happen to know his schedule?"

"Yes, I have it right here."

"Great. Can you tell me what day the Grace Chapel Inn is scheduled for inspection?"

"Actually, I don't see it here."

"It would be an add-in. Mr. Penberthy may be taking over the inspections for another gentleman who fell ill this month, and our inn would be one of those."

"Oh, I know what happened here. Mr. Penberthy couldn't fit all of Mr. Delaney's inspections into his schedule. He's only doing some of them. If you got a letter that didn't give you a date, that means your inn is one of those that didn't fit."

"But the letter doesn't say my inspection is canceled."

"Technically, it isn't canceled," Ginny said. "It's probably better to say it's postponed. Mr. Penberthy hopes to get to all the inspections, but, just between you and me, he's already overbooked. If you're not on the list, it will be really difficult for him to be able to squeeze you in."

"Oh. Okay." Jane thought about Ginny's comments for a second, then said, "Do you think I can have him call me back to confirm that?"

"Sure. But as I said, his schedule is very tight. I don't know when he'll get a chance to call you."

"Well, I'm here day and night."

"Okay. I'll give him the message that you called."

Jane gave the secretary her call-back information, thanked her, then hung up the phone with a frown. "We didn't make it onto the actual inspection list."

"So he's not coming?" Louise asked.

"I don't think so. He's added in as many of Mr. Delaney's inspections as he could, and the rest of us have to wait, I guess, for Mr. Delaney's return."

"It makes perfect sense to me," Louise said.

"It does to me too," Jane agreed hesitantly.

"If it will make you feel any better, I could help you in the evenings this week to get everything ready just in case an inspector should show up anytime soon," Alice said.

Jane tossed the letter to the counter. "No. I'm being paranoid. Mr. Delaney had surgery. His replacement, it seems, couldn't fit us in. They aren't sure when they will get to our inspection, but they have to do an inspection; so they couldn't say it was canceled." She shook her head. "I'm not going to upset myself about this. That would be stupid."

• • •

That day, as Jane spent time with Ethel and Florence checking sign-up sheets and discussing the show, and Alice took over Louise's work in the back flowerbeds, Louise continued working with the talent-show participants.

She practiced with the dance team from the majorettes.

She spent time with Vera helping choose background music for the skit her fifth-grade class would perform.

She practiced a soothing accompaniment for Nia Komonos' reading.

She met with the church choir director, who provided her with sheet music for the songs they had selected.

She also spent a long session with the ANGELs group trying to work out the exact nature of their performance.

When four shrubs arrived on Thursday, Jane was busy with Florence and Ethel, and by prior arrangement the plants were put out of sight behind the garden shed. Working as a team, Louise and Alice planted the shrubs, and afterward Louise called Craig to let him know none of the flowers had arrived. He assured her they would be there by Saturday, but Saturday came and went without a delivery. Jane was so busy she didn't notice the new shrubs in the back flowerbeds anymore than she had noticed the freshly tilled soil. So Louise wasn't especially worried that her surprise would be ruined.

Walking to church on Sunday morning, Jane asked about the situation with Myra and Rosalind, and Alice said there was nothing new to report except that Rosalind was bubbling with enthusiasm, keeping up her commitment to the hospital as a volunteer and happier than Alice had ever seen her.

Waiting for the service to begin, Louise prayed for both Myra and Rosalind. Hearing of Rosalind's abundant energy and enthusiasm, she felt guilty that she had made so many promises that she just couldn't seem to keep. She thanked God that everything was working out in spite of her inability to do the tasks herself. She apologized for making promises, then having to solicit help to keep them, but she didn't feel any sort of relief from the guilt. She told herself to let it go, that admitting the shortcoming and promising to do better was enough, but the feeling nagged at her. She didn't want to think she was getting too old to meet her commitments. She didn't want to stop making commitments. But obviously she had miscalculated somewhere.

Leaving the church, she smiled at Rev. Thompson. "Good morning. How are you today?"

"Louise, I couldn't be better. But you must be exhausted. I'm hearing music coming from your house at all hours of the day and night. How are you keeping up the pace?"

The pastor's observation helped her to see that she had created a schedule that would be hard for anyone, and Louise smiled slowly. "I have two very good sisters who are helping me."

She pointed at Jane, who was speaking animatedly with Ethel and Florence. All three women were smiling as if they sincerely enjoyed putting together the talent show. Florence positively glowed, and Louise knew Jane's irrepressible personality was responsible for that. With Jane's enthusiasm supporting her, Florence probably felt she could do anything.

"I've seen Alice working in the back gardens. Is she thinking of giving up nursing for agriculture?" The pastor chuckled at his own question.

"Not a chance. Actually, I came up with the idea to do some plantings to surprise Jane, but then I got bogged down with the talent-show practices, and Alice picked up the mantle."

Rev. Thompson smiled. "You do have two wonderful sisters."

"Yes, I do."

"And you're a good leader."

Louise laughed. "Because I've started projects I couldn't finish?"

"No, because you delegate," Rev. Thompson said with a smile. "Delegating, sharing, working together, that's what life's all about. The three of you seem to have that system working brilliantly."

Louise found herself standing a little taller. Not proud of herself, not proud of her sisters, but proud of her family. "Thank you, Pastor Ken. Our father had a lot to do with our respect for each other and our ability to work together."

"Your father must have been a wonderful man." The pastor shook his head. "Hard shoes to fill."

"That's why we were lucky to find you."

"Ah, the diplomat emerges again," Rev. Thompson said, just as Jane walked up to him and Louise.

"What are you two laughing about?"

"I was just telling Pastor Ken what a wonderful job he is doing."

"And I was telling Louise what a wonderful diplomat she is."

"So I've walked in on a mutual admiration society?" Jane asked.

"Yes, save us from our sugar sweetness," Rev. Thompson said.

"Okay, I have just the topic to change the subject," Jane said. "Florence did a tally of the acts for her talent show last night and came up with a realistic schedule, and we still feel we're two acts short."

"You would never know it by me," Louise said with a laugh. "I swear every resident of town has practiced in our parlor."

"Yes, but two acts dropped out."

The pastor frowned. "Really? What a shame."

"Both of them had unexpected commitments pop up. What really concerns us all is that we have to fill those slots," Jane said, clearly dismayed.

"Is there any way I can help?" he asked.

Jane grinned. "Yes. Sing. One song. That's all we're asking."

Rev. Thompson laughed and took a step back. "Not me, Jane. I only sing in church and in small groups."

"Please," Jane persisted.

He shook his head. "No, I don't want to sing in front of a group that large . . . or ruin the show."

"Don't you have *any* talent we could use?" Jane teased.

"Sorry. The well is dry. Unless you would like me to give a sermon, I can't help you."

"Okay, you're excused. Thanks just the same," Jane said. "Well, Louise, I think it's time for us to head home."

"Yes," Louise agreed. "Good day, Pastor Ken."

"And to you, ladies," he said.

Louise saw Alice in the crowd and asked Jane to walk with her to the group of ANGELs among whom Alice stood. Jane had handled Rev. Thompson's demurral gracefully, but when in greeting the ANGELs she seemed distracted, Louise guessed that the shortage of acts was beginning to wear on her.

Things seemed to worsen when Jane returned

from answering the phone at dinner that evening. From the expression on her face, Louise could tell that the news she'd heard in the phone call wasn't good.

"The choir just discovered that they made the finals in a regional competition scheduled for Memorial Day. They previously had indicated that a conflict would be unlikely because they were long shots, but now . . . They don't want to drop out of the show completely, but they've asked to do only one number because of having to divide their preparations." She squeezed her eyes shut. "So now the show will be even shorter."

Chapter Thirteen

When Alice walked into the dialysis unit on Monday morning, she was greeted by the pop of a flashbulb.

"Darn it! That woman just ruined my shot."

Alice blinked to get her bearings and realized that she was the woman who had ruined someone's photo by inadvertently stepping in front of a camera. She held her hands up in surrender as a way of acknowledging her "transgression." Across the room, Myra and Rosalind were posing for pictures. They stood behind a bank of microphones that had been set up in front of an art grouping on a side wall. The reception chairs that typically sat in that space had been removed to give Myra and

Rosalind more room and probably to create a more visually appealing scene.

With bright lights glowing, reporters from the local television station and the Potterston newspaper were questioning them, and between questions the newspaper photographer was snapping pictures.

Standing by the reception desk, Brett Swanson smiled and motioned for Alice to join him and his children. "Come join us over here, Alice."

Alice stepped between camera wires and around cameramen to reach the family. "Good morning, Brett," she whispered, afraid of once again disturbing the scene. "Hi," she added, leaning around Brett to speak to his children.

"Hi," the pretty blond girl and lanky boy replied simultaneously.

"I'm sorry, Alice, I probably never introduced you to Lori and Kurt," Brett said, referring to the teens.

Alice smiled. "Nice to meet you both."

"You too," the teens replied.

"Where's Jeff?" she asked, looking around.

Jeff peeked out from around his father's thighs. "I'm here," he said, then he grinned.

Alice stooped down. "Hiding from the cameras?" she asked with a chuckle.

"I don't like the lights."

"I don't like the lights either," Brett said, "but it's part of the process. So what are we going to do about that, Jeff?"

"Pretend they're not here."

"Exactly."

"So what's going on?" Alice asked Brett when Jeff disappeared behind his father again.

"A little press conference. Once the word spread about Rosalind's generosity, both the paper and the TV station called. Myra feels that if her situation can inspire just one other person to consider donating, then she has to be involved with the interview too."

"That makes sense," Alice murmured. "And all this is quite impressive." She agreed that Rosalind's generosity could inspire more donations, but Myra's transplant wasn't a success yet. If something went wrong, publicity could do more harm than good.

"You're impressed?"

Alice bit her lip, then said, "This time tomorrow this could be a national news story."

Brett laughed. "Only if we're lucky. That kind of exposure could net a lot of donors."

"Do you think it's a good idea to get your hopes up like that?"

"We don't expect hundreds of people to volunteer. Not everyone can. But you never know. We might inspire somebody."

"Being in the limelight doesn't bother you?"

"I don't believe it's going to get *that* much attention," Brett said. Then he grimaced. "Unless something goes wrong."

"Then we'll just have to pray harder that nothing will," Alice pointed out gently.

Brett nodded. "Yes, and the odds are in our favor, Alice." He grinned. "Look who I'm lecturing—a nurse. You *know* the odds are in our favor."

He was right. Alice was aware that the procedures were so far advanced now that the donation process was downright simple by medical standards. Rosalind was a healthy woman. Despite her years of dialysis, so was Myra. They were the poster couple for a kidney transplant.

So, why, Alice wondered, did she have an uneasy feeling about this scene?

Jane spent the morning cleaning. Though James E. Delaney was supposedly ill and probably couldn't do her inspection, she didn't trust the fact that her letter hadn't actually, specifically said the inspection was canceled. If she was lucky, a kinder, gentler inspector would visit Grace Chapel Inn. He would arrive today as indicated in the original notice, see that the inn was spotless and give it a glowing report. If she was unlucky, James E. Delaney would arrive holding his side, barely able to walk, let alone cheerfully inspect a bed-and-breakfast. He would drag himself through the inspection and fail the inn based more on the fact that he was still in pain than on any imperfection. "Hold on, Jane," she said to herself aloud. "You're getting carried away." She had just finished the last of what she considered necessary cleaning and was standing in front of the refrigerator taking inventory for a trip to Potterston for groceries when a quick succession of knocks rattled the frame of the open back door.

Thinking it might be her inspector, she stepped away from the refrigerator so she could see who was there. A tall, balding man stood on the back porch. Though he carried a clipboard, his blue coveralls didn't look like the clothing a typical inspector wore.

"I got your flowers here, ma'am."

"Flowers?" Jane asked, walking to the back door.

He looked at his clipboard, then up at her again. "Two trays. Looks like lots of impatiens."

"Impatiens?" she asked, glancing through the screen door at the tray the deliveryman had set at his feet.

"Kinda hard to kill those," he said with a laugh.

"Yes, I guess." She shook her head. "But I didn't order them."

"Are you"—he peered down at his clipboard again—"Louise Smith?"

Jane opened her mouth to reply at the same time that Louise came sailing through the swinging door. "She's not Louise Smith. I am."

Jane turned from the door. "Louise, did you order these flowers?"

Walking past Jane and opening the screen door so she could sign the delivery confirmation sheet on the clipboard, Louise said, "I'm sorry, Jane. This was supposed to be a surprise."

"You bought me two trays of flowers as a surprise?"

Louise handed the clipboard back to the deliveryman, who turned and left the porch to get the other tray of flowers from his truck.

"Alice and I have been cleaning out the back section of the gardens, getting them ready to add a few things. In fact, we've already added some new shrubs."

"Really?"

"Yes. I know you had pronounced the back flowerbeds fine with only the perennials. But I also know you had hoped to get back there sometime and really make the section special." She paused and sighed. "So I decided as a way to give you a boost of confidence for the upcoming inspection, I would add some new shrubs and plant some annuals. When I got behind schedule, our dear sister agreed to help, and she has done much of the preparatory work."

Jane didn't know what to say. Louise was a generous woman by nature, so the gift itself didn't surprise her. The amazing part was that Louise understood that beautifying the flowerbeds in the back of the yard could lift Jane's spirits and give her confidence. And she agreed with Louise that Alice was a "dear sister."

Finally, Jane said, "I'm so touched, Louise. That's very sweet of you both."

"Yes, well," Louise said sheepishly, "I had hoped to present the completed flowerbeds to you as a surprise. And that might have been the case, but obviously our deliveryman didn't know that the trays were supposed to be put behind the shed."

Jane grinned. "I can always pretend I don't know."

"Or since it's after eleven o'clock, and the time for today's scheduled inspection has come and gone, you could change clothes and help with placement this afternoon."

"I could do that," Jane agreed, then she grinned again. "You are so sweet, Louie!"

Louise sighed. "Now you're pushing it."

That evening as Louise straightened the parlor and waited for Florence to arrive for her practice, she silently thanked God again for her sisters. She and Jane had spent a lovely afternoon up to their elbows in the freshly spaded dirt, placing flowers around the azaleas, rhododendrons, and red-maple shrubs. After deciding to go for a less formal effect than the one Craig had sought in his sketches, they'd taken their time reconsidering placement and argued a bit about where to put what, but they also laughed . . . a lot.

When Alice arrived home that night, it was she who was surprised by the flowerbeds. After changing out of her nurse's uniform, she let Jane and Louise lead her back to the far corner of the yard and preen over the beautiful piece of work they had done. Alice was truly impressed, and she sincerely praised Louise's choices. In return she received her sisters' praise and gratitude for her part in the gardening success.

Though Louise chose to give Craig most of the credit, she couldn't help but feel a thrill of pride that she had been part of creating something beautiful. She also had created something for her and her sisters to do as a team. Something that was fun. Something that reminded them of how lucky they were to have each other.

Later, when Florence arrived, chipper, cheerful and ready to sing, Louise greeted her happily. Though they were six days away from the actual show, Florence's rendition of "Memory" was coming along nicely, and Louise hoped that they would be able to begin practicing "All Shook Up" tonight as well.

"Are you ready to run through 'Memory'?" Louise asked, poising her hands above the piano keys.

"Ready," Florence said confidently.

They breezed through the song with ease. Florence's rendition would never compete with a professional's, but it was a special performance nonetheless. The emotion of her portrayal made up for the fact that though Florence had natural talent, her voice had not been trained. All in all, Louise was quite proud of how far Florence had come in her practices.

When the song ended, Louise beamed. "That was lovely," she said with enthusiasm.

"Great!" Florence said, obviously delighted. "So now we can start on 'All Shook Up.'"

"Yes," Louise agreed. She shifted her music and after a moment of studying it, said, "Ready?"

"Yes, I am," Florence said happily, and Louise began to play.

Before they even got through the first verse, Louise's enthusiasm was quashed. Florence just didn't sound right with the rock-and-roll number, and as someone who had worked with many singers, Louise knew that a song like this one would be trouble for Florence.

She removed her fingers from the keys, though Florence sang another few words before she realized Louise had stopped.

"What's wrong?"

"Florence," Louise said kindly. "You're doing such a special performance with 'Memory' that I have to wonder if it's a good idea to do another song."

"Of course it is!" Florence said, her eyes wide with dismay. "We've scheduled this song in the program to provide an upbeat feeling at the beginning of the show. It's not just a good idea for me to sing this song. It's a necessity."

"Okay," Louise said, deciding that she possibly had been hasty in her assessment. After all, she'd cut off Florence without even letting her sing an entire verse. "Let's try it again from the top."

Again, she prepared to play. Florence nodded for Louise to begin, and her fingers fell to the keys.

Florence still sounded dreadful. Nevertheless, sticking to her decision to let Florence sing an entire verse, Louise kept playing. As she approached the end of the first verse, Louise chose to continue, assuming that after an entire song of being so far off key, Florence couldn't possibly deny that this song was wrong for her, especially since she had just sung "Memory" with such passion.

She allowed Florence to sing the whole song and wasn't surprised when the room fell totally silent for several seconds after Florence finished and the last note had faded away. She didn't want to be the one to say the obvious. So she let Florence speak first.

"That was wonderful."

Louise turned on the bench. Positive she had heard incorrectly, she said, "Excuse me?"

"Thank you, Louise. You were fabulous as always, and I now have two really great songs for the show."

Louise was speechless, and she felt slightly dazed. How did one tell someone so confident that at least half of her confidence was misplaced?

"I know. I know. You think the song's a little young for me."

"Not at all. It's from our generation. It's very

appropriate to show that we may be a little older but that we still have energy and vitality."

Florence absolutely beamed. "That was my point in choosing it."

"However, Florence," Louise began, still trying to come up with the correct words, "your voice—"

"Has never sounded better, thanks to you," Florence said. "I've been doing the exercises you told me about when we were practicing 'Memory,' and I can hear the improvement in 'All Shook Up.'"

"Those exercises are important," Louise responded, if only because those exercises should have strengthened Florence's throat muscles. "However—"

"However! However! However!" Florence sputtered. "Why do you keep saying however?"

"Because I think we have some problems."

Florence seemed to deflate. "Problems?"

"Voices and songs need to go together," Louise said, scrambling for a way to present this so Florence wouldn't be insulted, or, worse, lose the confidence she needed to be able to perform her other song.

"But you've already said that it was appropriate for me to sing 'All Shook Up.'"

"Actually, I suggested that it was appropriate for someone our age to sing that song, but not everyone—"

"You're saying my voice can't handle it?"

"I'm saying that we have only six days until the

show," Louise said, finally thinking she had found her approach to make an explanation that Florence could accept. "And you'll need much more practice to get this song right."

"No. No, Louise, don't placate me," Florence said, suddenly sounding sad and tired. "I get it. We worked over a week on 'Memory' and it's barely passable. I'm not a superstar. I'm not anything."

Blindsided by the unexpected remark and the turnaround in Florence's mood, Louise was saddened by her outburst. "Oh, Florence," was all that she could say.

Florence swallowed and Louise could tell she was holding back tears. "I'm sorry, Louise. You know what? Maybe the whole talent show was a bad idea. We just barely have enough acts. Technically, we need three more to have two full hours. Originally, I had wanted three hours worth of performers, but now I can barely get two. In addition, we're finding out I'm apparently worthless, so we can cut two more numbers. Which means we're now five acts below the number needed to fill two hours. The whole stupid show is pointless."

Louise drew a quiet breath. She had seen performance anxiety any number of times. She also had seen starlets and stars throw fits to get compliments or their own way. She didn't sense that Florence's outburst was either performance anxiety or an attempt to get compliments.

Louise shifted on the bench until she was facing Florence. "What's going on, Florence?"

Florence swallowed. "It's nothing," she said, fussing with her music, stacking it in her manila folder and then making sure every page was exactly even with the one above it.

"*Something* is wrong."

Florence drew a breath and suddenly smiled at Louise. "It's nothing. I'll pull this show together without my songs." She waved her hand in dismissal. "We don't need me. I'll find other people."

"Your rendition of 'Memory' is truly very good."

"It's passable. I'm not star material."

"Most of us aren't," Louise said gently. "But even though you'll never perform at Carnegie Hall, Florence, you're very good. You should be proud of that."

Florence brightened a little more. "Really?"

"Yes," Louise insisted.

"You're sure?"

"Yes."

Florence drew another deep breath. "I want to believe you. I really do. But I've never actually been good at anything."

"That isn't true. Everybody's good at something."

Florence shook her head. "Not me," she said, her voice soft and light, as if she didn't care. "I have a cousin who is a decorator in the Washington, DC, area." She glanced up at Louise. "She's so wonderful that she doesn't just make lots of money, she also wins awards."

Louise cocked her head. "Jane wins awards for her cooking."

"I have another cousin who is a bestselling novelist."

Louise's eyebrows rose. "Really?"

Florence nodded. "His father, my uncle, wrote for the *New York Times*."

Louise felt her mouth fall open slightly. "Oh, I didn't know that."

"I have another uncle who was in a president's cabinet."

"Wow!"

Florence smiled as if she'd finally forced Louise to see the point she had been trying to make all along. "I'm not special."

Though Louise understood what Florence was driving at, she didn't agree. She thought for a few seconds, considering how to make her argument, and finally said, "Well, you're certainly not a member of a president's cabinet. I don't know if you could write a novel. I also don't know anything about your cousin's decorating skills, but, Florence, not everybody was made to be special in the way you're describing. Yet we're all special in God's eyes, and that's an amazing truth."

"I know that, Louise," Florence agreed quietly. "But just . . . just for one day . . . I would like to know what it feels like to be that other kind of special."

Louise said nothing and Florence picked up her manila folder. "I don't think you can really understand my situation. Look at your family; each and every one of you has *something*. Alice is a professional, kind and generous and community oriented. You're gifted in music. Jane is a successful chef who could probably move anywhere in the world to showcase her talents. Each of you has something, does something better than most others. Each of you understands and praises the others." She paused as if frustrated that she couldn't seem to make her point. "My family was rarely supportive like that, and I don't have a talent that sets me apart."

Louise again thought of the day she spent with Jane and how they had ended up surprising Alice, who walked around the flowerbeds, praising the gardens as if they had been planted by angels. Her heart went out to Florence.

Florence turned to leave and Louise said, "Wait. Where are you going?"

"Home. I've got to call your Aunt Ethel. She's the one who's been most successful with signing up talent. So she's the one who will have to figure out how to get five more acts for the show."

"Three more acts," Louise corrected, turning toward the piano. "We may only have six days until the show, but you have the talent to learn that song and sing it well."

Florence's eyes widened. "Really?"

"Yes, it will take practice. Lots of practice."

"I don't care."

"But I know you can do it, Florence." Louise paused and caught Florence's gaze. Before she spoke she prayed that she was doing the right thing. If six days wasn't enough time for Florence to learn this song, without forgetting the one she'd learned the week before, all of Louise's help could actually do Florence more harm than good.

"We're simply going to have to practice every day."

Chapter Fourteen

Tuesday morning Jane allowed Ethel and Florence to make the usual rounds of neighborhood businesses on their own. Undoubtedly, they would check the sign-up sheets, find no new names and go to the Coffee Shop dejected and ready to obliterate their sorrows with a cup of tea and a pastry. Ethel would eventually perk up and eagerly plan a new strategy that at this late date stood little chance of succeeding, if only because the talent show was only a few days away. Everybody had been tapped. Many people had simply refused. Some said no for the very good reason that they didn't feel they had talent. Others had company for the weekend. Still others didn't wish to work with Florence. Jane couldn't think of many Acorn Hill residents who hadn't been asked, or a strategy that could possibly get anyone to change his or her mind and perform.

Jane loved her aunt, and in this particular circumstance even admired the way she could continually muster energy for a project that seemed to be falling apart at every turn. But today Jane simply wasn't up for another pep talk or, worse, to see the odd look of disappointment that would periodically appear in Florence's eyes.

Pausing outside Sylvia's Buttons, Jane took a moment to admire the window display. A small sign in the left corner of the window said SPRING FANCY, and Jane smiled because that's exactly what the exhibit was. With pastel colored gingham tulips tucked into pale-green velvet that was spread to look like grass, and with a swatch of blue silk cascading around like a brook, the display was an exhibition of exquisite fabrics, spring colors and Sylvia's wonderful imagination. Looking at the display, Jane knew lots of people would have stopped by to admire Sylvia's handiwork, and because of that she knew Sylvia was privy to news other Acorn Hill residents might not know. That was why Jane needed to speak with her this morning.

She stepped into the shop and called, "Sylvia?"

"Back here."

Jane made her way through the small shop, which was, as always, buried in fabrics. She found Sylvia at a table, tape measure around her neck and pins in her sweater. Her pretty strawberry-blond hair was piled on top of her head, and as Jane approached, Sylvia removed her reading glasses. "What brings you here today? No talent scouting to be done?"

"On the contrary, we don't have enough acts for a two-hour show, so Aunt Ethel and Florence are out looking." She shrugged. "I couldn't do it another day."

"Florence getting to you, or is it Ethel?" Sylvia said with a laugh.

"Neither," Jane answered honestly. "They've both been a lot of fun. Today I need a break from rejection."

Sylvia nodded knowingly and perched her glasses on her nose again, then went back to sewing.

"What are you working on?" Jane asked.

Sylvia pointed down at the garment with her chin. "This?"

Jane nodded.

"It's a costume for the grandson of a friend who's in a play of some sort being put on in a park somewhere."

Jane laughed. "Well, that's interesting . . . and certainly specific."

Sylvia shook her head. "It's a grandma surprise," she explained before she went back to work in earnest on the outfit that to Jane looked to be Elizabethan. Probably for a grandchild who was in a high school or college play.

When Jane didn't say anything, Sylvia added, "My friend wants her grandson to steal the show."

Jane studied the garment again. Made of bright, ruby-colored satin, the outfit was nothing if not eye-catching. "Well, he certainly will in that. It looks wonderful."

"Thanks."

Rev. Thompson entered, and Sylvia and Jane greeted him.

"Good morning, ladies. Don't mind me. I'd like a few minutes to look around."

The pastor disappeared among the shelves, and Jane turned back to Sylvia. "So, nothing new around town?"

"Nope. Everybody's getting ready for the holiday."

Jane sighed. "I have an ulterior motive for coming in this morning."

Sylvia peeked up at Jane expectantly.

"I know that everybody's already made his or her decision about performing in Florence's talent show." She took in a big breath for courage because if she got the wrong answer it would really ruin her day. "But have you heard any gossip about whether people plan to attend this thing?"

Sylvia peered up from her work again. "Actually, I can't say that I have, one way or the other." She let the costume rest in her lap. "I see why you're asking. You could be enduring this big talent search for nothing."

Jane sagged with defeat and dropped into a chair that was half buried in tapestry fabric. "Darn it!"

"This really seems to have you down."

"I know. I feel terrible that Aunt Ethel is going to all this trouble to round up acts and constantly staying positive when we might be staring down the barrel of absolute failure. But I feel worse for Florence."

Sylvia frowned. "Florence is a very strong woman. She'll shrug this off."

"You know, everybody thinks that," Jane said, casually glancing around to make sure she couldn't be overheard as she considered confiding in Sylvia about what she'd heard Florence tell Louise. Not seeing Rev. Thompson and guessing he was in the back of the store, she said, "I overheard her talking to Louise the other night when they were rehearsing. I couldn't hear most of what she said, but I kept hearing a quiver in her voice that made me downright sad."

Sylvia moved the costume to the table in front of her. "Quiver?"

"As if she was going to cry," Jane said.

"Was her singing that bad?" Sylvia asked carefully.

"No. The song I heard certainly needed work, but I'm sure Louise could bring her around in a few practices."

"So you think that means she wasn't upset about her singing."

"Right. And if she's not upset about her performance, perhaps it's the rest of the talent show. It's her idea. She doesn't want it to fail."

"I can understand that," Sylvia said.

Just then, Rev. Thompson stepped around a tall stack of material. "Didn't mean to listen in, but I can understand that too," he said. "It's human nature to want to succeed. How bad is participation in the show?" he asked Jane.

She turned in her seat. "I don't really like to tell tales out of school, but this talent-show business is public knowledge. We had hoped for an impressive show, and now because of unexpected circumstances, we barely have enough material for two hours."

"Yes, you mentioned on Sunday that two acts dropped out, but I didn't realize things were so bad."

"What's worse," Jane said, "is that I have a sudden, dreadful concern that few, if any, will attend."

Rev. Thompson appeared to consider that, but he didn't say anything to Jane. Instead, he turned to Sylvia as if to change the subject. "I was hoping to pick out the material for the curtains I wanted to have made, but you look busy. Maybe I should come back?"

Sylvia smiled gratefully. "That's very considerate of you, Pastor. I do need to get this out today."

"Okay, I'll be back tomorrow."

"Great," Sylvia said.

The pastor said his good-byes and left the shop, and Jane felt even worse than she had when she entered. When even the church leader couldn't seem to give a word of encouragement about finding new talent or boosting attendance, Jane knew the show could be in big trouble.

That evening, when Jane and Louise told Alice they were walking to the back garden to check on the new plants, Alice decided to go with them. Jane carried a watering can to add a little moisture to the soil, and considering how big the gardens were, Alice decided she should carry some extra water just in case.

As they strolled slowly through the grassy back-yard, Jane and Louise fell into a discussion about Florence and the talent show, and Alice mentioned how similar their situation was to Myra and Rosalind's.

"Their hearts are in the right place," Alice said. "They want to send a good message. The media is paying attention, but my fear is that if something goes wrong, the whole thing could backfire."

"The same appears true with Florence," Louise said, sounding saddened for her. "She says she wants to feel special, but I'm inclined to think that she just wants to feel she's a part of something."

"So she planned the talent show," Jane said. "And now she faces the risk that it could flop."

"Yes," Louise agreed. "And instead of feeling a part of the community, she's going to feel estranged." Louise sighed. "It's hard for me, because I want to fix this for her, but there's only so much I can do."

"Same here," Jane agreed. "I can't force people to participate when they have other obligations or feel they don't have talent."

"And I can't do anything to help Rosalind and Myra's situation," Alice said, shaking her head. "I can't determine how people will react any more than I can make sure the surgery goes well."

The three sisters stopped at the border of the beautifully tended garden. Dahlias, hollyhocks, mums, daisies, geraniums, pansies, and impatiens created a riot of shapes and colors that delighted each one of them.

Jane reverently said, "It's too bad we can't fix and arrange everything else the way we did with this garden."

"Yes," Louise said. "It was work, but it was all predictable work. We tilled the soil, planted the plants, and now we have a splendid addition to the garden."

"But you can't do that with people. It makes me wonder why life sort of pulls us into difficult situations with others."

"To lead us toward prayer," Alice said. "I always tell the ANGELs that the situations you can't fix are the situations you're in charge of praying for."

"Father used to say that," Louise observed. "A lot."

They watered the plants, discussing the flowers and continued care for the garden, and as they returned to the house, Louise said, "I think I will look into Florence's music some more before her practice tonight."

"And I'll call another committee meeting for the talent show. I'll have Aunt Ethel and Florence over for brunch tomorrow, and I'll go over every detail of their recruiting practices with them to see if there's anybody we possibly missed," Jane said.

"And I'll try to see both Myra and Rosalind tomorrow. Wednesday is Myra's normal dialysis day," Alice explained, "so I should automatically see her in my regular routine. Rosalind might be a little harder to find."

Alice left Louise to her music and Jane in the kitchen with a pen and paper creating a list of things she could do to ensure that the talent show was well attended. The program had not been promoted to the fullest because it had been assumed that family members and friends of performers would attend. However, with so few people interested in performing, Jane wondered whether they would have to do something special to get people to come to the show.

Alice climbed the steps to her room ready for a shower before she went to bed with a book. When she finally turned out the lights that night, she realized she was feeling much better about the situation with Myra and Rosalind. She had to admit it was easier for her to surrender the surgery to God's hands than it was for Jane and Louise to surrender something like a talent show, where at least part of the responsibility was theirs.

Jane welcomed Florence and Ethel into the inn the next morning for brunch.

"Will Louise be joining us?" Florence asked happily.

"No, I'm afraid she's in town this morning."

Ethel shook her head. "She's such a busy woman. She needs to slow down."

"She loves to stay active," Jane said, then directed Florence and Ethel into the dining room.

"The dining room?" Florence said almost reverently.

Jane laughed. "Yes. We have some special things I think we need to discuss, but I also feel we need to be a little pampered before we jump into more work."

"I couldn't agree more," Ethel said, leading the way into the formal dining room.

Eight chairs sat around the mahogany dining table, the seats padded with subtle green-and-ivory damask to match the green walls. In place of the Swedish mints that typically sat on the table, Jane had set a bowl of white roses.

"So fancy," Florence breathed.

"A little something to lift our spirits."

Ethel narrowed her eyes. "You must have really bad news."

"No, not bad news. I want to talk about advertising. I know we had discussed in our original meetings that we didn't need to advertise because the show sort of advertises itself as we recruit acts, but I've been wondering if that's enough to get people to attend the show," Jane said, deciding to come right to the point.

To Jane's surprise Ethel laughed. "You don't have to worry about that. Lloyd printed tickets and has been handing them out like candy because the program is free. We're a hit."

Florence gasped. "Really?"

Ethel sighed impatiently. "Of course. Mentioning it must have slipped my mind, but you know I'm not going to let a detail like tickets fall by the wayside."

"I never thought of it, since we aren't charging admission," Florence admitted.

"Well, I thought of that too," Ethel said, then fluffed her hair. "But there was a little matter of refreshments. To know how much to order we had to know how many people to anticipate. I handled it."

Jane smiled. The show was going to be a success. There was no reason to worry. "So this really will be a relaxing brunch."

"Yes, indeed," Ethel said with a laugh. "What did you make for us to eat?"

• • •

When it was time for her break from the dialysis unit, Alice walked to the reception area. "Hi, Pearl," she said to Pearl Muncie, the administrative assistant for the unit. "Can you tell me if you have a schedule for hospital volunteers?"

Pearl looked up with a smile. Her short red hair was combed off her face, and her blue eyes sparkled. In her mid-twenties, Pearl was old enough to be a responsible worker, but young enough to breathe energy and enthusiasm into the department. "We don't have any volunteers in this unit, Alice."

"I know," Alice said. "I was wondering, though, if Rosalind Westwood was working elsewhere in the hospital today."

Pearl gave Alice a confused look. "Rosalind's *in* the hospital."

Alice frowned, not comprehending. "So she's here?"

Pearl laughed. "No, no. She and Myra are in Philadelphia, preparing for the transplant."

Alice gasped. "So soon?"

"The way I understand it, the surgery team had an unexpected opening, and things just sort of fell together. The transplant will be tomorrow."

The news was so unexpected that Alice needed a moment to process it. "Oh, I see," she said, feeling almost dizzy from the news, but in a way not really surprised. She knew Rosalind had begun the testing procedures and health screenings immediately after she offered her kidney to Myra. She also knew that it was important to move as quickly as possible.

"What a boost for the donor program," Pearl said as she walked to the filing cabinet behind her desk. "Rosalind is so cool." She faced Alice again. "I mean, not only is she willing to donate a kidney to someone she barely knows, but she also isn't afraid of the publicity." She shook her coppery curls as she laughed.

Alice knew that Rosalind really did have everybody's best interests at heart. Still, Alice couldn't help seeing the other side of the story. If something went wrong, anything, even the slightest thing, the story could be blown out of proportion and the publicity surrounding Rosalind's generosity could have a very negative effect.

Jane took her last bite of homemade red-velvet cake. She savored the final morsel, knowing she was probably only going to get a salad for supper that night because she, Ethel and Florence had each eaten enough calories at their brunch for at least two meals.

Florence sat back on her chair. "Thank you very much, Jane. Brunch was delicious, but more than that, this time to relax has made me feel very confident about the show."

"You're welcome," Jane said.

"And thank you too, Ethel," Florence said. "It never even crossed my mind to consider refreshments or that we would need something of a head count."

"You're welcome from me too," Ethel said, rising. "Taking the head count by passing out tickets is the kind of thing that's second nature to me." She smiled proudly. "Now, let's show Jane our appreciation by helping to carry these things into the kitchen."

"Aunt Ethel," Jane said with a laugh, "help with the dishes would be the perfect thank you."

"Sounds good to me," Florence agreed, rising from her chair.

The three women sorted and collected the beautiful china. Ethel carried the cups and saucers. Jane carried the plates and silver. Florence brought several of the serving dishes.

"Just set them on the counter while we gather everything," Jane instructed, setting her china on the open spot above the dishwasher.

Ethel and Florence did as Jane said, then followed her into the dining room, where they gathered the remainder of the serving dishes, linen napkins, salt and pepper shakers, cream pitcher and sugar bowl.

"Set those on the kitchen table," Jane said as she returned to the kitchen, "and I'll put them away later."

"Okay," Florence said. "Do you want the table-cloth?"

"No, it's fine. Besides," she said with a grin, "you gals have done enough. Thank you for coming. I never would—"

A quick burst of knocks at the back door interrupted her. She paused, turned to see who had knocked and saw a tall man standing beyond the screen.

"Sorry," she apologized for the interruption to Ethel and Florence before she walked to the door. "Can I help you?" she asked the man.

"Irwin Penberthy," he said, then flashed an ID that Jane didn't really get time to read. "I'm here for the scheduled inspection."

"But that was supposed to be yesterday."

Irwin Penberthy looked at Jane over the top of his glasses. His thin face was drawn in a scowl of disapproval. "You should have received a letter. From me. I sent them out personally. I remember yours was on the list."

"It said the inspection was—"

"Don't say canceled," Irwin said sharply. "I made very certain I didn't even come close to saying your inspection was canceled."

"But your secretary told me you couldn't fit me in."

"I couldn't *then*," Penberthy agreed coolly. "But now I can. Are you going to let me in?"

Chapter Fifteen

Irwin Penberthy stared at Jane through the screen door as, on the verge of panic, Jane glanced around her kitchen. Dishes from brunch sat on the counter above the dishwasher. Salt and pepper shakers, the cream pitcher and sugar bowl lined the table. The coffeepot was half-filled with cold coffee. Pots filled the sink.

Still, the kitchen itself was clean. Cluttered, to be sure, but essentially clean. The same was true with the dining room. Those were the only two places Mr. Penberthy needed to inspect, so she did not have to go into full-blown panic mode. After all, this wasn't James E. Delaney, the man who looked for excuses to go into other places in an establishment. Even if Irwin Penberthy did, though, Jane assured herself, he would find those other places clean, not as they had been on Monday, but clean.

She drew a strength-inducing breath. "Of course, you can come in, Mr. Penberthy. Welcome," she said, motioning him into the kitchen, where she introduced him to Ethel and Florence. "We clearly weren't expecting you, but," she said, with an effort at a grin, "that might work in my favor since you'll see that even when cluttered my kitchen is clean."

As Penberthy looked around, Jane couldn't help watching his face. With every section of clutter he viewed, the lines on his face deepened until he was scowling.

"See here, young man," Ethel said. "Grace Chapel Inn is about the cleanest establishment in the county. There's no reason for that scowl."

Jane felt her panic returning. The last thing she needed was for Irwin Penberthy to have a run-in with Ethel.

"Aunt Ethel, don't you think it's time for you and Florence to check on things in town?"

"Why?" Penberthy asked suddenly. "Are you trying to get rid of her because you're hiding something that you're afraid she'll let slip?"

Jane gasped. "Certainly not! I just think that having fewer people in the kitchen would make the inspection go much easier."

"Humph," Penberthy said, removing his clipboard from under his arm and a pen from the inside pocket of his seersucker suit jacket. He shifted his glasses in such a way that he could read looking down, which also caused him to peer up at her over the rims as if she were a student being reprimanded by the high school principal.

"I've been yanked from Dauphin County because of Mr. Delaney's unfortunate illness. My workload is now double. I never told anybody an inspection was canceled, yet everywhere I arrive, I find disorder and a lack of discipline. There is nothing, Ms. Howard, that can make this inspection go easier."

• • •

Alice had lunch that afternoon with Sandy Minor, one of the other nurses in the dialysis unit. After her conversation that morning with Pearl about Myra's transplant, she had said a quick prayer that everything would go well, then totally and completely took her mind off Myra and Rosalind—not because she was becoming indifferent, but because putting things in God's capable hands was much better than worrying about them.

Rosalind and Myra's choice to submit themselves to publicity confused her, and she was sure that was why she was inclined to have negative feelings about it. But the decision to be interviewed by the paper and television station about the transplant had many, many benefits. The publicity was necessary, and Alice couldn't allow herself to think about it in negative ways.

So she put it in God's hands and focused on lunch.

But when Alice and Sandy finished eating and walked their trays to the collection area, Alice could overhear the murmured comments of the other hospital workers in the cafeteria.

"Rosalind didn't think this through. I don't care what anybody says. All surgery is risky."

"But that's exactly Rosalind's point. The laparoscopic surgery isn't as invasive as the former procedure. The risks are minimal."

"What will she do if her other kidney fails?"

"Who's paying for this?"

"She doesn't even really know Myra."

"What about her own kids?"

"Did you see that spread in the paper? If you ask me, Rosalind's just looking for publicity."

"No way! We all know Rosalind has a heart of gold."

There were good comments and bad comments, but, unfortunately, there were too many of the latter. Alice knew it was human nature to worry, but it almost seemed as if people were looking for ways to criticize.

Walking back to the dialysis unit with Sandy, who liked to chat nonstop about her children, Alice said another prayer that everything would work out.

Penberthy made a quick succession of checkmarks on the sheet on his clipboard.

"My kitchen usually isn't in a state of disorder," Jane said hastily, hoping he would erase a few of the angry slashes he had just made on the clean, white sheet.

"So, you normally don't have company?"

"Land's sake!" Ethel said with a laugh. "Jane always has lots of company. She's one of our best-loved residents because she's always got fresh sweet rolls or cookies or something."

Penberthy looked at Jane over his glasses again. "You encourage visitors."

"What kind of person discourages visitors?" Florence demanded. "We're neighbors—"

"Who pop in all the time," Penberthy finished for her as he made a few notes on his page. "And I'm guessing you pop in a lot."

"Which just goes to show," Ethel put in, "that Jane's kitchen is so clean she doesn't mind company popping in."

"Popping in with germs," Penberthy said. "In a cold or flu epidemic, visitors are an establishment's worst nightmare."

"They don't mingle with the guests," Jane said quickly.

"Except during the tea parties," Ethel said, "which are held in the parlor. Lovely things—"

"So your guests and the people from the town mingle?" Penberthy asked, scowling at Jane.

Florence looked scandalized. "Of course we mingle. Our town is part of the inn's charm."

Penberthy turned to Jane. "You need to be answering some of these questions, not depending upon your guests."

Jane swallowed. "I'm more than happy to answer your questions. But you're supposed to inspect the kitchen and dining area, not grill visitors about what goes on here."

"I'm permitted questions," Penberthy said, again making notes on his sheet. "And I can inspect any area I wish if I find just cause. Especially those places that might adversely affect the kitchen and dining area." He glanced around again. "How close is this tea-party parlor to the kitchen?"

Jane nearly breathed a sigh of relief. "The two areas aren't close at all."

"So the main contamination of your 'town visitors' comes from the kitchen."

"There's no contamination," Jane said, now getting as angry as Florence appeared to be getting. "Restaurants have vendors and suppliers and delivery people coming and going all the time."

Penberthy looked over his glasses at her again. "And you would know this because . . . ?"

"Because Jane worked in one of the most popular restaurants in San Francisco," Ethel said, puffing up with pride.

"Really?" Penberthy said, his face showing no trace of his being impressed.

Jane took a breath, wondering how one man could put so much condemnation in one little word. She also wondered how working in a restaurant could possibly be a bad thing in Penberthy's mind.

"Yes," Jane said, deciding not to offer any more information than that. From here on out she would only answer questions, not volunteer information.

"Well, Ms. Howard, for someone who worked in a restaurant, you seem incredibly careless about your kitchen."

"I'm not careless."

"You let people just wander in," he said, pointing

at Florence and Ethel as if they were hazardous waste rather than visitors.

"They don't help with food preparation," Jane said, her voice firming and becoming businesslike. She wasn't going to deal with this fellow on any level but a professional one. "No one touches the dishes after they are washed but me or my sisters, who are co-owners of this bed-and-breakfast. They know the rules. We are very careful."

Before Mr. Penberthy could respond, Rev. Thompson rushed in through the back door. "Hi, everyone! I have wonderful news." He marched directly to the silverware drawer and quickly extracted several spoons. "I have an act."

Everyone only stared at him.

"I can play the spoons," he said, waving Jane's everyday silver. "'Stars and Stripes Forever.' Listen."

As Jane watched in horror, the pastor began manipulating the spoons he had taken from the silverware drawer. He patted them together. He patted them against his shoulder. He patted them against the little spot above his knee. Each place he patted the spoons produced a different sound, as if he had practiced finding the notes for his song before announcing he could play it.

When he had finished, he grinned. "Isn't that great?" He next looked at Mr. Penberthy, and the two exchanged greetings, Penberthy's less than cordial.

Ethel was the first to find her voice. "It's wonderful," she said, though her tone lacked the enthusiasm he was probably expecting. "I know exactly where I'll put you in the lineup."

"Lineup for what?" Penberthy asked.

"The talent show this weekend," Rev. Thompson replied. "The acts have been practicing in the inn's parlor. And afterward, if you're lucky, Jane brings you into the kitchen for a snack." He looked at Jane and winked.

Jane looked stunned.

"Really," Penberthy said, and Jane sunk into a kitchen chair. After all the years she'd spent serving other people, this man was going to have her head on a platter.

Returning from her trip downtown, Louise had entered the house through the front door and heard a commotion in the kitchen. She hurried there to see what was going on. She could have sworn she heard the sound of someone playing the spoons. The noise was so out of character she knew something had to be wrong.

When she pushed through the swinging door and saw Ethel and Florence wearing scowls of disapproval, Rev. Thompson looking confused, Jane looking shell-shocked and a tall man with a clipboard making notes, she suspected that the man with a clipboard could only be an inspector and that for some reason he seemed perturbed.

She had no idea that Rev. Thompson had contributed to the stranger's sour mood.

She walked into the room with her hand extended to shake the inspector's. "This must be Mr. Penberthy."

He gave her a suspicious look. "You know who I am?"

"I put two and two together when I stepped in just now. Though I have to say," she added confidentially, "that your letter left us in doubt. We weren't sure if the inspection had been postponed or canceled."

"It never said canceled," Penberthy insisted angrily. "And I don't appreciate my missives being criticized because *you* can't understand them."

Louise had enough life experience to know when to retreat. She stepped back, away from Penberthy's glare and also out of the inspection. This was, after all, Jane's purview. She needed to be the one doing the talking. Still, Louise thought, as she glanced around, there were things she could do.

"Pastor Ken, Aunt Ethel, Florence, why don't we leave the inspection to Jane and Mr. Penberthy?"

Jane cast Louise a look that most definitely thanked her but at the same time was somehow a plea for further assistance.

Louise smiled helplessly. Getting Florence, Ethel and the pastor out of the kitchen was about the only thing she could think of. If Jane wanted her to do something else, she had no idea what it was.

With a shrug to let Jane know she hadn't gotten her message, Louise herded the three visitors out of the kitchen and left Jane alone.

Chapter Sixteen

Escorting the guests through the dining room toward the front door, Louise saw that crumbs from brunch were still on the table. Glancing toward the parlor, she saw sheet music scattered about, as well as dust dancing in the sunlight pouring in through the window. She remembered that the house hadn't been dusted since Monday because of Jane's work with Ethel and Florence, and she suddenly guessed what Jane wanted her to do.

The inn was really in fine shape, and none of these minor problems alone was enough to cause the inn to receive a poor inspection, but because their inspector was a scowling Irwin Penberthy, Louise realized that they could be in trouble.

"Everybody's staying!"

Ethel, Florence and Rev. Thompson stopped in their tracks. "Excuse me, Louise?" Ethel said.

"Mr. Penberthy is here to inspect the inn."

"Yes, we know," Ethel said with a sniff. "He made quite sure we knew that."

But Rev. Thompson groaned. "I didn't pick up on the fact that he was the inspector. That's why he wasn't really thrilled with somebody playing with your clean spoons."

Louise frowned. "Probably not."

"I think we also might have made matters worse when we took offense at his criticizing our being in the kitchen," Florence said, with a shake of her head.

"Yes," Ethel agreed. "It just makes me so mad that we weren't quicker on our feet. Jane has been nice enough to help us with the talent show, and we've not only taken her away from the project she needed to be focused on, we've given her inspector a very bad impression."

"We can fix that," Louise said hurriedly. "Pastor Ken, if you don't mind, I'm going to put you in charge of dusting."

He held up his hands in amicable surrender. "I've handled a dust cloth lots of times."

"We left crumbs on the dining room table and I'm sure there are some on the floor," Florence reported unhappily. "So I'll clean up there and run the vacuum."

Louise shook her head. "No vacuum. We don't want Mr. Penberthy to know that we're going ahead of him cleaning. We want him to think he's finding things as they usually are. The vacuum noise would alert him."

"So what do we do?" Florence gasped.

"We'll do things the old fashioned way. Florence, I'm giving you straw-broom detail."

She smiled slowly. "You still have one of those?"

In spite of her trepidation, Louise laughed. "Yes." She turned to her aunt. "Aunt Ethel, you be the advance person. Go into every room looking for things that are lying around, like my sheet music. Straighten up whatever is messy or hide whatever you find that shouldn't be out."

Ethel laughed. "Hide things?"

"I don't mean hide them as if we're hiding something we don't want the inspector to see, but hide in the sense that you're putting something away that's out but doesn't need to be out."

Ethel looked puzzled but nodded.

Louise found a dust cloth for the pastor and a broom for Florence and then followed Ethel into the parlor. "Put all the sheet music into the piano bench. I'll straighten it out later."

"Okay," Ethel said amicably. "Where are you going, dear?"

"Upstairs. I have a date with a few bathrooms. If crumbs or scattered sheet music will make him look harder for trouble or give him the motivation to inspect things in the inn that he might not otherwise inspect, an even slightly soiled bathroom can't possibly be good."

"Understood. I'll make sure things move along down here," Ethel said with determination.

"And quickly," Louise said as she scurried toward the stairs.

• • •

Irwin Penberthy took his time inspecting the kitchen. He made a lot of sounds like, "Uh-huh," and, "Um-hum," and, "Ohhhh." Those were interspersed with an occasional, "Well, now," and, "Isn't this interesting?" and Jane didn't think any of the terms were demonstrations of pleased surprise.

"Let's go on to the dining room," he finally said, pocketing his pen.

"Don't you need to make notes?"

He shook his head. "I'm just about certain I know what I'll find there, and if it's the same as the kitchen, that will determine whether I feel the need to move on through the house."

"But you really only need to inspect the kitchen and dining room," Jane cautiously reminded him.

"I believe we've already discussed that. I'm granted leave to enter any area of the bed-and-breakfast that I feel may be problematic if my discoveries so warrant."

Jane tried to smile as she motioned for him to follow her.

Much to her surprise, when they pushed through the swinging door into the dining room, it was clean. Every brunch crumb was gone. The floor looked to have received a recent cleaning, and the hutch had been dusted. *Louise!* Jane realized as she hid a smile. Maybe this inspection wouldn't go poorly after all.

She walked Penberthy through the dining room

and didn't protest when he asked to see the parlor, which was also spotless, as were the living room and even the front entryway. Unfortunately, because Penberthy was looking for trouble, she was sure he would ask to see the bathrooms next, and Jane held her breath.

But rather than ask to see the bathrooms, he took his pen from his jacket again and began marking things on the clipboard. "We can go back to the kitchen now."

Jane breathed a silent sigh of relief. His not wanting to see the upstairs was a good indication that he hadn't found any reason to go upstairs. She would have to provide a special thank-you to Louise for this. But first she wanted to have Mr. Penberthy leave with a glowing recommendation despite the fact that his first impression of the inn wasn't a good one.

She thought of things she could offer him and remembered there were several tasty treats left over from brunch that he might enjoy.

"Mr. Penberthy, now that you've seen the inn, can I interest you in some homemade red-velvet cake? It tastes of chocolate, not velvet, by the way. Or if you haven't yet had lunch, maybe a salad or a sandwich?"

Penberthy looked affronted. "Are you trying to bribe me?"

Jane gasped. "No! The inspection is over. I have no need to bribe you."

"The inspection may be over, but I haven't yet written my final report."

"But you know the inspection results. I know you do. It's in your voice."

"Which is exactly why you're trying to influence me by offering me lunch."

"I'm not trying to influence you."

"Good, because I'm not changing my report."

Though Jane had been sure his report would be positive, neither his words nor his tone was good. Her knees weakened, and her chest tightened with trepidation. "And what is your report?"

"I find your establishment to be acceptably clean."

Though "acceptably clean" wasn't the glowing praise Jane was accustomed to, it was better than some of the other things he might have chosen to write. Jane felt the strength returning to her limbs, until he added, "However, you seem to have no idea of how decorum and order facilitate sanitation. With the way you have neighbors and friends in and out of your kitchen—some of whom are at liberty to handle your silverware—it's clear that you aren't running as tight of a ship as you need to be running."

"But I—"

"Worked in a big San Francisco restaurant?" Penberthy said scathingly. "So you feel you know more than the country bumpkins back here in Pennsylvania?"

Jane's eyes widened with shock. It almost seemed that no matter what she said, he misinterpreted her words. "That isn't what I was going to say at all."

"Good, because from where I'm standing you don't know beans about running a restaurant." He handed her a copy of his handwritten report. "Good day, Ms. Howard. And if you have guests for this weekend—"

"We're all booked—"

"Let me suggest you call them and tell them you've been closed by the Commonwealth of Pennsylvania."

Louise had just finished saying good-bye to Rev. Thompson, Florence and Ethel, all of whom had been resting on the front porch, when she heard the slam of the kitchen screen door.

Not liking the sound, she hurried into the kitchen just as Jane sank into one of the kitchen chairs.

"He closed us down."

Louise gasped. "What?"

"We're closed," Jane repeated. "It was a discretionary thing. He said the kitchen and dining area may have been clean, but I clearly didn't understand the relationship between decorum and sanitation."

Louise's brow wrinkled in confusion. "I'm not exactly sure I know what that means."

"It seems to mean that people really aren't supposed to be able to arbitrarily come and go in a kitchen that's used to feed paying guests."

"But this is also our home, and there are no guests right now. More than that, though, the kitchen *is* clean. It's always clean."

"As I said," Jane said, her voice dull with shock, "it was a discretionary thing. As an inspector, he can look beyond the cleanliness to potential problems. He feels we're riddled with them."

"So what do we do?"

"We clean everything and request another inspection."

"But that could take months if they're slow to respond."

"It will probably only take weeks."

"But we have guests."

"We have no choice, Louise, but to cancel their reservations."

Dumbfounded, Louise sank into the chair across from Jane. "All this because Pastor Ken grabbed a few spoons?"

"No, I think it was more that. He didn't like having to do this inspection. When he didn't hit it off with Aunt Ethel and Florence, I knew he was going to give us trouble. Then Pastor Ken gave him the opportunity he wanted to close us down. But it's not their fault. Right from the beginning I could tell he was looking for something. I just let down my guard because he seemed to find everything clean."

She took a quick breath and smiled bravely. "Thanks for going ahead and making sure that things were in order."

Louise swallowed. "You're welcome," she said, but her words were spiritless. She might have gone ahead of Jane and the inspector making sure everything was clean, but she wouldn't have had to if she hadn't drawn Jane into the talent-show project. Worse, Louise knew the inspector wouldn't have found Ethel, Florence and eventually Rev. Thompson in the kitchen at all if Louise hadn't brought Jane into the project. This failure, Louise feared, was largely her fault.

"Jane, I—" she began, but the uncomfortable silence in the kitchen was interrupted by a loud bang. Jane vaulted off her chair as Louise ran to the window.

Louise frowned. "I think Mr. Penberthy's car backfired."

Jane drew a quick breath. "At this point, my brain is too fried to care—" Jane began, but Louise was halfway out the door.

"My brain isn't fried," she said and quickly made her way down the back steps to the driveway where the inspector had parked his car. Looking inside the open passenger's window, she saw him turning the key. His face was red from frustration.

"Mr. Penberthy," she said, smiling sympathetically. "It looks as if you are having a bit of trouble."

"Forget it, Mrs. Smith. You aren't going to influence my decision any more than your sister did." He pumped the gas frantically again as he twisted the key. "I don't know what it is with you people thinking you can bribe me."

Louise gasped. "Bribe you?"

"Well, why else would you come out here?"

"To *help* you," Louise said, striving to stay in control. No good would come from losing her temper. "We have a phone in the inn. You're welcome to come inside and use it."

Reaching inside his jacket pocket, he grabbed a cell phone, pulled it out and snapped it open. "No thanks. I don't need you. I don't need anyone. *That,* lady, is the key to success. You would be wise to learn it."

Chapter Seventeen

After work, Alice raced up the steps of the front porch. Eager to tell her sisters the news of Myra's transplant, she pushed open the door.

"Louise! Jane!" she called, tossing her purse onto the check-in desk. After spending an entire shift with the staff of the dialysis unit, all of whom were in varying stages of relief and excitement about Myra's transplant, Alice felt a hundred percent better about the situation.

Her colleagues' enthusiasm and confidence in the procedure had rubbed off on her as they shared stories of successful transplants about which they were familiar. Soon Alice became as enthusiastic as her coworkers about Myra and Rosalind's decision to be so public and vocal about what they were doing. With success rates so high, having the local media follow both a donor and a recipient through the process was sure to inspire other donors.

"Louise! Jane!" she called again.

Again, nobody answered. Wondering if they were in the kitchen, Alice made her way there, but she still didn't find either sister.

Deciding to freshen up before she went looking for them in earnest, she retraced her steps, grabbed her sweater and went upstairs.

On the way to her room, she noticed that Jane's bedroom door was closed. Alice frowned. Jane's not wishing to be disturbed was very odd, because it was suppertime. In fact, now that Alice thought about supper, she realized that she hadn't seen any sign of meal preparations.

With a sigh, she walked into her own bedroom and changed into shorts and a comfortable top.

When Alice left her room, Jane's door was still closed. Really puzzled, she decided to look for Louise.

She didn't have to do too much searching. Louise was in the kitchen when she arrived. Her face was drawn in concerned lines as she hoisted a large pot to the front burner of the stove.

She laughed. "You're cooking? Jane must be sick."

"At the moment I'm just getting water ready for spaghetti. As for Jane, she is sick, but not physically," Louise said as she put a cover on the pot. "She's taking a nap, sick at heart. Our inspector arrived unexpectedly today."

"Our inspector? I thought he was recovering from surgery."

"He is. The gentleman—and I use that term loosely—who wrote us the letter about Mr. Delaney's being ill is our replacement inspector. What he failed to mention in his letter was that if his schedule freed up, he would fit as many of Mr. Delaney's inspections in as he could. He showed up today at the end of a brunch Jane had prepared for Aunt Ethel and Florence, and he wasn't happy to discover they were helping Jane clean up."

"Having help is against a regulation?"

"Not exactly, but his meeting with Aunt Ethel and Florence seemed to put him in a bad frame of mind. Then having Pastor Ken come into the kitchen, help himself to spoons from the silverware drawer and play 'Stars and Stripes Forever' on his knee really made his mood sour."

Alice tried to picture it and couldn't. All she could say was, "That doesn't sound good."

"It might have turned out okay," Louise said with a shrug. "I took Aunt Ethel, Florence and Pastor Ken out of the kitchen, and we decided to go ahead of Jane and Mr. Penberthy, dusting and straightening, especially in the dining room, where they'd just eaten brunch."

"Makes perfect sense to me," Alice said.

"It did to us too, and, in fact, Mr. Penberthy seemed to find everything in good order. Then Jane offered him something to eat, and he accused her of trying to bribe him."

"Bribe him?"

"Jane was appalled at his accusations too. But Penberthy is a very suspicious man, and he took everything she said the wrong way. He wrote up the inn for the minor infractions he had found as if they were far beyond what they really were . . . and closed us down."

Alice's mouth fell open. "What?"

"He closed us down." She paused to draw in a breath. "When Jane told me, I supposed there had to be a misunderstanding, so when Mr. Penberthy's car wouldn't start, I ran out and offered him the use of our phone."

Alice closed her eyes in despair. "And he accused you of trying to bribe him too."

"He is nothing if not consistent," Louise said, crossing her arms on her chest as she leaned against the stove. "He pulled out a cell phone and dismissed me."

"That's it?"

"Well, the tow truck from Dairyland arrived a few minutes later. When Harlan couldn't get

Penberthy's car to start by tinkering under the hood, he towed it to the shop."

"Are they there now?"

Louise shrugged. "I guess. Mr. Penberthy was clear that he didn't wish for my interference. So I haven't checked up on him. I'm done trying to help."

Alice headed for the back door. "Well, we have guests this weekend and Jane keeps a spotless kitchen. I won't let him close us down because he's snippy."

Louise said, "Good luck, Alice, but don't get your hopes up. I can't see you having any more success than I had."

Alice nodded and hurried out the door, promising herself that she would do as Louise suggested and not get her hopes up. It was a stretch at best to think she would have any more success than her sisters had achieved, but she had to try.

She drove to Dairyland, the town's combination convenience store and gas station, where Harlan Green also ran the towing service and did automobile repair.

Pushing open the glass door, Alice said, "Hi, Charlotte," to the teenage girl who was behind the counter. "I'm going to go in back and see Harlan."

"Sure, Miss Howard," Charlotte said with a smile. "Go ahead."

"Thanks." Alice went down the aisle toward the glass door to the garage. Before she pushed it open, she took a deep breath and looked inside. Harlan was under the hood of a relatively old car and a man in a seersucker suit sat at a table against the wall reading a magazine.

Alice straightened her shoulders, pushed open the door and walked to the man with the magazine. "Mr. Penberthy?" she asked.

He looked up with a smile. "Yes."

"I'm Alice Howard."

His smile immediately faded. "Oh."

Alice forced herself not to swallow, because she knew it wouldn't be a good idea to show nervousness in front of this man. After all, who was he? He was simply another human being, another child of God. She would treat him with respect and he would treat her with respect.

"I'm sorry for disturbing you, but my sister Louise just told me about the inspection, and though I can see how you would have gotten a false impression of the inn, you only got that impression because of a series of unfortunate and atypical events."

"I got that impression because your sister allowed someone off the street to rummage through the drawer containing the same utensils used by the guests." He paused. "I'm not an idiot."

"Oh my goodness!" Alice said with a laugh. "I'm sorry if something I said made you believe I thought that. It's obvious that you're an intelligent man who knows his job. In fact, as an independent observer, I was coming down here to tell you that you didn't make a mistake. The inn just didn't put its best foot forward today because of a series of unexpected circumstances."

"That's perfectly understandable."

Hearing his accepting words and kind tone of voice, Alice felt as if a burden were lifting. "Really? You understand?"

"Of course, I understand."

Alice breathed a full-scale sigh of relief. "That's great."

"All your sisters have to do is apply for another inspection."

Alice felt her expression crumble. "Apply for another inspection?"

"That's the procedure," Penberthy said and went back to reading his magazine.

"But we have guests this weekend."

He didn't bother to look up. "I guess you're going to have to call them and cancel."

"But we . . ." She almost said, "need the money," but she pulled back at the last second. That was none of his business and really not part of an inspection. Besides, she had the oddest feeling he would somehow use that against Grace Chapel Inn or Jane if she mentioned it.

She looked around. Harlan still had his head under the hood. When she realized Mr. Penberthy could be stuck at the garage for much longer than he imagined, inspiration struck.

"It appears that you're going to be in Acorn Hill for a few hours. You have plenty of time to stop at the inn again. By then all the problems you found will be straightened out." She paused, thinking of a way to sweeten the pot. "It will save you another trip to Acorn Hill sometime next month."

"Sometime next month Mr. Delaney will have returned." He flipped the page on the magazine. "This isn't my problem." He spared her a glance. "It's yours."

Alice stared at him in disbelief that anybody could be so mean-spirited. Louise was right. There was no talking to this man. Not because he couldn't see reason. No. He could see reason if he wanted to. The problem clearly was that he didn't want to.

She turned and began to walk away. As she did, Harlan pulled himself out from under the hood of Penberthy's car.

"Good afternoon, Miss Howard," Harlan said. He was a young man, only in his twenties, with dark hair and equally dark eyes. A lifelong member of Grace Chapel's congregation, he had married a woman who was a former member of Alice's ANGELs.

"Good afternoon, Harlan. How are Donna and the kids?"

"They're great. Billy wants to be a mechanic when he grows up. Our two-year-old, Maddy, is going to be as smart as her mother."

Alice chuckled. "Well, they say parents are the first teachers. If your kids want to be just like you, then I would say you're doing something right."

Harlan grinned.

Penberthy cleared his throat.

"Any news on my vehicle?" he asked stiffly, as if angry that he wasn't Harlan's top priority.

"You bet, Mr. Penberthy. I'm on the case," Harlan said. "Miss Howard and I go back a long way."

Penberthy was unimpressed. "That's nice, but I need to get going."

"That's okay, Harlan," Alice quickly said, not wanting her presence to cause any trouble for Harlan. "I need to get moving too. Tell Donna I said hello."

"Will do, ma'am," Harlan said before he turned to Penberthy. "I'm real sorry, Mr. Penberthy, but you've got some problems with your alternator."

"Whatever," Penberthy said angrily. "Just fix it. If you're asking if I care what it costs the answer is no. This car has been in my family for nearly thirty years, and I want to keep it another twenty."

"See, there's your problem," Harlan said carefully. "You've hit antique status and that means that I have to special order your part."

Nearly at the door, Alice heard Penberthy gasp. "What!"

"I'm sorry, sir. I'll put in an order for the necessary replacement, but I'm not entirely sure when we'll get it. My advice to you is to call a friend and have him or her come and pick you up."

"I can't call a friend; my friends work. And they're in Dauphin county, too far away for a quick drive. No one wants to take time off to come pick me up."

Alice turned abruptly and walked back to where Harlan stood talking with the inspector. "Mr. Penberthy," she said, smiling sweetly, "you're welcome to stay with us."

Penberthy's face fell as if he was horrified that she'd even made the suggestion. "I closed your inn. *Closed!*" He repeated. "As in, it-is-not-a-fit-place-for-people-to-stay. If I won't let guests stay in your inn, I certainly won't stay there myself."

Alice felt the heat of embarrassment rising up her cheeks, but she also experienced a swell of righteous indignation for Jane. What must this man have put her poor sister through!

Dismissing Alice, Penberthy turned to Harlan again. "I can't believe you can't get the part. This car is not *that* old," he insisted.

"I didn't say I couldn't get the part," Harlan said. "I said I didn't know how long it would take to get the part. Service departments don't stock parts for every vehicle still on the road, and they don't stay open twenty-four/seven. If I call, it has to be tomorrow. Then they have to contact their supplier and have one shipped."

"So we're talking tomorrow?"

"Maybe. If the shop's still open when I call." He scratched his head. "But most likely we're talking day after tomorrow, which is Friday. If we're not lucky, we're talking Tuesday, because even if the part's shipped on Saturday there are no deliveries on Sunday. Even if there were, I don't work on Sundays and Monday's the holiday."

Just then, the door from the convenience store opened. Fred Humbert stepped inside. "Hello, Harlan," he said, walking over to the trio talking by the raised hood of Penberthy's car. "Hello, Alice."

Alice said, "Good afternoon, Fred," at the same time Harlan said, "Hey, Fred, what's up?"

"My car's going to need to be inspected next week and I was wonderi—"

"Excuse me," Penberthy said, glaring at Fred. "You may not have noticed it, but Mr. Harlan and I were having a conversation."

"It's not *Mr.* Harlan," Harlan said heatedly. "It's just plain Harlan. Harlan is my first name. And you and I weren't having a conversation, you were trying to get me to do something that can't be done."

Though her situation was dire, Alice suppressed a smile. Harlan was nothing if not practical and honest.

"You're a mechanic. Fix my car," Penberthy demanded.

"I don't have the part, Mr. Penberthy," Harlan said. "Let me suggest you call a friend."

"I told you. My friends work. I can't call one of them."

Once again Alice could only imagine what this man had put poor Jane through from the way he was treating Harlan. Still, Harlan wasn't a person who allowed himself to be pushed around.

"Then it looks like you've got a bit of a problem, Mr. Penberthy."

"Not really." Penberthy sniffed. "I simply need the name of a hotel. I can stay the night."

Harlan shook his head in disgust, but Fred brightened. "Well, sir, you are in luck. Acorn Hill boasts the best bed-and-breakfast in the state, Grace Chapel Inn. It's run by Alice here and her sisters," he said, motioning to Alice, who held her breath, not sure how Penberthy would react. Now that he knew his car couldn't be fixed, maybe he'd be more agreeable than he had been when she first made the offer for him to stay at the inn.

But Mr. Penberthy bared his teeth.

"Really? The best?" He snarled. "I'll have you know I just closed that inn down today. I'm an inspector," he said and pulled out his ID. "And in my book the place isn't fit for guests."

Fred looked as astounded as Alice, who stood dumbfounded that anybody could be as rude as Irwin Penberthy was.

Harlan picked up his rag and rubbed the grease from his fingers. "I'm going to my office to call for your alternator. You might want to go to the park and scout out the bench you'll be sleeping on tonight, because if you don't want to stay with the Howards at Grace Chapel Inn, there's nowhere else to stay in Acorn Hill."

Penberthy held Harlan's gaze. "Maybe I'll do just that."

"Be my guest," Harlan said. He tossed his greasy rag to the fender of Penberthy's car and headed for his office.

Fred turned to Penberthy. "You may want to rethink your idea of sleeping in the park. From what I figure, it's going to rain tonight."

Realizing that she would have to put her own concerns aside and provide the shelter Penberthy would need, Alice found her voice. "Yes, Mr. Penberthy. Please reconsider staying with us."

Irwin gaped at her. "I *closed* your inn. I *cannot* stay there."

Alice took a breath and straightened her shoulders. Like Harlan, she knew when enough was enough. "I'm sorry you feel that way, Mr. Penberthy, because our inn is a wonderful place to stay," she said, keeping her voice soft and even. She wouldn't let this man push her to the point where she got angry, though she did intend to defend her sister and their bed-and-breakfast. "In spite of what you believe, it's also clean. If you choose not to stay with us, it's your loss."

With that she turned and walked out of the garage and into the convenience store. She strode directly to the freezer section and pulled out a half gallon of Rocky Road ice cream and brought it to the counter.

"Is that all, Miss Howard?" Charlotte asked.

"Yes, thank you, Charlotte, that will be all."

Charlotte rang up the purchase and Alice began the trip back to the house. She had a feeling it would be a long night.

Chapter Eighteen

Alice walked into the kitchen in time to see Louise dump the contents of her now steaming pot into a colander in the sink.

"Spaghetti," Louise said. "It's one of Jane's comfort foods."

Alice stopped suddenly. She was aware of Louise's somewhat limited cooking skills and wondered if her sister's spaghetti might make Jane even more upset. Still, it was a time to be positive. "I brought Rocky Road ice cream" was all that she said.

"Another good idea," Louise agreed, as she pulled the colander of spaghetti from the sink.

"I guess she's not out of her room yet."

"No," Louise said. "Why don't you go up and see if you can get her to come downstairs to eat?"

Alice held her ice cream aloft before putting it in the freezer above the refrigerator. "This should tempt her down."

Louise sighed. "I don't know. She was distraught when she went to her room."

Alice nodded, then left the kitchen and made her way to Jane's closed bedroom door. She knocked once, then said, "Jane, honey. It's Alice. May I come in?"

She waited a few seconds for Jane's response. When Jane said nothing, she raised her hand to knock again, but the door opened before she could.

"I'm fine, Alice," Jane said, opening the door enough that Alice could see the bright eggplant color of the room, the small armless couch filled with pillows and the silky duvet on her low-slung contemporary bed. "I've faced worse professional setbacks."

"But this time you're not in it alone. This inn is the responsibility of all three of us. So Louise has made spaghetti, and I bought Rocky Road ice cream. We'll talk while eating the spaghetti, and I'll bet before we get to the Rocky Road, we'll have an answer."

Jane smiled. "Wow! Spaghetti *and* Rocky Road. Very tempting."

"You know how setbacks go, Jane," Alice said, turning serious. "They pop up when you least expect them, but they pop up for everybody. You can't control them."

"But I was supposed to be prepared."

Alice shook her head. "Louise read that letter and interpreted it as meaning the inspection was postponed indefinitely. She didn't see the post-ponement as a delay from the original date. She understood the letter to mean that somebody would get in touch with us to set a new date. We all read that letter. We all got the wrong impression. You even called Penberthy's office for clarification of his letter. If anybody made a mistake here, it's Mr. Penberthy with his poorly written letter."

Jane laughed at that. "He should be ashamed of himself."

"Or he should take a Comp 1 class at community college," Alice said, then took Jane's hand and eased her out of her room. "Spaghetti awaits."

They walked down the stairs and into the kitchen, where they discovered Louise had set the table. "I'm so sorry you're upset, Jane," Louise said the second they stepped into the room.

"It's not your fault," Jane said. "As Alice pointed out, we all read that letter. We all believed the inspection had been postponed, not delayed."

"Just a shade of difference," Alice said.

"And just enough for us to be taken by surprise," Louise agreed. "But that's only part of why I'm sorry. You would have been prepared today if I hadn't dragged you into the talent show."

"You didn't drag me," Jane said with a slight shake of her head. "I volunteered. Besides, I've been having fun. That's why *I* feel so guilty. I've been having fun when I should have been making sure everything was in order for the inspection."

"Still, it was my fault you were involved in that," Louise said. As she spoke, a rumble of thunder shook the house. She waited until it finished before she said, "That was unexpected."

"Not really," Alice said with a laugh. "I met Fred briefly this afternoon, and he warned about rain. He thinks there's a storm coming tonight."

A flash of lightning illuminated the kitchen window, then the thunder roared again.

Jane's eyes widened. "Did he say it would be a big storm?"

"Let me think." Alice's brow furrowed as she thought. "Sorry. I just remember him saying it was going to rain."

This time when the lightning flashed, the kitchen lights flickered. "Let me get some candles just in case," Jane said, walking toward the pantry.

"Good idea," Louise agreed.

As Jane retrieved the candles and a lighter for them, Alice and Louise checked the table to be sure they had everything they needed to eat dinner. Jane set lighted candles on the two countertops and brought another candle to the table.

"If the power goes out, we'll be able to see our way to the counter," she said with a laugh. "And we have this one," she added, waving the third candle, which sat in a pretty glass holder, "just for atmosphere."

They sat at their usual seats at the table, said grace, and passed the spaghetti and sauce around.

Louise had also prepared salad with Italian dressing and thawed a loaf of bread from Jane's freezer.

Alice inhaled deeply. "Louise, this smells wonderful."

"Jane gets the credit for the bread. It was in the freezer."

"Just waiting for a day like this one," Jane pointed out. Then she too inhaled the delicious, spicy aromas rising from their feast. Rain began to pound against the window. Wind blew rain-scented air through the screen door and to the table. The napkin beneath the warm bread in the basket fluttered. The candle flames flickered.

"I better close the door," Alice said with a laugh, rising from her seat. "Or we'll lose our candles."

At the door, she glanced outside. "The sky is really dark."

"We haven't had a good rainstorm in a while," Louise said. "I think we were due."

"Probably," Alice said, closing the door.

As Alice returned to the table, Jane asked, "So what are we going to do about the inspection?"

Alice smiled. With the rain pattering against the window, the scent of warmed bread mixing with the spicy Italian sauce for the spaghetti, and the three sisters seated around the table, the kitchen was cozy. Jane had gotten the message and was sharing the burden the way they had always intended it should be shared.

"Well, I think we need to take a look at his inspection sheet and address the issues. When I went to Dairyland, I happened to see Mr. Penberthy," Alice said, deciding it might not be a good idea to let Jane know she hadn't run down for ice cream but to try to change his mind. "And he told me that we need to apply for another inspection."

"That's what he told me too," Jane said.

"He told me that that could take weeks," Louise added.

Alice nodded. "Things like this happen in business. We do the best we can, but we can't predict when we're going to get an ill-tempered inspector. So we will deal with it."

"Yes," Louise said. "We will deal with it."

"Exactly," Jane said.

"So, we're in agreement, then. We'll call tomorrow for a new inspection and address the issues on the sheet as we're waiting for the new inspection date."

"Yes," Louise said.

Jane nodded.

"Just one more thing," Louise said. "I've contacted our expected guests. No one was to arrive before Friday, so I was able to call and give each of them the unhappy news in time for them to make other arrangements. As much as technology can frequently be more trouble than it's worth, it was very nice to have a cell-phone number for the

Oxfords, who were already on their way from Minneapolis. Because they were on the road, I gave them the numbers for a few other bed-and-breakfasts, and though they were disappointed, at least their trip wasn't ruined."

"There was nothing else to do," Alice said. "But I have something more positive we can talk about so that we can really enjoy Louise's delicious dinner."

"What's that?" Jane asked.

"Myra and Rosalind are in Philadelphia. The transplant was actually scheduled for today."

"Oh my," was all Louise said.

"That's wonderful!" Jane said.

"Yes, it's wonderful," Alice agreed. "You both know that I have been a little skeptical about all the publicity concerning this transplant. But today the staff in the dialysis unit had such confidence in the procedure that my worries have been alleviated."

"Actions always speak louder," Louise said.

"Agreed," Alice said. "No one even tried to convince me not to worry. Instead, they were all simply thrilled with the fact that Myra was getting a new kidney. When they talked, it was of how bright her future would be and how happy Myra's children would be to have a more active mom."

"That's great," Jane agreed.

"So, will there be a follow-up on their story in the paper?" Jane asked before taking a bite of her spaghetti.

"According to the staff in the unit," Alice said, "reporters will be waiting at Rosalind's home for her when she returns. Then they will do a piece about the possibility of her going back to work the following day."

Louise gasped. "She's going back to her volunteer work the following day?"

Alice shrugged. "If all goes well, she might be well enough to do that."

Jane shook her head. "She's very courageous."

"Yes," Alice said, "and she's doing what she always does in her volunteer work—not making a big deal out of her situation. By letting the press interview her at work, she's serving as an example to the people who might be able to donate a kidney. By her example, she's showing them exactly what can be done. Then in case anybody's considering it, she'll alleviate some of their concern."

"You know," Jane said, "that Rosalind's way is the way Father taught."

"Yes," Louise agreed. "He lived his life as an example. And he changed lives, one person at a time, simply by living out his faith."

"Yes, he did," Jane said. "We have a tendency to think of living out our faith in terms of spiritual things. Rosalind is reminding us that faith can also be lived in very practical ways."

"But still sacrificial," Louise noted. "None of what Rosalind is doing is easy."

"No, none of it is," Alice agreed, "but that's just

the point. We often want living a life of faith to be easy. Sometimes it's just plain hard."

"Yes," Jane said at the same time that the front doorbell rang. Her brow furrowed. "I wonder who that could be?"

Louise rose from the table. "I'll go and see." A rumble of thunder followed Louise out of the room, and, feeling uncomfortable having Louise go alone to greet a wet, probably stranded visitor, Alice also rose. "I think I'll go with Louise. You never know who a storm will bring to your door."

Jane laughed. "I'm sure it's no one sinister. Probably just someone looking for a place to get out of the rain for the night. Too bad we'll have to turn him away. But you two can handle it. I'm eating my spaghetti before it gets cold."

Alice chuckled at Jane's perspective as she pushed through the swinging door and made her way to the front entryway.

Louise was standing at the door, holding it open. Though the front porch had a roof, the rain was falling so hard that Alice was sure it was probably splashing to the door. Alice couldn't believe that Louise wouldn't invite the caller in, if only to save herself from getting wet.

She approached, ready to suggest that they ask the guest in, but when she saw Irwin Penberthy standing on the threshold, she stopped.

"Mr. Penberthy?"

He inclined his head. "Miss Howard. I was just

telling your sister that I know I can't stay at your inn as a paying guest since I closed it today. However, I have nowhere else to go."

Alice just stared at him. She had no idea what he wanted her or Louise to say. He'd closed them down. Perhaps this was a test. Would an inspector try to trick them into letting him stay only to turn around and use their kindness against them?

She didn't know. However, she did realize that this particular inspector was a man who went strictly by the book. He wasn't an especially forgiving man, and she didn't think he believed in cutting anyone any slack.

If they invited him to stay, they could be putting the final nail in the coffin for Grace Chapel Inn.

"I'm not exactly sure how you think we can help you, Mr. Penberthy," Louise said a bit stiffly.

"Look," Penberthy sputtered, his eyes darting wildly from Louise to Alice and back to Louise again. "I get it big time that everybody in this town will be angry that I closed you down. And I shouldn't be here, but there is nowhere else in this tiny little town to stay."

"But we have been shut down," Louise insisted, apparently sharing Alice's worry.

For several seconds Penberthy simply stared at Louise. Louise didn't say anything. Then from behind Alice Jane said, "Let Mr. Penberthy in, please."

Louise turned from the door. "Jane, Mr.

Penberthy closed us down. We cannot accept him as a guest."

"Then we'll allow him in as a friend," Jane said, nudging between Alice and Louise and reaching out to grab the wet sleeve of Mr. Penberthy's suit coat. "Friends don't pay, so he isn't a guest of the inn. He's a friend spending the night."

Clearly uncomfortable, Mr. Penberthy nonetheless let Jane guide him into the foyer.

"Please put your umbrella next to the coatrack," she said, pointing to the container by the door. "You can store your briefcase beneath the desk until after supper. Then I'll show you to a room." She paused to smile. "Unless you would like to freshen up before you eat, Irwin."

She used his first name, Alice was sure, to give support to the invitation to stay at the inn as a friend.

"Thank you, Jane," he said, faltering a little at the use of her first name. Still, he apparently had caught on that the only way he could stay at the inn was as a friend, not a guest. Desperately needing a room, he was willing to do whatever it took.

"I would like to dry off a bit before I eat."

"Right this way then," Jane said, leading him up the stairs.

Alice and Louise watched them climb the steps together. When they were out of sight, Louise turned to Alice. "What do you think?"

Alice laughed. "I don't know. I sort of feel like

the lamb sitting down with the lion, only I'm not sure this particular lion has been converted yet."

Louise shook her head as she chuckled. "Jane asked him to stay as a friend. That should take care of any grounds he might think he has to write us up for an additional infraction."

"Yes, but what if he does a secret inspection in the meantime?"

Louise shrugged and turned to walk back to the kitchen where their supper was getting cold. "He's already shut us down. What's he going to do? Double-super-secret shut us down?"

Rolling her eyes, Alice said, "You have a very odd sense of humor sometimes, Louise."

"Maybe," Louise agreed, entering the kitchen, "but I think what Jane's doing is living out her faith the way Rosalind has. Jane's the person Mr. Penberthy hurt the most," Louise said. "The decision to allow him to stay took great courage from her. Now, what we have to do is support her."

"And make sure none of us regrets this," Alice said, taking her seat at the table.

"I think we have to leave that particular aspect in God's hands," Louise said.

Knowing Louise was correct, Alice closed her eyes and said a quick prayer that Jane's sacrifice wouldn't result in even more trouble for the inn.

Chapter Nineteen

Louise stepped into the kitchen the next morning and found Jane busily mixing batter.

"I'm making cinnamon French toast with apricot syrup."

Louise's mouth watered, but her eyes narrowed. "You're treating him like a guest."

"I considered that," Jane said, "but then I also realized that if one of my real friends was staying here, I would work to make sure his stay was as comfortable as the stay of any other guest. I also realized that I would even show off a bit with a recipe or two." She grinned. "So the bottom line is I'm showing off for a friend."

"Just promise me you aren't trying to impress him."

"Not any more than I try to impress you and Alice or Aunt Ethel, Sylvia and Florence." She paused, then released a dramatic sigh. "Cooking is what I do, Louie."

"So this is a stress-management technique?"

"Yes."

"You better mean that."

Jane nodded. "I do," she said brightly, then she frowned. "I don't." She sighed heavily as she set the batter bowl on the counter. "Louise, this is our one shot at getting him to change his report."

"Or we could make things worse. Bluntly put,

Mr. Penberthy doesn't seem to be a nice man. He's angry over being forced to do Mr. Delaney's inspections, and now he's stranded here because his car has broken down. Even though it's common knowledge that Mr. Delaney nitpicks, at this point, I think we would be better off with someone persnickety than someone grouchy who's been made even more angry by a car that won't start."

"I won't do anything drastic or obvious," Jane said. "I just want the chance to show him that we do run a clean, organized business."

"Okay, but—"

As Louise spoke, the kitchen door abruptly whipped open and Ethel stumbled inside, pushed by a gust of wind. "This storm is really something! Fred says it won't let up until lunchtime." She closed her umbrella and set it by the door, then patted her hair, checking for damage. Satisfied that her hair was in place, she walked to the stove, where Jane stood, laying thick, batter-coated slices of bread into a baking pan.

"What are you making that smells so delicious?"

"This is cinnamon French toast," she said, nodding at the bread she was setting in the pan. "What you're smelling is the apricot syrup that I have warming."

Jane pointed to the small pot at the back of the stove, and Ethel leaned toward the pot and inhaled appreciatively.

"I hope you made enough for thirty, because the

elementary school won't open for us to practice in this storm."

Jane spun away from the stove. "What?"

Louise looked shocked. "I thought the maintenance work on the auditorium had been completed early so that we could do our final practices there."

Ethel shrugged. "Apparently, they don't want us tracking through the front lobby with wet shoes," she said, as if it were the most ordinary thing in the world. "And since we're only timing the acts this morning, Florence and I thought we could do it here."

Louise watched a series of emotions cross Jane's face. At first she appeared shell-shocked. Then she looked to be digesting the information. Then it seemed as if she might argue. Then she became accepting.

Louise, too, thought that they had no choice but to accept the situation. Though Ethel and Florence hadn't consulted them about using the inn, Louise didn't see that they had had a choice in the matter. The show had to be timed. Grace Chapel Inn was the only place all the acts could congregate to perform one after the other.

In addition, Louise couldn't help wondering if having a flood of visitors might be the hand of God at work. A crowd at the inn would just about guarantee that Irwin Penberthy would not change his mind. As Louise had already pointed out to Jane, trying to change the mind of a grouchy man might do more harm than good. Their new situation might be God's way of showing them they were better off waiting for James E. Delaney than they were trying to impress Irwin Penberthy.

"That will be okay . . . I guess," Jane said.

"We have an unexpected guest, Aunt Ethel," Louise said, explaining Jane's hesitancy. "And I believe Jane may not wish to upset him."

Confused, Ethel faced Jane, who took a long breath. "He's a friend," she said, glancing at Louise, "but Louise and I are also involved with the talent show." She swallowed. "So we'll do whatever we need to do to make it work."

"Well, of course you will, dear," Ethel said breezily, making her way to the table. "When will this delicious breakfast be ready?"

"Twenty minutes," Jane said. "But, really, I can't serve the same thing to all the people who are coming."

"Could you warm up some muffins or something?" Ethel asked, referring to the fact that everyone knew Jane always had goodies in the freezer for last-minute company. "That would be appreciated on a day like this."

"I could probably make muffins from scratch while you are busy."

"That would be so nice," Ethel said.

"Are you sure, Jane?" Louise asked.

"Yes. There's only one condition."

Louise inclined her head, indicating Jane should let them know what it was.

"Everybody stays out of the kitchen."

Considering that having too many people in the kitchen had been Penberthy's biggest problem during the inspection and that they didn't want him adding anything to his report, Louise thought that was a fine idea.

"I will see to that," Louise said.

Jane smiled her relief. "Thanks."

Ethel rubbed her hands together with glee. "This is why I love rain. It always inspires people to do special, wonderful things. Thank you, Jane; we're going to have such fun today."

Louise wasn't entirely sure she would regard the upcoming day as fun. If Harlan didn't have the inspector's car ready, the day could turn out to be an even bigger disaster than yesterday.

Irwin Penberthy awakened to the sound of rain outside his window. For a few seconds he enjoyed the soothing pitter-patter. Then he realized the pleasing lavender scent of his pillow was unfamiliar.

He bolted up in bed and fumbled for the glasses he had left on the nightstand. After putting them on, he blinked to adjust his vision and looked around.

Jane Howard had called this room the Sunset Room when she brought him up the night before. Irwin hadn't wanted to be pleased, and, in fact, he'd kept his approval of the room to himself, but he liked what he had seen when she first opened the door for him.

The ragged faux paint in the simple terra-cotta color so perfectly accompanied the creamy antiqued furniture and the impressionist prints on the wall that he felt surprised and calmed. The colors and décor were soothing. His mattress was comfortable. After a shower in his private bath, he'd slipped under the covers and let the sounds of the storm and the tranquility of his room lull him to sleep.

But last night he'd also been out of sorts. First, because his car was not working. Next, because this town appeared to have the most incompetent mechanic on the face of the earth. Then, because there was no place to stay other than the inn he had closed.

He was so desperate that he had been willing to compromise, maybe even amend his report with the promise from the Howards that they would correct the way they ran the place. But because Jane so eagerly invited him in as a "friend," he felt that compromise was no longer required.

That was a good thing because now that he was properly rested and ready to face the world again, he wasn't predisposed to be kind to people who didn't deserve kindness. They ran an inn, a place for people to stay. Guest comfort and safety had to come first, and from what he'd seen he didn't believe the Howards understood that. They were so busy living their social lives that there was no way they could be showing proper attention to their guests.

He concluded that he had done the right thing in closing the inn, and he was glad he hadn't compromised his decision in order to get a place to sleep.

Satisfied, he rolled out of bed. Of necessity, he dressed in the clothing he had worn the day before and made his way downstairs. Even before he descended halfway, chatter filtered up to him from the lower floor.

He shook his head in wonder. These women would never learn. Only twenty-four hours after he'd yanked their license for having personal company in their kitchen, they were entertaining someone again. He'd done the world a service by shutting them down. Clearly, they were far too disorganized to run a business.

With every step he took toward the first floor, the noise became louder. He swore he heard horns, specifically trombones, warming up, and he frowned.

Too confused to let this go uninvestigated, he followed the sounds of the music and found a trio of trombone players in the living room.

"What's going on?" he asked one of them.

"Practicing," a jovial fellow replied. "We haven't played together since high school. It's been a blast."

Penberthy frowned again as he looked at the three gentlemen before him. Their median age appeared to be fifty, which meant high school had been a long time ago.

He shook his head with disgust. "I suspect you need plenty of practice then."

To Irwin's surprise the three men laughed.

"You better believe it!" one gentleman said through his laughter. "Of course, if we sound awful, we'll probably get a laugh, and that might be better than trying to pull off a serious performance."

Penberthy gasped. "Are you kidding? Why would you want people to laugh at you? And what are you practicing for anyway?"

But the three trombone players didn't hear him this time. They liked the idea of getting a laugh so much they were busily discussing its merits.

He shook his head. Maybe the Howard sisters weren't the only people in Acorn Hill who didn't understand decorum.

Crossing the foyer, he made his way to the parlor. Louise Smith sat on the piano bench. Beside her was a young lady of about fourteen. Engaged in an animated discussion about the sheet music in front of them, neither saw Irwin.

None of the others in the room saw him either. He was ignored by the woman the Howards had introduced the day before as their aunt Ethel. The Florence woman he'd also met ignored him too, as she busily gave instructions to a dark-haired woman who looked to be in her mid-thirties.

Jane Howard was listening intently to the weather prognosticator from the garage as he explained something to her, and in the corner, the pastor conscientiously practiced playing spoons on his knee.

The practicing people had nothing in common, save the ability to ignore the other acts around them. Sheet music was everywhere. People bobbed and weaved through Irwin's line of vision. Cups sat on coasters on the tables scattered throughout the room. Napkins held half-eaten muffins.

To him the scene was a nightmare of noise and messiness, and once again Irwin knew he had done the right thing in closing down this place.

He turned and walked out of the parlor, past the trombonists and to the front door. Grabbing his umbrella from beside the coatrack, he caught the doorknob in his other hand. He needed to get out before he decided to add anything else to his report. If he truly believed the Howard family incapable of running a business, he could write the kind of report that could preclude these women from ever opening their inn again. But that was a decision better made when he wasn't stressed out over his car. Or maybe it was something he should put in his notes for James Delaney when he did the follow-up inspection.

Something to think about.

With his umbrella protecting him from the rain, Irwin walked to Dairyland. He opened the door to the convenience store, and the scent of fresh coffee greeted him. His stomach growled. He poured himself a cup of coffee, counted out the exact change to pay the young woman behind the counter and walked into the garage, where he found Harlan sitting in his office at a desk cluttered with papers.

Talking on the phone on what was probably a personal call if his big grin was any indication, Harlan had his feet on the highest stack of papers and the chair pushed almost to a reclining position.

To his credit, when Harlan saw Irwin, he said, "Gotta go. Talk to you later." He disconnected the call and bounced to his feet.

"Mr. Penberthy. How are you this morning?"

"Skip the pleasantries, Harlan. Is my car done?"

Harlan remained stone-faced. "I told you yesterday, I had to call for your alternator."

"And you said it would be here today."

"I said it *might* get here today. Besides, no deliveries have come yet. Even you must realize it wouldn't be here at ten in the morning."

Penberthy squeezed his eyes shut in frustration. "So you're saying it's not here."

"I warned you about that yesterday," Harlan said, then had the audacity to chuckle at Irwin as if he were a dimwit. "Mr. Penberthy, this is Acorn Hill,

Pennsylvania. When I need something I call a parts-service company in Potterston that gets regular deliveries, and they send parts to me. Sometimes they have those parts in stock, sometimes they have to order what I need."

"This is very important."

"Well now, I can see that's true, and if they had your alternator in stock, we'll get it in later today, probably before eleven," he said, grinning proudly.

"You didn't ask the parts supplier if my alternator was in stock?"

"No need," Harlan said. "If they had it, it will be here today. If they didn't, it will get here the day after they get it."

Penberthy's mouth fell open. "You don't follow through?"

"No point in following through," Harlan said, sounding as if Penberthy's questions were stupid. "If he's got it, it will be here. If he doesn't, it will get here the day after he gets it." He frowned. "I'm not sure what part of that explanation doesn't make sense to you, Mr. Penberthy."

Penberthy inhaled a long breath to keep from saying something he would regret. The entire town was crazy. Or lazy. Or disorganized.

Well, by eleven he should know if his part had been in stock. Considering that an alternator was a fairly common item, he was certain it would arrive.

"I'll be back at eleven," he said. Then he turned and left the garage. He walked through the convenience store toward the exit, but before he could depart, the clerk stopped him.

"Excuse me," she said, motioning toward Irwin's cup of coffee.

"I paid for this!" he said through gritted teeth. Didn't anybody in this town pay attention?

To his surprise the pretty young clerk smiled. "I know. You were in such a hurry before I didn't get a chance to tell you refills are free."

Irwin stopped dead in his tracks and backpedaled to the counter. "Refills of coffee are free?"

"Yes."

"You give away coffee?"

"No. You paid for your coffee."

He took a quick breath. "Right."

"So help yourself to another cup before you go."

"I think I might just do that," Irwin said. He downed his now-cooled coffee and poured himself a second cup to take to a park bench. He wasn't going back to Grace Chapel Inn, rain or no rain.

But at eleven, Harlan didn't have good news for him. There was no alternator with the morning's deliveries.

"I'm sure it will be here tomorrow."

Because it was a common part, Irwin was sure it would be in the following day too. But that didn't help him figure out what to do today.

"I heard the Howards are letting you stay with them," Harlan said, breaking into Irwin's thoughts. "If I were you, I'd just stay there another night.

You said yesterday your friends were busy, and Jane's quite a chef."

"So I've heard, but I don't wish to wear out my welcome, or to endure the noise of all their company." But he also didn't want to risk spending too much time with the Howards for fear they would try to change his mind with all their saccharine niceness.

"See, that's your problem," Harlan said. "If those folks invited you to stay, you're welcome for breakfast, lunch and dinner." He glanced at his watch. "In fact, I'm guessing if you went back right now, you'd be just in time for lunch."

When Penberthy said nothing, Harlan shook his head. "You big-city people kill me. You don't even understand good old-fashioned hospitality."

"All right, let me put it to you another way, then," Penberthy said. "I don't want these women being nice to me so that I'll change my mind about their inn."

Harlan shook his head. "Not in their nature to do something like that."

Irwin said, "Humph." In his experience that was *everybody's* nature.

Harlan shook his head again. "It seems to me you're being stubborn."

"I'm not stubborn. I'm cautious."

"Stubborn, I say. You'd rather be stranded than accept the Howards' kindness." Harlan turned his attention to a car behind him, reaching beneath the hood for the clasp that opened it. "Suit yourself."

Chapter Twenty

Jane kept herself busy that morning preparing a lunch for the talent-show participants. She refused to let herself think about the fact that Irwin Penberthy hadn't eaten breakfast. She told herself he could be one of those people who didn't eat first thing in the morning. She told herself that maybe the scent of cinnamon didn't entice him as it did so many other people.

But despite her attempts at positive thinking, she felt discouraged. She had failed the inspection, and even though she told Louise she wouldn't try to entice Penberthy into reconsidering his decision, his not appearing for breakfast was more than a slight. It seemed proof that he thought poorly of her kitchen and proof that she was letting everybody down.

The door to the kitchen opened and Ethel strolled in. "Jane dear, do you—" Jane's aunt stopped abruptly. "My goodness! What's wrong?"

Jane tossed a dishtowel onto the counter. "Nothing."

"Oh, come on now. It's written all over your face that you're upset." She paused, then kindly said, "It's the inspection, isn't it?"

"Of course it is."

"Jane, these things happen."

"I know all about failure . . ." Jane began, but Ethel laughed.

"I'm not talking about failure. I'm talking about getting a grouchy inspector. I know this has to have happened to you before in San Francisco. You don't work in a restaurant for years without meeting up with an inspector who treats you unfairly."

Jane took a breath. "As a matter of fact—"

"So you've had unfair inspections before."

Jane nodded.

"And how did you handle them?"

"Well, usually, the inspector didn't close the restaurant, just wrote us up. So I could fix the problems and go about my work the way I always did."

"That's what you need to do now. Keep everybody out of the kitchen," she said with a self-deprecating grin. "Even me. And that 'fixes' the biggest problem he had with the inn. Then go about your business the way you always do."

Jane took a quick breath, then smiled. "You're right."

"Actually, I nearly forgot the most important thing of all. You have to give this over to God. Stop whatever you're doing, then go to your room or out to the garden and pray for a few minutes."

"I'll do that," Jane said, then stepped into her aunt's open arms for a quick hug. "Thanks, Auntie."

"Don't thank me. You answered your own question. Go out to the garden to pray, then come back in and do what you always do, the way you always do it." She paused to smile at Jane. "And be yourself. If Irwin Penberthy doesn't like you, that's his loss. By the time you apply for the repeat inspection, he'll be out of the picture anyway."

After Ethel left the kitchen, Jane slipped out the back door and took a walk to the gardens. She opened herself up to the beauty that surrounded her, the peace of the area and the town itself. As she stood in the sun, which was finally peeking out from behind the retreating storm clouds, she released Grace Chapel Inn's future and Mr. Penberthy into God's hands.

Irwin returned to the inn. He had no intention of fraternizing with the Howard sisters, but he remembered that they had a library. He would find a good book and content himself with reading for the rest of the day.

Satisfied, he entered through the front door, tucked his umbrella by the coatrack and made his way back to the library. He was about halfway to the room when a delicious aroma hit him and his stomach growled.

Darn it! He'd missed breakfast, and Harlan's news had caused him to forget about grabbing lunch before he returned. He was starving.

He tried to take a few more steps toward the library, but hunger won out, and he went in search of the fabulous scent. He looked into the parlor and saw people scattered about on all the available seats, balancing paper plates on their laps.

"Oh, good afternoon," one of the trombone players he'd seen earlier said. "Jane's got some soup and some really great sandwiches in the dining room. Go on in. Help yourself."

Irwin half smiled at the audacity of this guest who felt comfortable inviting another guest to eat the Howards' food.

The people of this town needed a lesson in manners, Irwin thought, but he was hungry and he continued following the aroma until he stood outside the dining room. All the chairs had been removed from around the table, which was set as a buffet. The food smelled so wonderful that Penberthy's stomach growled again.

As he stood contemplating the table, Jane Howard noticed him standing in the doorway.

"Mr. Penberthy!" she said, sounding aghast. "How long have you been standing there? Grab a plate. The food's not fancy, but this lunch was last-minute."

"I see," Penberthy said. Unable to help himself, he added, "Do you often have this many people in your house?"

Ethel laughed. "Oh my, no! But this is a special week."

Florence all but jumped in front of the Howards' aunt to take over the conversation. "Yes, it is. I thought it would be a great idea to have a talent show on Sunday night, and Ethel is helping me arrange it."

"Yes," Ethel agreed, "and Louise is doing all the accompaniment."

"And Jane's done most of the organization," Florence said. "She put together the order for the acts. She also got Sylvia—of Sylvia's Buttons—to fix up costumes."

"How nice," Penberthy said as he picked up a plate. He suddenly realized that enduring the explanation of the talent show by Ethel and Florence prevented any of the Howards from talking to him. He didn't have to risk any one of them trying to get him to change his report.

Taking a ham-and-cheese sandwich from the tray, he said, "Tell me more about this talent show."

Florence beamed. Ethel seemed to stand taller. Each woman caught one of his arms. "Sit with me," Ethel said.

"No," Florence said, "he should sit with me. It's my idea."

"Why don't we find chairs together?" Penberthy said, adding macaroni salad to his dish.

"Fine," Ethel said, glaring at Florence.

"Wonderful," Florence agreed, smiling a superior smile at Ethel.

In the end, they sat together on the sofa in the parlor. Because the trombonists had finished eating, they gave up their seats in front of a handy coffee table, and Penberthy not only had food and people to keep the Howards at bay, he had a comfortable seat.

"So what else about the talent show?" he asked before biting into his sandwich, which turned out to be delicious. He had never eaten bread like this before and guessed chef Jane had probably made it. Still, he refused to let himself be impressed.

"It's something the entire town is pulling together," Ethel said. "Florence started it and elicited Louise's help."

"And Louise brought Ethel in," Florence said.

"Louise also added Jane," Ethel said, "because we needed someone to break ties when Florence and I didn't see eye to eye."

That made Penberthy laugh. He could imagine that these two didn't always see eye to eye.

"The three of us basically brought in the acts—" Ethel tried to continue.

"But Louise is the real star," Florence said, interrupting. "She takes a personal interest in all of us." She smiled shyly, which confused Irwin until she said, "She wants each of us to sound his or her best. She's spent a lot of time with me."

"Well, that's very nice," Penberthy said, looking at Florence. Irwin suspected she wasn't somebody easy to get along with, yet Louise Smith hadn't simply convinced her she needed to work to be her best, she'd somehow gotten Florence to appreciate it.

Not that Penberthy was impressed. He refused to be impressed.

Irwin didn't see any of the three sisters again until everyone had finished eating. Then Jane appeared in the doorway with a clipboard and announced the order of the performances. Everyone was to stay in the living room, dining room or front hall and only come to the parlor when called to do his or her act.

Everyone happily complied, and Penberthy decided that now was the time to find the study that had belonged to the Howards' father and grab a book. He rose from his seat, said his good-byes to Florence and Ethel, and began walking to the study.

But before he entered, the eclectic mix of acts stirred his curiosity, and on an unexpected impulse, he began looking for a back way to the parlor. He stepped softly across the front hall and into the kitchen without being seen by Jane, who was alone, cleaning the mess from lunch.

A quick wave of regret washed over Penberthy. Considering the caliber of the food and the raves about Jane's cooking, he deduced that Jane must have prepared lunch. Now she was cleaning up alone because he'd shut her down for having people in her kitchen. He took a quick breath to get rid of the guilt. After waiting for just the right moment, he sneaked by her when her back was turned and returned to the front hall.

But as he stood at the open door to the parlor and listened to the not-quite-acceptable voice of one of the men participating in the show, then heard Louise's praise for his enthusiasm, Penberthy's conscience pricked him anew.

There was nothing in the guidelines that said Jane couldn't have help. Her kitchen simply wasn't supposed to be as busy as a trading post. And certainly the pastor shouldn't have felt free to dig into the drawer for instrumental spoons. Still, Penberthy knew he shouldn't have been so hard on Jane for allowing her aunt and Florence to help her clean up the day before.

As he pondered this, he heard Florence and Louise chatting. From what they said he gathered it was Florence's turn to sing. Before Louise began to play, however, she said encouraging words to Florence. She reminded her that her true gift was her vulnerability when she sang. She told her to allow the emotion to give her voice passion.

"Then," Louise said, "the words won't matter. The notes won't matter. People will feel you are communicating with them, and they will hear beauty."

As Penberthy leaned against the reception desk, he heard Florence sigh. Then he heard the piano as Louise began to play. Then Penberthy heard Florence, and he knew Louise Smith was one of the most brilliant teachers he had ever encountered. Not because she made Florence sound wonderful, but because of the authentic emotion he heard in Florence's voice. Her honesty took the song to the level of feeling that the composers had intended.

She sang with the voice of someone up in years and the emotion of someone whose life probably had known its share of regret. The performance touched Irwin so much that he had to sit.

As he located a chair, Jane hurried in to finish clearing the table.

"Oh, Mr. Penberthy," she said, obviously not expecting to see him.

He smiled sheepishly. "I've been listening."

Jane laughed. "I don't know whether I should scold you for eavesdropping or apologize. Some of our talent isn't all that talented."

"Have you heard Florence?"

She shook her head.

"She's not extraordinarily talented, but her performance is amazing."

"Louise is bringing out the best in performers." Jane smiled.

Having witnessed Louise's kind heart and now seeing Jane's work on behalf of her neighbors and friends, Penberthy almost felt contrite. But he reminded himself of what Jane had signed on for when she agreed to run this bed-and-breakfast. He couldn't feel sorry for her. He certainly couldn't be soft on her. The smart thing to do would be to leave, so he didn't have to see the results of his conscientious adherence to the rules. After all, it was for the good of the bed-and-breakfast that Jane must master the decorum required to run such an establishment.

"To say your sister brings out the best in people is an understatement," Penberthy said. He took a quick breath. "But I'm getting a little uneasy eavesdropping. I think I'll go to the study."

"Good idea," Jane agreed. "My father acquired many of the classics. I'm sure you'll find something you'll enjoy."

Irwin spent the afternoon in the study. Around six, Alice poked her head in the door and announced that dinner would be at six thirty, if he needed time to freshen up. Penberthy thanked her but told her he wasn't very hungry and would be having a sandwich later at the Coffee Shop. When he asked for suggestions on where to buy a few things for his unexpected stay, Alice gave him directions to the pharmacy.

On his way there to buy the toiletries he would need, he remembered Florence's mention of Sylvia's Buttons. Sylvia, he recalled, was the person helping with costumes for the talent show. He wondered if her shop might be a source of clean clothes, so after his trip to the pharmacy, he walked to Sylvia's Buttons.

A strawberry-blonde wearing reading glasses greeted him. "Hi, what can I do for you?" she asked, tugging on the tape measure around her neck.

"I'm sorry. I thought this might be a clothing store. It appears, though, you're a seamstress."

"Yes, I am. But I also have some clothes for sale—things I made, if you're interested."

"I would love a pair of trousers and a clean shirt."

"Coming right up!" Sylvia said brightly. She ducked behind a rack and came out holding a pair of denim pants and a T-shirt.

He shook his head. "Do you have an oxford-cloth shirt and khakis?"

"Not exactly," Sylvia said, obviously thinking about what she had on hand. "But close."

She ducked behind the rack again, and when she returned she had a pair of beige trousers and two short-sleeved shirts. "You can have your choice."

"Actually, if the shirts fit, I would like to have both."

"Great!" Sylvia said. "Dressing room is over there." She pointed him in the right direction, and Penberthy found that the clothes were a satisfactory fit.

With his purchases in hand, he left Sylvia's Buttons and took his time walking back to the inn. He didn't wish to spend any more time than necessary with the Howards. Not because he had shut them down, but because their behavior clouded the issues surrounding why he had closed them down.

Though it might be true that the Howards were good people, and even true that he had stretched the rules in criticizing Jane about the traffic in her kitchen, it wasn't right for an inspector to second-guess a decision.

Satisfied with his reasoning, he made the turn onto the sidewalk that led to the inn's front entry. He saw a candle burning on the porch and heard the low voices of the sisters as they chatted. He paused.

"So everything went well with Myra and Rosalind?" Jane asked.

The sister Penberthy had seen the least, Alice, replied, "So far so good."

"And Rosalind is home?" Louise asked.

"Yes. I saw a piece about her on the news."

Not feeling he was interrupting anything too personal, Penberthy began to walk toward the porch again.

"It's just all happened so fast that it seems odd," Jane said.

"Yes," Alice said. "I wonder if that's why my sense of unease has returned."

Louise laughed. "Alice, you and Jane and I are uneasy about this because we're not accustomed to things going smoothly."

Penberthy stopped. Louise had opened the door for any one of them to segue into a conversation about their poor luck in getting him for an inspector. He knew they would say something horrible about him if given the chance. Well, he would just pause and listen, and the next time he was tempted to feel guilty, he would remember this.

"That's true," Alice agreed. "The technology alone boggles my mind."

Penberthy cocked his head. Alice hadn't jumped on the opening created by her sister.

"And we're all still impressed with Rosalind. It's not every day that someone donates a kidney," Jane said.

"Yes, new technology or not, transplants are still a miracle to me," Louise said.

Penberthy took a quick breath. No wonder they weren't feeling sorry for themselves. They were worried about a friend. He took the final steps that would put him in their line of vision.

"You know someone who had a transplant?" he asked quietly.

Alice straightened. "Oh, hello Mr. Penberthy; we were talking about a patient at the hospital."

"One of the hospital volunteers agreed to donate a kidney to someone she barely knew," Louise added.

"She was doing it as a complete act of charity, so everyone who hears the story is amazed," Jane said.

"But that was exactly the point. Kidney transplants shouldn't amaze us," Alice said, picking up the story again. "Transplant procedures are improved, and the risks have been minimized."

Penberthy shook his head. These women weren't cut out to run a business. They were generous and kind, clearly intelligent, too, but they just didn't get it.

In fact, Penberthy finally understood the real reason why he had closed this place. The Howards didn't put their business first. The bed-and-breakfast wasn't their primary concern. One moment the talent show was; now, a kidney transplant for someone they hardly knew was the object of their discussion. Irwin didn't know why he'd worried that they would try to change his verdict. These women didn't care enough about their business to try to change his mind.

"Well, your hospital volunteer's generosity is very nice," he said. "Very nice." Now he felt a different instinct. Because of what he had seen of Louise's and Jane's kindness, he liked the Howards, and he didn't want to recommend to James Delaney that the inn be permanently closed. He wanted to help them. After all, they had helped him by giving him someplace to stay. "But I would think you have more important things to worry about."

Louise grimaced. "You mean the talent show? Jane told me you listened in on some of the acts."

"I mean your business," Penberthy said. "Did you ladies ever stop to think that perhaps you focus a little too much on other people?"

Alice gasped. "No!"

Penberthy took a long breath. "Look, I like you

ladies. So does everybody in this town. But at some point you have to realize your business and your guests come first, not a talent show, and most certainly not somebody you don't even really know. You need to get the people of this town to respect Grace Chapel Inn as a business and not to impose on you for things like practices or to expect you to entertain and feed everyone simply because you have the space."

He sighed heavily, not liking what he had to say but believing it was the truth. "If you don't soon start looking at your business as your primary concern and get the people of this town to respect the inn as a business, you may be in more trouble than you imagine."

Chapter Twenty-One

The next morning as Irwin Penberthy walked to the kitchen, he heard quiet chatter. Pausing to listen at the door, he realized the Howards were seriously discussing what he had told them the night before. Jane wondered if he was right, if they really did give liberties to the townspeople and in doing so had inadvertently put their guests second. Alice agreed that putting the business first was a reasonable demand on an inn where people expected quiet and privacy. Louise admitted that she had many times noticed that Grace Chapel Inn was far from quiet.

Hearing that they were coming to the appropriate conclusions, Irwin decided not to disturb them and instead made a trip to the Dairyland garage, where he discovered his alternator hadn't arrived.

"But," Harlan said, "I called the auto-parts store, and the alternator has arrived there. If they ship it today, we'll get it Tuesday."

Irwin opened his mouth to say something, but Harlan waved his hand to stop him.

"Mr. Penberthy, you've waited long enough. I told them not to send it. I'll drive to Potterston and pick it up. Your car will be ready today around one."

"Well, I, I . . ." Irwin sputtered, clumsily restraining the angry words he was about to say.

It occurred to Irwin that Harlan finally seemed to understand that *he* had to solve the problem. But it hadn't been easy to get Harlan to realize that. Had he not nagged Harlan, Harlan might not have made the follow-up call. Had Harlan not made the follow-up call to check on the status of the alternator, they wouldn't know the part was in, and Harlan probably wouldn't have volunteered to drive to get it.

Pushing worked. Holding people accountable worked. The Howards might need to be pleasant and accommodating to their guests, but it was equally important to get the people of the town to respect their business.

"Okay," Irwin said. "I'll be back at one."

• • •

Alice spent the morning weeding the garden, and when she returned to the kitchen, Louise was pouring herself a glass of lemonade, and Jane was standing over a huge bowl of dough.

"Are you working out your frustrations?" she asked with a chuckle.

"No, I'm all done being frustrated," Jane said as Louise walked to the table and took a seat.

"I've been pondering what Mr. Penberthy said last night, and I still feel uncomfortable with it."

"Me too," Alice agreed, turning on the faucet to wash her hands. "As we said this morning, what he said seems to have merit. We do want to put our guests first—"

"And I think we do," Jane put in.

"I do too," Louise agreed.

"Then it's unanimous. None of us feels we've put our activities ahead of our guests."

"So even though this morning we agreed to think about Mr. Penberthy's suggestions," Louise said, "now that we've considered them, we've decided that he's wrong."

"I wouldn't say he's wrong," Alice said thoughtfully, "I think it's more that he's misguided."

"Or maybe a better way to say it is that he doesn't have all the information," Jane added. "In fact, I'm sure of it."

"I'm not sure how we handle that."

"I don't think we have to," Jane said, giving her

dough a final punch before she covered it with a clean dishtowel. "He won't be our inspector next time around. As far as I'm concerned, we only have to treat Mr. Penberthy with respect until he leaves."

"And hope that we can counter whatever he puts in his report," Alice added.

"Yes," Louise agreed. "Since he's leaving this afternoon, we won't inadvertently give him any more wrong impressions."

Alice agreed, but she also knew the damage had been done. Sometimes it only took one exaggerated inspection report to forever sully an inn's reputation. That meant that when they encountered their next inspection, they would have to work that much harder to overcome whatever Irwin had said. With James E. Delaney's reputation, that wasn't going to be easy.

Satisfied with Harlan's plan to fix his car, Irwin spent the morning reading in Daniel Howard's library. At noon, he thanked the Howards, said good-bye and reminded them one more time to think about his advice about not being so accommodating to the people of the town. Then he was off to Dairyland. As he breezed past the counter in the convenience store, he said good-bye to Charlotte and stepped into the garage.

His car was exactly where Harlan had left it, and the hood was still up. Another car sat in the second bay. Its hood was also open.

"Harlan?" he called.

Harlan jerked out from under the hood of the second car. "Oh my gosh! Mr. Penberthy!"

"Don't tell me you forgot me," Penberthy said with a laugh, thinking that couldn't possibly be true.

Harlan said nothing, but his face turned beet red.

Irwin felt his own blood pressure begin to rise. "You *did* forget me!"

"I'm sorry, Mr. Penberthy. But when Annabelle Rivers brought her car in, I sort of lost track of everything else."

"Oh, I get it. I'm not a pretty girl, so—"

"It's not that," Harlan interrupted. "Annabelle Rivers is nine months pregnant. She could go into labor any day. When her car broke, her husband got a ride to work and she called me. I dropped everything to fix her car. They can't risk being without a vehicle if her time comes in the middle of the night."

"I suppose I understand."

Harlan shuffled his feet. "I don't think you do, Mr. Penberthy. You might see that I needed to fix Annabelle's car, but I don't think you've figured out yet that I missed the shop in Potterston. It closed at noon."

Penberthy gasped. "Are you kidding me?"

Harlan shook his head. "I'm sorry. Look, I know this is my fault, and what makes it worse is that Monday is Memorial Day. I won't get that part until Tuesday. So why don't you call a friend and have him or her take you home. When I get the part on Tuesday, I'll fix your car immediately, and I won't charge you for labor. All you'll have to pay for is the alternator."

Penberthy only stared at him.

"You can even use my phone to call a friend," Harlan said apologetically.

"I have a cell phone," Penberthy said through gritted teeth. "If I had wanted to call someone, I could have called two days ago. But I *don't* want to call someone. Don't you people around here understand anything? It's an imposition to call someone and ask him or her to drive nearly two hundred miles roundtrip to get me. Particularly since I would have to ask them to drive another two hundred miles on Tuesday to pick up my car. I don't impose on my friends."

He took a long breath and calmed himself. Yelling at Harlan, satisfying though it was, didn't solve anything.

Finally Harlan said, "If that's what you really believe, I feel sorry for you."

"Sorry for me!" Penberthy spat. "Because I'm considerate of my friends? You people in this town kill me. It's the imposition of the townspeople on the good nature of the Howards that got them closed down. And now I understand why. You don't think of anybody but yourselves."

With that he stormed out of the garage, and

returned to Grace Chapel Inn. He didn't bother with the bell. Why should he? He was beginning to feel as comfortable in the inn as he was in his own home. Instead, he put his things next to the coatrack, then walked through the foyer and into the kitchen, where the ladies were having lunch.

"I'm back."

"Irwin," Louise said, turning on her chair to face him. "What's wrong?"

"Harlan got involved in fixing the car of a pregnant woman who is due any day—"

"Annabelle Rivers," Alice supplied, then apologized for interrupting.

Penberthy nodded. "Yes. Anyway, he got so involved with her car he forgot about mine. It seems the parts store in Potterston closes at noon." He swallowed. "If you don't mind, I'm here until Tuesday."

Alice glanced at Jane, who glanced at Louise, who took a slow breath. Penberthy knew why they were concerned. It seemed that every day he stayed here, his opinion of the inn worsened. He nearly told them that he would stop adding things to his report in return for another few nights' stay, but he couldn't do that. He had to be honest. If he continued to find more reasons why this inn shouldn't be open, he was duty-bound to document them.

"Of course you can stay," Alice said, but Irwin heard the uneasiness in her voice. She rose from her seat. "Let me get you a bowl of the soup we had for lunch."

Thinking quickly, because he needed to find a way to balance the scales, Irwin said, "I can't stay here for nothing. I would like to do something to help out around here."

"We need a backstage timekeeper for the talent show tomorrow," Louise said cautiously.

"I'll do it," Irwin said. He didn't bother to point out that when presented with the opportunity to get some help with anything she wanted, Louise didn't ask for something for herself or for the inn. She asked for help with the town's project. He knew she recognized that he couldn't pay to stay. He also realized Louise had probably figured out that a request for help with the inn could be construed as his giving them assistance beyond the scope of what he was permitted to do as an inspector.

The next day Irwin was on his own when the Howards left for church. He had intended to sit in the library and read, but he wasn't one who typically stayed away from Sunday services. After only a few minutes of uneasiness, he hurried upstairs and changed into the suit he had worn the day he arrived. A few minutes later, he cautiously entered the back of Grace Chapel, where he sat in the last pew.

The building itself was deceptive. It appeared to be nothing but a simple, white clapboard structure. But seated in the back, where he could examine the building and its features at his leisure, Irwin saw that the interior was quite handsome and that the stained-glass windows were spectacular. The rich music of the organ relaxed and uplifted him.

A short time later he became attentive and pensive when Rev. Thompson began to talk about kindness. It was the second time he heard the story of the organ donor, and he had to admit he was moved by it. Who wouldn't be? In this day and age, a person didn't often hear of another person being so generous.

"'Give, and it will be given to you,'" the pastor quoted Luke 6:38. "'A good measure, pressed down, shaken together . . .'" His voice boomed through the small church. "But the purpose of giving isn't to receive. And the purpose of that passage isn't to convince us to give so that we will receive. The purpose of that Scripture is to remind us that giving is a circle."

The reverend paused and shook his head. "Giving connects us. It turns a stranger into a friend and can make a friend family."

Irwin frowned. He wondered if this was why he continually fought feelings of friendship for Jane, Louise and Alice. Technically, he had been the recipient of a generous dose of giving this weekend. He would be a fool not to admit that, and he would also be a fool if he didn't recognize that having strangers extend such kindness to him was affecting him.

Though he would never have dreamed of it, this weekend he had been without a place to stay. Why? Not because his car broke. He was "homeless" because he didn't have a friend he could call upon to come and get him. He didn't want to put out any of the people he considered his friends. He couldn't. He knew none of them would react well to being asked to make such a long drive.

Instead, people he didn't know—the very people who owned the inn he had just closed—had opened their doors to him.

A new thought tiptoed into his brain. Maybe he and his friends weren't respectful of each other's time and talents as much as they were isolationists, keeping each other at an arm's distance and seeing each other, being kind to each other, only when convenient—which wasn't often.

At the end of the service, he hurried out of church. As he had done with dinner the night before, he found lunch on his own. He did so not because he didn't wish to associate with the Howards, and not even because he didn't wish to be further indebted to them, but because he felt odd, uncomfortable. He'd never before considered that the way he and his friends lived their lives was flawed. In fact, he'd always believed the way he lived his life was considerate, appropriate, civilized.

A few hours later, he showered and dressed for the talent show, unexpectedly excited to have the role of timekeeper. Wearing his suit and his dress shirt, which Jane had kindly laundered, he stood in the foyer, ready to go to the elementary school.

One by one, the Howard sisters joined him. Jane, who wore a stunning blue dress that brought out the color of her eyes, arrived first.

"Though I'm not in the show, I will be backstage getting everybody ready to go on," she explained twirling once to show off the flared skirt. "Plus, I had a big part in pulling this production together. I want to put my best foot forward, not just for myself, but for the town. Many of the people in attendance tonight will be guests from out of town."

Second came Alice, who had dressed more casually in white slacks and a sunny yellow blouse.

"Not in the show," she said with a laugh. "Not keeping track of acts, handing out lemonade or even doing the timekeeping."

Irwin chuckled. "That's me. I'm keeping track of the time."

"And I'm going to be in the front row, very comfortable as I watch the performances."

Irwin laughed again.

Finally, Louise descended the steps, wearing a beautiful black sequined dress. From the way she looked, Penberthy thought she should have been playing with the Philadelphia Orchestra rather than at a small-town talent show.

"You look wonderful, Louise," he said, watching her walk down the steps.

"Why, thank you, Irwin."

"I don't think this town understands what a gem it has in you," Irwin said.

Louise shook her head. "You have a lot of opinions about our town. I'm not sure how you got them, but I'm sure you're wrong in some of your assumptions. In fact, my sisters and I have been thinking a lot about your cautions about allowing our friends and neighbors to come to Grace Chapel Inn," Louise said, approaching him. "And we're going to respectfully disagree."

Penberthy's eyes widened. "Disagree?"

"Yes," Louise said. "I came home to be a part of this community, and basically what you're asking us to do is to deny that we are part of something larger than ourselves."

"I feel that way too," Alice put in gently. "It seems to me that the townspeople are a part of the charm of the inn." Alice walked to stand beside Louise. "When Jane hosts a tea party, for instance, and we invite the mayor and Aunt Ethel, they entertain our guests with wonderful stories of the history of the town."

"Guests do love those tea parties," Jane said with a laugh. "Everyone comments as much on the marvelous stories Aunt Ethel tells as they do the tea."

Before Penberthy could reply, the doorbell rang

and Florence entered without waiting for someone to answer the door. "I hope you don't mind my coming here," she said to no one in particular. Wearing a simple floral dress, and with her hair covered in a shimmering scarf, she didn't really look ready to perform. "But I'm so excited, I couldn't wait another minute. I thought it would be smart if we all arrived together."

Alice laughed. "You can ride to the school with us then."

"That's a great idea. Don't let me forget to get my dress out of my car. I don't want to perform in this old thing," she said, pointing at her print dress.

"See?" Penberthy whispered to Louise as the phone rang. "She's even nagging you for a ride to the show."

As Alice answered the phone, Louise sighed and faced Irwin. "She's not nagging. She's looking for support. We're giving it."

"At the expense of your business?"

"Giving her a ride to the show has nothing to do with Grace Chapel Inn," Louise said. "I'm hoping James E. Delaney doesn't feel the same way you do about the people of the town, because now more than ever I feel you're wrong."

Louise turned to Alice, who had hung up the phone. "Last-minute problem?" she asked, obviously noting the odd expression on Alice's face just as Irwin had.

Alice pressed her lips together, then quietly said,

"Something's wrong with Rosalind. She's been admitted to Potterston Hospital."

"Oh my goodness!" Louise gasped.

"Oh no!" Jane said. "Alice, I'm so sorry."

"I've got to get down there," Alice said. "I've got . . ." She swayed as if about to lose her balance.

"You can't drive," Louise said, taking her sister's arm to steady her. "Look how upset you are."

"And you can't take her," Jane said to Louise. "You're the accompanist."

"And you can't drive me," Alice said to Jane. "You're in charge of getting the acts onto the stage."

Everyone glanced at Penberthy. He shook his head. "I don't have a car. And even if I did, I'm timekeeper."

"I have a car," Florence said unexpectedly. "I'll drive Alice."

"But Florence," Louise said with another gasp. "You can't go. This show is your idea."

"And I practiced a long time, and I would have done a great job," Florence agreed. "But if you think this through, Louise, I'm only one of the acts. That's it. If I want you focused on the music and Jane focused on getting the right people on stage, then I have to do this." She paused and smiled. "That would probably be my best contribution."

Louise said, "Are you sure?"

Florence said, "Yes. I've never been more sure of anything in my entire life."

Chapter Twenty-Two

Alice took the front passenger seat of Florence's car as Florence slid behind the wheel.

"Now don't you worry about a thing," Florence said to Alice. "You don't even have to talk. Pray for your friends if you want to."

Alice nodded. "Okay."

"Okay," Florence said brightly.

Alice stared at her companion for a few seconds, then she said, "Thank you, Florence, and I'm sorry you have to miss the show."

"As I told Louise and Jane, I'm only one of the acts."

"Yes, but I know this show meant a lot to you."

"And I know these people mean a lot to you," Florence countered. "Let me do this for you, Alice."

Alice nodded, then turned to look out the window, clearing her mind so she could pray for Rosalind. But she couldn't help thinking about Florence. It seemed her counseling sessions with Pastor Ken had worked, not just because Florence put someone else's need ahead of her own, but because she seemed so happy doing it.

As the purple-velvet stage curtains opened, Irwin Penberthy stood in the wings with Jane. She held a clipboard. He held a stopwatch. After Florence left to drive Alice to Potterston, he, Louise and Jane had brainstormed and decided that even if it took every ounce of their creativity, this show would last long enough for Florence to drive to Potterston and return. Irwin's job had become vitally important—he had to make sure the show ran its full two hours.

If an act somehow ran shorter than its practice time, Irwin would give Mayor Tynan a thumbs-down sign, indicating that he should tell a joke or two before introducing the next act. That, Irwin was certain, would keep the show on track.

Grace Chapel's choir opened the talent show with an uplifting song of worship. When they were through, Irwin helped Jane usher them off the stage before he gave Mayor Tynan a thumbs-down.

The mayor walked out onto the stage and calmly faced the packed auditorium. Irwin couldn't believe there were this many people in little Acorn Hill, but he remembered Florence had said something about providing Sunday-night entertainment for out-of-town guests, and Irwin suspected many of the people in attendance were visiting for the holiday. He didn't have time to dwell on attendance, however, because Jane had the next act on deck in a matter of seconds. The mayor finished his jokes, and the show went on.

At intermission, exhausted, Irwin stole away to get a break from the pressure of making the acts stretch to fit the necessary two hours, and also to get himself out of the way of the performers making last-minute adjustments to costumes, hairdos and makeup.

As he walked into the front lobby of the school, where Ethel and Lloyd served lemonade and cookies, he overheard comments confirming that many of the people in attendance were guests of the Acorn Hill residents.

"Such a wonderful choir!" he heard one woman say. "I think they could compete with the big choirs we have in Philadelphia."

Charlotte, the teenage clerk from Dairyland, faced the older woman with a smile. "Yes, Aunt Agnes, they are wonderful."

To the left of Irwin a man said, "Those trombonists were hysterical." He accompanied Fred, the weather prognosticator, to the table with the cookies. Because Fred and his companion looked so much alike, Irwin was sure he was a relative. "I can see the people of Acorn Hill have retained their wonderful sense of humor."

"Yes, we have," Fred agreed. "I think we all realize that every once in a while it's good to laugh at yourself."

"I can't believe how your pastor's rendition of 'Stars and Stripes Forever' had everybody rolling in the aisles," another guest said with a laugh.

Irwin found himself smiling too. Remembering how the pastor's performance had cracked him up, he reached for a cookie.

Standing behind the refreshment table, Ethel sniffed and said, "Good evening, Mr. Penberthy."

"Good evening, Mrs. Buckley." He nodded to acknowledge the mayor. "Mayor Tynan."

"I can see you're enjoying the show, Mr. Penberthy," the mayor coolly observed. Backstage, the mayor may have been cooperative and even somewhat friendly, but here in the crowd, where he could be seen and heard, he obviously wanted to show he wasn't happy with Irwin.

Irwin suddenly felt unwelcome. He knew they were all angry with him for closing the inn, but Ethel and Lloyd seemed angrier than was warranted. He didn't want to think that the Howards had told everyone in town that Irwin had warned them about being too friendly. If they had, that also meant everybody knew he had suggested putting some distance between themselves and the local residents.

Still, that was the only explanation for the cold shoulder he was getting, and it made him wonder about the kindness and supposed goodness of the Howards. Yes, they had taken him in, but at what price? To make him the object of gossip?

Harlan walked up behind him, and Irwin remembered that in his frustration on Saturday he had told Harlan that the townspeople were part of the reason Irwin had closed down the inn. It was Harlan who had told! Anger welled up in Irwin. After all Harlan's nice talk of taking care of a pregnant woman and even fixing Irwin's car for nothing, Harlan was nothing but a gossip. The people of this town sickened him.

"Where's Alice?" Harlan asked.

"The volunteer who donated a kidney for a transplant a few days ago was admitted to the hospital," Ethel explained.

"That doesn't sound good," Harlan said.

"Alice went to check on her," Lloyd said.

"Florence drove her," Ethel said.

"Florence?" Harlan said, his face puckering with confusion. "Isn't this show her idea?"

Ethel simply said, "Yes." Then she cast a glare in Irwin's direction. "If someone else had volunteered to use her car to take Alice, she would be here right now."

Suddenly everything fell into place for Irwin. Harlan hadn't gossiped. Ethel and Lloyd, and probably every other person involved with the show, weren't mad at him for what he'd said about the town. If these people were angry with him, it was because they thought he should have suggested to Florence that he use her car to take Alice to Potterston Hospital. He couldn't believe they felt he should have done that, but then he realized he *had* been the most logical choice to drive.

In fact, he had been so obviously the choice that he wondered how or why he hadn't thought to offer to drive Alice, but as quickly as he thought that, the answer came to him. Once again the problem lay with the way he and his friends inter-acted. They were so "considerate" of each other's schedules that he wasn't accustomed to doing favors.

Florence, however, hadn't missed a beat. As the potential drivers were eliminated, she had jumped in and volunteered, even though it meant missing the talent show that Irwin knew she had been dying to perform in.

Worse, he had nearly accused Jane, Alice and Louise of gossiping about him, and he *had* men-tally accused Harlan of gossiping.

Irwin quickly finished his lemonade, crushed his paper cup, and tossed it into the trash. "I guess I better get back to my post."

"I'll see you there, Mr. Penberthy," Lloyd said, but there was no warmth in his voice.

Irwin arrived backstage with five minutes to spare before the second half of the program began. He met Louise as she was making her way to the piano in the left rear corner of the stage.

"You're doing a beautiful job," he said.

Louise stopped walking and smiled at him. "Thank you."

"You know, the consensus in the lobby seems to be that I should have been the one to drive Alice to the hospital."

Louise frowned. "But you don't have a car."

"I could easily have used Florence's or Alice's."

"True. But we were all in such a state of shock that none of us was thinking clearly." She gave him a kindly smile.

Irwin nodded and Louise walked away. But as Irwin watched her go, a terrible wave of guilt washed over him. He'd closed Grace Chapel Inn. He had harangued Louise and her sisters for treating the people of the town too well. He'd stayed at their inn for free. And then he'd missed the real opportunity to pay them back for all their kindness to him.

Yet Louise easily excused him.

She hadn't pointed the finger, preached him a sermon or used his misstep as a chance to get even. She'd absolved him. And he had a sneaking suspicion that if he told Harlan he'd accused him of being a gossip, Harlan, too, would tell him to forget it.

Now more than ever, Irwin was determined that the show would run long enough for Florence to perform. If he had to get on that stage himself and do an act, this show would last until Florence returned.

But the second hour seemed to go faster than the first. No matter how hard Mayor Tynan tried to stall, Irwin could see he was running out of material. Things seemed to go downhill from there. The dancers danced faster and Louise played faster to keep up with them, cutting a full thirty seconds from their routine. Pastor Ken's second spoon song only lasted just over two minutes instead of the three it had timed in practice, and Fred's solo didn't add a second. No one had remembered to remove the choir's second song from the program, and suddenly an entire five minutes disappeared from the schedule.

Irwin was sweating when, two acts from the end, Alice walked up behind him and tapped him on the shoulder. "How are things going?"

"Alice!" he said. Feeling a wonderful rush of relief, he impulsively hugged her—*much* to her surprise. "How is your patient?"

Seeing Alice, Jane ran over. "Yes, Alice, how is Rosalind?"

"Rosalind has a cold. She came to the hospital to have herself checked out as a precaution. That's it. She's fine," Alice said. "Unfortunately, the story got blown out of proportion."

"I'm sorry that happened, but I'm very happy it wasn't something else," Jane said, then she glanced around. "Where's Florence?"

"Parking the car."

Jane looked down at her clipboard. "We have one-and-a-half acts' worth of time to get Florence on stage. Irwin, I'll get her in the dressing room to change into the dress she brought for her performance. Can you get the next act on stage yourself?"

"Absolutely." Making the note on his clipboard, Irwin added, "Thank goodness she gets to perform! I thought for a minute I was going to have to go out on stage and tell jokes until she got here."

Jane laughed. "With your stage fright?"

"How do you know I get stage fright?" Irwin demanded.

"I saw all the blood drain from your face when you first looked out at the audience." Jane shook her head as Florence appeared in the hall by the dressing room. "I'll see you in a minute. I've got to make sure Florence is properly zipped and buttoned."

Irwin laughed and Jane rushed back to Florence. As he watched her walk away, Alice lightly tapped his arm.

"Deep down inside, you're a real softie."

Irwin couldn't help it; he laughed again. "What a thing for you, of all people, to say."

"Why? Because you closed our inn?" She shrugged. "You thought you had good reason." She shrugged again. "I don't happen to agree, but I recognize your right to your opinion."

"Helping with the show certainly doesn't prove I'm a softie."

"No, but the way you're rooting for Florence does. Deep down, Irwin, you have a good heart."

He shook his head. "Not even close. I'm hoping for Florence to get a chance to perform because I should have thought to use her car to drive you to the hospital myself." He didn't want to get credit for something he wasn't doing. "My reasons for rooting for her are selfish. I'm feeling guilty."

"Irwin," Alice said with a laugh, "has anybody ever told you you're much too hard on yourself?"

"No."

"Well, you are. And maybe that's the reason you're so hard on everybody else."

With that she walked away. The act on stage concluded, and Irwin scurried to get Alice's ANGELs to the stage. Right before their performance began, Florence appeared in the wings, Jane on her heels.

"Your dress is fine. Your makeup looks great," Jane said as if ticking off items on a to-do list. "This is going to work."

"But I didn't want to finish the show," Florence said nervously, wiping her palms down the sides of her pretty green chiffon dress. "I don't want to be the last performance everyone sees, the one they remember."

Irwin set down his clipboard and took Florence's hands. "You're going to be great."

She gave him a worried look. "Do you think?"

"All right, I'm going to come clean and admit that I listened in on your practice on Friday." He glanced at Jane. "Ask Jane. She caught me eavesdropping."

Jane grinned. "I did."

The ANGELs finished and began noisily trooping off the stage. As they walked around Irwin, he squeezed Florence's fingers to make sure he had her attention. "And I thought you were wonderful."

Jane's grin widened. "He did. He told me."

"So go out there," Irwin said as Mayor Tynan walked on stage to introduce her, "and knock 'em dead."

"Okay," Florence said.

Florence took the stage. The lights dimmed. Slowly, dramatically, Louise began to play. And Florence sang like an angel.

Chapter Twenty-Three

Florence was the belle of the after-show party at the school. She was so proud of herself that she glowed.

Standing on the sidelines, watching Florence accept her congratulations, Louise was proud of her, too, and even shared in the sense of accomplishment that Florence felt. Florence's stellar performance was a success for both of them, not merely because Louise had coached Florence, but also because Louise had kept going even when the going got tough.

Louise silently thanked God that He hadn't let her back out of her commitment to the show or to Jane's flowerbeds. There was no feeling like the fulfillment one experienced in doing good deeds, not for acknowledgement, but for the benefit of someone else.

Even more important, Louise had learned that enlisting the help of Jane, Ethel, Mayor Tynan and even Irwin hadn't been a failure. It had only meant lots of people were able to bask in the joy of the accomplishment. Louise hadn't merely learned to go the distance; she'd also learned that sharing the journey made it fun for everyone.

"Are you ready to go?" Jane asked, sidling up to Louise.

"I'm tired and my feet are crying to get out of these shoes, but I'm still wound up."

"We'll make tea," Alice said, joining her sisters, "and sit on the front porch. I think we could all use a few minutes off our feet," she added with a chuckle.

"Good idea," Louise said.

As she turned to go, however, she heard Florence say, "I think our next production should be *South Pacific*. I've been practicing 'I'm Gonna Wash That Man Right Outta My Hair,' and I think that show could be a real moneymaker."

Louise froze. Alice glanced at Jane. Jane burst out laughing.

"What do you think, Louie?" Jane asked through her giggles.

"I think tomorrow's another day, Scarlett," Louise said, nudging her sisters in the direction of the door.

On the way out, they met Irwin and offered him a ride back to the inn.

He glanced at the starry sky. "If you don't mind, I'd like to walk."

Alice shrugged. "It's the perfect night for it."

"Yes," he agreed, looking at the heavens. "It is."

The ladies made the quick drive to their home. Alice started a pot of tea. Jane arranged a platter of vanilla wafers, and Louise reached for mugs from the cupboard.

Suddenly Jane said, "Do you think Mr. Penberthy was tricking us by telling us he wanted to walk when he really wanted to go back into the party?"

"What a silly thing to say," Louise said, chuckling as she shook her head. "Irwin wouldn't trick us. Especially not to go back into the party."

"Oh, I don't know," Jane said. "I think we've all got Mr. Penberthy wrong. From the way he manipulated those acts tonight, working to keep the show running until Florence returned so she could perform, I'll bet he's far different than any of us knows."

"I agree," Alice said with a nod. "But I also suspect he learned a few things about himself tonight. From what he told me, I don't think he was even aware of who he was deep down until wanting to help Florence forced him to behave differently. My guess is he's walking home because he wants some time to reflect on it all."

"I suspect he felt bad about not thinking to drive Alice to the hospital," Jane said.

"I know he did," Louise said. She paused and sighed.

"He's hard on himself."

"Much too hard," Jane agreed.

"But that explains why he's so hard on the people he inspects," Alice said. "If he won't accept anything but perfection from himself, it's not a stretch to see that he also expects perfection from everybody else."

"I wonder where he grew up," Louise said as she put the mugs on a tray to take to the front porch.

"We never thought to ask," Alice said.

Jane shrugged. "He's not overly talkative."

"Or maybe we didn't appear interested," Louise suggested. "After all, we were busy." She picked up the tray holding the mugs. "I'll see you girls on the porch."

"I'm going with you," Jane said, lifting her plate of wafers and following Louise to the door.

"I'll be out when the tea is ready," Alice called after them.

She joined them a few minutes later. Louise watched as she poured the fragrant tea and then took a seat on the swing.

"We were still discussing Mr. Penberthy," Louise explained, "and all the reasons we didn't extend him the friendship we generally do to our guests."

"As you said, we were busy," Alice said, then took a sip of her tea.

Louise inclined her head in agreement. "Or perhaps God didn't want us interfering. Maybe He wanted Irwin to come to his own conclusions."

"Who's drawing conclusions about what?" Irwin called as he walked toward them on the front sidewalk.

"It's nothing," Louise said casually, not wanting the poor man to know they had been discussing him.

"Inn secret?" Penberthy asked with a laugh as he joined them on the porch.

"We don't have any secrets," Alice said, scooting over on the swing to make room for him.

He declined her offer with a slight shake of his head. "You're right. You and your inn certainly have no secrets. That means I really shouldn't have been surprised that the people of your town feel free to come and go as they please."

"We're not going to argue that with you tonight, Irwin. I still think that's part of the inn's charm," Jane said.

"Tonight I'm not going to argue, either. Tonight I agree. The people of this town *are* part of the inn's charm."

Alice, Jane and Louise all glanced at him. "Really? You agree with us?" Alice asked.

Penberthy took a breath that brought him up to his full height and seemed to return him to his more serious mood. "For whatever reason, I drew a bunch of bad conclusions about the people of this town. I kept seeing them as taking, but tonight when Florence gave up her opportunity to perform, I began to see that everybody in this town, in his own way, gives back." He chuckled and shook his head. "You all need each other."

"That we do," Louise agreed, smiling into her mug because she had come to that conclusion herself, just in a different way. Where Irwin saw getting help as a blessing, Louise understood that the ability to give help was the blessing.

"I must have been under the influence of my cold medicine when I made the first inspection."

Jane's brow furrowed. "But you don't have a cold."

"Sure, I do." He pulled his copy of his report from his jacket pocket and tore it up. "First thing in the morning I will make a new inspection, and I'm positive the results will be quite different." He turned to walk to the front door. "I'm going to bed."

When he had been gone long enough to be out of earshot, Jane said, "Well, what do you know?"

"Can you believe that?" Alice asked.

But Louise casually rose from her seat. "I'm not surprised. I've always believed in the kindness of strangers."

Epilogue

Jane arranged the gleaming silver tea service and carried the tray into the parlor, where Irwin Penberthy sat with Ethel and Lloyd, discussing the art show that all three had seen in Wilmington.

Ethel sat on the sofa between the men. On a nearby chair, Louise also participated in their conversation. Rosalind Westwood and Alice were seated near the small table brought in to hold the sandwiches and desserts.

Jane paused in the doorway admiring the scene, aware of the perfect atmosphere created for afternoon tea. Furniture was polished, lace-covered tea tables were set with sparkling china, and even the delicate sandwiches and rich desserts added to the genteel ambience.

The Howard sisters had begun the tea parties as a special surprise for Muriel Fairchild, a former guest visiting from England. Jane researched them and at first was guided by the typical conventions, but over time a few of the traditions shifted and changed until now the tea parties at Grace Chapel Inn were a combination of tradition and whatever Jane considered interesting. As long as the words *refined* and *elegant* could be used to describe such entertainments, Jane knew she could change a sandwich or dessert or even use a theme to make her tea parties special events.

She walked into the parlor and set the tray on the table. Scones with clotted cream were arranged on a serving dish. They sat beside a platter of cucumber tea sandwiches, cranberry fingers, and apricot-ham tea sandwiches. Carmel-toffee squares and strawberries dipped in chocolate rounded out the tea as dessert.

"It was such a surprise to run into you," Ethel said, catching Irwin's hand and giving it a squeeze.

"Wilmington is an easy drive," Irwin said with a chuckle. "It's good for the soul to get away for a while, but if I can combine my relaxation time with an art festival, then I come back doubly rested."

"I've been to that festival," Louise put in. "I love that the works are so diversified. There's everything from water colors to metal sculptures."

"I've bought jewelry there," Jane said, easily entering the conversation as she lifted the teapot. Only a few weeks before, if someone had told her that Irwin Penberthy wouldn't merely return to the inn as a guest, he would return as a friend, Jane probably wouldn't have believed it. Yet here he sat, happy to be a guest, chatting with Ethel, Lloyd and Louise as if they were longtime acquaintances.

"Tea, Aunt Ethel?" Jane asked with a smile.

"Yes, thank you, dear," Aunt Ethel replied, but she stopped abruptly when Myra Swanson entered the room. "Oh my goodness!"

"Good afternoon, everyone," Myra said sheepishly. "You said not to bother knocking, just to come in." She shrugged. "So here I am."

"And it's wonderful to have you," Louise said, rising. She walked to the doorway and linked her arm with Myra's. "Thank you for coming."

"It isn't every day a girl gets asked to tea."

Rosalind and Alice rushed to greet Myra. "How

are you?" Rosalind asked at the same time that Alice said, "You look wonderful!"

"I feel terrific," Myra said, responding to both of them.

"We're so glad," Alice said as she took Myra's arm to guide her to a seat.

"I don't have to be treated like an invalid," Myra said with a laugh.

Inspired, Jane turned and offered her the teapot. "Why don't you serve tea, then?"

Myra set her purse on the chair. "I would love to."

Myra poured tea for Rosalind and Alice, moved to Louise, Lloyd and Irwin, then finished her serving.

"Ah, tea," Irwin said. "The world may think it's becoming more civilized, but any society that ignores such a comforting ritual is regressing, if you ask me."

Alice and Louise chuckled, but Lloyd nodded. "That's why it's so good to have a place like Grace Chapel Inn."

"And three women running it who aren't afraid to try new things," Ethel said, smiling at Jane, then Alice, then Louise.

"I'll toast to that," Irwin said, gently lifting his teacup in a salute. He caught Jane's gaze and smiled. She smiled back. It had been a stretch of her faith to offer him a room after he had shut down the inn, but she had done it. As a result, she'd won a friend for life.

"I'll toast Jane, Louise and Alice too," Lloyd said, raising his cup.

"To my sisters," Louise said.

"My sisters," Alice and Jane echoed.

"And to friends," Jane said, looking around the room. "Friendship has been a blessing for us all."

Red-Velvet Cake

Cake:

¼ pound butter
1½ cups sugar
2 eggs
2 tablespoons cocoa
2 ounces red food coloring
2 cups sifted flour
1 teaspoon vanilla
1 teaspoon salt
1 cup buttermilk
1½ teaspoons baking soda
1 tablespoon vinegar

Preheat oven to 350 degrees. Cream together butter, sugar and eggs. Mix cocoa and food coloring, then add to cream mixture. Mix and alternate vanilla, salt and buttermilk with flour. Mix and fold in (do not beat) baking soda and vinegar. Pour into two nine-inch pans, greased and floured, with wax paper on bottom. Bake at 350 degrees for thirty minutes.

Frosting:

1 cup milk
¼ cup flour
1 ¼ cups granulated sugar
¾ cup shortening
1 teaspoon vanilla

Combine milk and flour, and cook until thick (like a white sauce). Stir constantly. Cool.

Cream sugar and shortening until light and fluffy. Add vanilla and cream sauce. (Cream sauce must be completely cool.) Beat until icing becomes stiff.

Guideposts magazine and the *Daily Guideposts* devotional book are available in large print editions by contacting:

Guideposts
Attn: Customer Service
P.O. Box 5815
Harlan, IA 51593
(800)431-2344
www.guideposts.com

Center Point Publishing
600 Brooks Road ● PO Box 1
Thorndike ME 04986-0001 USA

(207) 568-3717

US & Canada:
1 800 929-9108
www.centerpointlargeprint.com